Max leaned down alr. of his beloved Ford . to come to terms with the looked up at Judd's face, al. ne could do was shiver.

"If you fucking laugh, I will choke you until you die," Judd said, his face flushed with embarrassment. He ran his fingers through the bush of pubic hair just above the labia and shook his head, a tear in his eye. When he finally spoke, his voice was quivering. "I just woke up and my dick was gone."

"You can pull your pants up now, man," Max said, rubbing his eyes. "No need to keep it out now that I've seen it."

"Max, what the fuck am I gonna do?"

Judd told the story of the voodoo woman and how he had stolen the pussy stick, leaving nothing out. He spoke in the hushed words of one recounting a guilty memory.

SCARY REDNECKS

& OTHER INBRED HORRORS

BY WESTON OCHSE & DAVID WHITMAN

INTRODUCTION

"You might be a redneck if ... "

How many times have we heard that? It's always followed by a punchline — usually, I must admit, a funny one. Those punchlines have provided a good living for southern comic Jeff Foxworthy. As funny as Foxworthy is, though, it's impossible to ignore the fact that he's putting muscle on the already substantial frame of one of the last remaining accepted stereotypical misconceptions: The Great White Redneck of the South.

The Great White Redneck lives in a trailer, drives a pick-up with a gun on the rack across the back window, and regularly attends exhibition events involving giant trucks. There's usually a battered car up on blocks in front of his trailer, but if not, look for a sink, a toilet, or an old swamp cooler somewhere nearby. The Great White Redneck's hygiene is suspect, his sexual proclivities degenerate and often illegal in most states, and according to most of those punch lines, his family tree doesn't have a whole lot of branches on it.

Foxworthy is certainly not responsible for this stereotype, and he is far from alone in keeping it alive. You'll see the Great White Redneck in movies and TV shows, always with a drawling southern accent. I'm sure I've been guilty of breathing life into the beast somewhere in my own work.

We should know better, of course. We should be able to look at these hollow stereotypes and laugh at them, not with them. We know people from the south are not like that — we've met and know them, we've worked with them, we've read them. Some of the most wonderful literature ever written has come from the south — Samuel Clemmons, Horton Foote, Flannery O'Connor, Larry McMurtry, William Faulkner, Joe R. Lansdale, Carson McCullers, on and on — it's a long list, and we all know that.

But somehow, that stereotype remains healthy. In a way, it makes us sadly predictable.

Along comes a short story collection called Scary Rednecks and Other Inbred Horrors. Doesn't exactly sound like a book that's going to suck the life out of that stereotype, does it? In fact, it appears to be just the kind of thing that will keep that stereotype up on its feet and walking around ... with its jeans dropped in the back and its hairy butt-crack showing, of course.

So who are the two guys responsible for *Scary Rednecks and other Inbred Horrors*? What are they up to and what do they have to say for themselves? What do they know about the American south and its people?

Weston Ochse was born in Wyoming, David Whitman in Pennsylvania. That hardly makes them southerners. However, very early in life, Weston was relocated to Tennessee, David to Florida, "which," David says, "isn't exactly what you would call the deep south, but there sure were a lot of what I would call Good Old Boys around."

If I'm not mistaken, Good Old Boys are a more refined breed of the Great White Redneck of the South. They appear to be quite prevalent in Texas. I'm not sure, but I think one way to tell them apart is by the size of their belt buckles.

Growing up in Tennessee and Florida, I'm sure Weston and David came into contact with plenty of people who could rightly be called "rednecks." And yes, there are rednecks, they do exist. Most stereotypes are not complete falsehoods, they are gross distortions — like all good lies, stereotypes usually include a grain of truth somewhere in their history. The biggest distortion about the Great White Redneck of the South is that he is not, by any means, southern. He is everywhere.

I live in California, and I am surrounded by rednecks. I'm serious, don't get me started, you'll wish you hadn't. They bear a frightening resemblance to all those comical stereotypes you see in the movies and on TV — except they are not southern.

Even though they've never left the county, many of them drawl when they speak, but a drawl and a southern accent are two entirely different things — the people I'm talking about drawl because they're too lazy to speak properly.

The idea that America's southern states are populated solely by rednecks is, of course, simply not true. But David Whitman and Weston Ochse, if not southerners by birth, were brought up in southern states. The stories in their collection are distinctly southern. They are solidifying the tissue that links southerners with rednecks ... aren't they?

They met when both subscribed to the Horror Writers e-mail list, and later decided to try collaborating. Although their styles are different, they discovered an interesting chemical reaction. David has been writing since childhood, when he wrote short stories and comic books. Weston, on the other hand, came to writing later, at the age of 30. While David's affection for the horror genre dates back to his childhood, Ochse's roots are in science fiction, his interest in darker fiction more recent. When they aren't writing, David is a psychologist and social worker, and Weston is an interrogator for the U.S. Army.

What would inspire them to put together a collection like this? Do they believe the stereotype to be true?

In a GothicNet interview with writer Brian Keene, Weston said, "I am from Chattanooga, Tennessee. I am white. I am Christian. I have blond hair and blue eyes. Shit, I am the poster child for all politically correct groups; I am the definition of the one to hate. ... I hate stereotypes."

So ... are they rednecks?

David calls himself "neurotic and sometimes introverted" and says he listens to jazz. Weston drinks wine and likes to watch Wolfgang Puck and The Christopher Lowell Show on television, for crying out loud. These are things that no self-respecting redneck would be caught dead doing in any part of the country.

So what's the deal?

"I think that rednecks are the last great heroes, sometimes," Weston says. "They think of the result rather than how they look. Rednecks are universal."

Universal, not southern. The redneck is everywhere, and, I believe, within all of us. Jeff Foxworthy's punchlines make us laugh, but every once in awhile, one makes us nod and maybe frown a little, doesn't it? Because it's just a little too close to home, right? How many of us have not, in some private moment when we knew we were unobserved, said our name as we belched? How many of us, when surrounded by children at some well-fed family event, have been unable to resist the urge to execute the "pull-my-finger" maneuver? There's a little of it in all of us, I think.

But does the collection contribute to the stereotype? Weston says, "I don't know."

While it certainly does not set out to shatter stereotypes, I think this collection contains enough humanity to avoid doing any damage in the other direction. Its primary aim is to entertain, which it does quite well. It's a darkly comic, sometimes hilarious, sometimes haunting and moving ride through a landscape both ugly and beautiful.

But still ... why that title?

"What we did play on," Weston said in the GothicNet interview, "was the prejudice of the public when we chose our campy title, Scary Rednecks and Other Inbred Horrors. It virtually guaranteed that someone would pick it up thinking, 'Hey, I have an uncle who is just like this.'"

Ah-hah! So that's what's going on! We've been played! Hell, I fell for it.

And good for them. It's precisely what we deserve for being so damned predictable.

–Ray Garton

CONTENTS

CATFISH GODS

BY WESTON OCHSE

Trey sat on the community dock, staring out across the green August water of Chicamauga Reservoir, his tanned legs swinging gently, fingers gripping the rough gray wood as thoughts of pleasure and mortality mingled within his thirteen year old mind. His grandfather had died six months ago and there were times when the heat and the bickering of his family and the memory of the loss became so much, he needed to be alone. He would sit and remember every word the old man had spoken; every action and every smile. He basked in the memories. All grandfathers are special, but Trey felt his was even more so. It was as if, the man's mere presence could calm the world. It was as if he was a God and when Gods die, one never forgets.

The dock was where Trey went when he needed to think; to remember. Other than his bed, it was the one place he spent most of his time. His first fight, his first bass, the first time he slid his trembling fingers along the curve of a breast as he massaged oil into the soft skin of an older high school girl, had all taken place on the dock. It was called the community dock, but had been abandoned by the city years before he moved into the neighborhood. Although access to the dock had grown over with tall weeds, a path had been pounded into the red Tennessee dirt by a faithful herd of eager children who now called it their own. It was a sacred place, one where parents never tread.

There was one month a year when you couldn't swim in the lake and this was the month. It made the interminably hot days long and filled with a hundred attempts to ease the constant boredom. The only good thing was that the mosquitoes had been all been killed when the TVA men lowered the water level by several feet, leaving the eggs to dry and die along the muddy beaches of the lake. The side effect, of course, was that long weeds grew up from the lake bottom as the sun, for the first time since winter, finally managed to plumb the depths, arousing the lake's deadly kudzu cousin. The weeds were as thick as a wrist and halted fishing, boating and now even swimming since Billy Prescott drowned last year. They said the weeds had wrapped around him a dozen times as if the leafy arms had reached out and snagged him, but that was just something the grownups said to scare the kids away.

Even Trey's thirteen year old mind, identified his freedom and the golden sunset against the green water as a rare time, a time he would remember when he was old and the lessons of school and the minutiae of life long forgotten.

The next day dawned ugly, the brightness of the summer sun dulled by the dish-water sky. The lake was slate gray and the waves seemed to reach up as if to try and free the oppressed light. Trey struggled out of bed and plodded into the kitchen. The coldness of the sky did nothing to alleviate the humidity, sweat immediately forming as a second skin. He poured himself a tall orange juice, and held the glass momentarily against his face. As he drank, he walked to the floor to ceiling window and eyed the driveway. Only the old Ford was left. His parents had driven to Laverne for a Sunday gathering, part business, part fun, they had said. He had been invited, but had pretended to be sick and promised to stay in bed until they returned. At thirteen, his parents had lengthened their leash, and today, was the first day they had ever let him free.

Trey grinned. They had planned it well, he and Greg. Today was their fishing day. They were going to try the loading dock across the inlet at the old TNT plant. It was the deepest place in the entire lake, except for the dam itself. Barges parked there weekly and loaded up the Army's secret stuff, creating rumors that were fun to propagate. If all the tales were even half-true, then there were fish down there as large as automobiles.

He'd dressed and was getting the gear together in the garage when Greg swung around the corner of the driveway, toting his favorite rod and an oversized tacklebox.

"What's up, Trey? You ready for a little fishing? Ready to catch the big one?"

Greg was three years younger, but a good friend nonetheless. When it came to fishing, age didn't matter anyway. As long as you were patient and followed a few basic rules, it was God's will that sent the fish your way. At least that's what his grandfather used to say.

"Go ahead and take the poles down to the dock, Greg. I'm gonna get the battery out of the car."

"Are you sure we ain't gonna get into trouble about this?" asked Greg, his blue eyes worried under his shag of red hair.

"Naw. They'll never even find out. They ain't supposed to be back until after dark anyway, and we'll be done long before that."

"What if we actually catch one of them beasts?"

It was Old Man Hassle that called them beasts, and Greg was at the age to believe everything the old caretaker said. Trey was pretty certain they wouldn't see any catfish that big, but twenty-five or thirty pounders were fairly common.

"Shit. If we bring one in, I'll just tell the folks I was feeling better. I'll tell them you and me went fishing from the dock. They won't be real happy, but Dad will be so impressed with the fish, he'll shut momma up."

Greg grinned from ear to ear, the dream of a huge fish and his best friend's intelligence were going to make this a day to remember.

They slid the yellow canoe from under the community dock and Trey pressed his sneaker against the foot pad that was the trolling motor's accelerator. He had snuck it from the downstairs storeroom. Its very presence among old boxes and broken tools was the genesis for the idea to fish by the TNT dock. It was really too far to paddle, but the small motor would get them there without tiring their arms. It had been a gift from his grandfather to his father, and had yet to be used. Trey felt a sadness in that, and saw his use of the old motor as a way to be closer to his grandfather. In his heart, he knew the old man wouldn't mind. He could almost see him now, standing in heaven, a martini grasped in his large hands looking down and wishing his grandson luck.

The water had white caps, brackish two-foot swells that made the going slow and difficult in the small boat. Greg held onto the front with both hands, and by the curve of his back, Trey could see the other boy's fear as he guided them around the larger clumps of weeds, both of them wary of getting them caught in the motor. Occasionally, they would pass a fish, held just under the water in the unrelenting grip of the weed, its eyes milky and rotten. The air was heavy with humidity, shirts and shorts already sopping with their sweat. The scent of honeysuckle drifted on the wind, mixing with the smell of rotting fish and the heady scent of the weed. Breathing was hard during any August in Tennessee, but upon the surface of the lake, it was near impossible as both boys alternately held their breaths against the foul smells of deadness and the sweetness of the surrounding forest.

Both boys had grown up on the lake, their summers filled with days where shoes and shirts were left indoors as they tried to become one with the sun and the water. When they weren't fishing or mowing lawns for some extra money, they were swimming around the community dock. Their favorite sport was underwater tag, spending more time holding their breath under than they did playing above. During those long games, Trey often imagined he knew how a fish felt, chased and cornered by a fisherman. He could hold his breath for over two minutes and would slither in and around the old wooden pilings, propelling himself from one end of the dock to the other in his efforts to escape the touch of his friends. The only greater feeling was when he shot to the surface for that breath of air that was required for another dive.

Often, when his mother and father were fighting and he found himself down on the dock, crying and wishing to be someone else's son, he would pray to the Gods of the fishes. He would beg to be released from his human bonds and become one with the water; a true fish. Their lives were simple and he envied the pleasure of the water, imagining himself too smart for the hook, plumbing the depths and coasting with the current. Trey had often thought, of all the fishes to choose from, that he would wish to become a catfish. Their lives were spent on the bottom, gliding and discovering the cast-off treasures of their human hunters. They were stately and moved with the purposefulness of kings. They lived long lives and grew to be immense. He remembered the picture he saw in the Guinness Book of World Records, the jaw of the fish large enough to swallow a small boy.

And then there were the stories of Old Man Hassle. He wasn't the only one who talked about giant fish, everyone had heard the rumors, but it was the old caretaker of the community dock who spoke of it more than anyone else. The lake was only about fifty years old. Still, divers would descend every few months to check the dam's integrity, searching for any cracks or holes in the millions of tons of concrete that could threaten the greater part of Chattanooga, sitting as a magnificent southern gem, just downriver. During the years, old wrecks of cars and trains were dumped along the base to add to the dam's width. These obtrusions were deadly to the divers, some becoming caught in the tangle of twisted metal as they inspected and pretended to be fishes. Even so, there was no end to divers who wanted to delve the lakes deepest depths. The pay was supposedly the highest of all and the list was long. Yet that list moved quickly as the divers went down, came back up and swore never to enter the lake again.

It was the catfish that sent them scurrying, arriving screaming and babbling as they surfaced. It was the catfish as big as Ford LTDs and Lincoln Towncars that swam up to stare at them as they inspected the aging concrete. People said it was all the old cars that bad been dumped down in the lake's depths that provided them with their source of measurement and it was this single thing that made people believe the stories. It was also what had people coming from everywhere to catch the mythical beasts.

Trey and Greg crossed the barrier from the haven of the

green weed and shallower water, to the black mysteriousness of the deep water. Still, they breathed a sigh of relief to be safe from Billy Prescott's fate. Greg turned in his seat and began preparing his rod, attaching a number six hook and opening a can of corn. As they moved to the hole, they found themselves in the shadow of an immense dock where the barges were loaded. They stared up at the pilings, easily three times larger than any telephone pole and covered with a black coating of tar that kept water from rotting the timber. The dock itself was at least a hundred feet above them, with a thousand stray wisps of fishing line from the large tires bolted to the side evidenced bad casts and impossible snags.

Trey cut the motor, they drifted momentarily and then stilled. The dock was protected from the wind by a small peninsula of trees, creating calm water where even the brown bubbles of pollution remained immovable. As Greg, dropped his line in the water, Trey turned and tightened the clamps on the motor. It would be his death if it fell over the side. Like the battery between his feet, the motor was off limits. As long as it didn't break or sink, however, he felt sure that his father would never find out.

It was mere moments before the smaller boy jumped up, screaming in delight as he reeled in a rather pathetic bluegill.

"Sit down, Greg. Are you stupid or something? You're gonna dump the boat," said Trey gripping both sides, attempting to steady the rocking.

"But I got one. I got one," said the younger boy, smiling happily.

"Shit, man. You got bait. After a few more of those, then we'll really start fishing."

Greg sat down and frowned a little as he removed the hook from the flapping fish. Like all kids with scars on their hands, he was careful to avoid the sharp spines along the small fish's back. He tossed the fish into the middle of the boat where it wiggled wretchedly.

"You know what Old Man Hassle said, don't you?" asked Greg, casting a line again.

"That old coot says a lot of things. I wouldn't believe too

much of what he says. My daddy says he's an old drunk, anyway," replied Trey, also tossing in a line. It was Old Man Hassle that gave Trey the idea to try the old Army Dock for catfish, but he wouldn't let his younger friend know exactly how much he really liked the old coot.

"Yeah, my mom says the same thing, but still, he's been around forever." Greg cursed as he missed the strike of a fish. He brought the empty hook back onto the boat, slid on a kernel of corn and tossed it back over the side.

"So what does he say?" asked Trey, pretty sure he knew the answer already.

"He said the biggest of all the catfish live down there," said Greg, pointing into the brackish water. "He said this is the place where they lay their eggs... where they grow new ones."

Trey had heard about the big ones, but the egg story was a new one.

"Old Man Hassle says it's the catfish that make the weeds grow," continued the smaller boy. "Like a fence to keep other fish out... and people."

Trey scoffed loudly. "That's plain stupid. How could fish make the weeds grow?" It was science, biology rather that made it occur. His biology teacher called it photosynthesis. It was the sun, reaching down to the lake floor, making long forgotten seeds blossom and bloom. "I think the old coot was drunk when he told you that. Anyway, it's the TVA men killing the mosquitoes. As far as the fish eggs go, they can grow anywhere. This isn't the only place."

"No. Really, Trey. Think about it? It makes sense. Old Man Hassle says they are Gods... Catfish Gods. He says they have the power to stop people from catching them if they want. It's the bad ones that we catch," said Greg, persisting in his stupidity.

"That makes no sense at all. It's plain stupid, Greg. How can a fish be a God?" Trey shook his head. "Why would you want to catch them, then? Catch a God?"

Greg frowned and turned in his seat, glancing slowly from at Trey to the fishing gear. He was a pretty strict Catholic and was going through catechism. Finally he smiled.

"Yeah, it is pretty stupid."

He grinned at Trey and the older boy could tell that his logic had sunk in. The smile was near to one of worship, but then he was used to them. The littler boy looked up to him, and more often than not, would do anything to impress him.

It took half an hour before they had brought in enough bluegill and crappie for bait. That was the fun about catfish. You never had to buy bait for them. Trey had learned long ago, it was the guts that they preferred over anything else. Disgusting as it was, it kept the girls from fishing for them. Once you got used to it and learned how to hold your breath, it was even okay for him.

Last year, after he had heard of the guts, right before the weeds took over, he had been in the same canoe fishing along the muddy flats just off shore from the houses. He was using his trout rig and was drifting guts from a large hook, the bait bumping along the bottom, held down by a large sinker. It was his first time using the guts, and he wouldn't have done it except he was fresh out of worms and had snagged all the lures he had stolen from daddy on the docks. He really wasn't expecting to catch anything, just enjoying the wind off the water and the sun, hoping for a tan that would carry him through the winter. When the fish first hit, he thought he had caught a snag, but when the 'snag' had began to pull the boat out deep, he knew it was an incredible fish. It took him an hour of alternately paddling and pulling, sure to keep tension on his four pound test at all times, before he finally reached the shore. It took another ten minutes for him to haul in the biggest fish he had ever caught. To this day his father hardly believes that his own son had brought in a twenty-five pound catfish on such microscopic line.

It was Trey's first catfish and catching it made him feel more than human. Soon, he found himself on the community dock, late at night fishing with trot lines laced with multiple hooks. He would sneak out, having left his rod and gear under his window, and make his way through the darkness to the dock. He rarely caught anything and would wake up near dawn, when the chill of the new sun made it too uncomfortable to remain near the water. His mother would 'cluck' at his sleeping, making him finally get up at noon, criticizing him for his laziness. Trey never gave away the truths of his nights, however. They were too special, communing with the sky and the water, thinking of all his grandfather had taught him about fishing and life. He enjoyed the peace and disjointedness he felt as he held the lines and pretended he was floating in the sky…the water; an integral part of the universe.

Trey had to gut all the fish while Greg stared away, pretending to ignore the pop of released flesh and the blood that seeped into the bottom of the boat, making the water a disarming pink. When Trey finished, he placed the corpses in a white plastic bag and piled the guts in a small bucket.

"Alright," he said smiling. "You can look now, I'm done."

"What? I was just staring at the water, Trey. Looking for some fish."

Trey smiled wider. He'd let it be and not mention the fact that there was no way his friend could see fish in the dark brackish water.

"Help yourself," he said gesturing at the pile that was already drawing green-bottomed flies. "It's time to catch one of your Gods."

Greg glared for a moment, wondering if it was an insult or a joke, then grabbed a length of purple intestine and placed it on the new rig—a triple ring, with a sinker offset from the large hook so the bait could drift a few tantalizing inches from the muddy bottom, while the weight held it down.

When they had let out enough line, they both leaned back and stared at the slow moving sky. On occasion, they would follow a particular cloud, watching as it changed shapes until finally disappearing into the kudzu covered forest that was their horizon.

Finally, Greg's pole doubled over sending him standing as he tried to control the dancing rod. The canoe rocked in the water and Trey struggled to still it by shifting his weight. Greg screamed at the top of his lungs as he began to reel furiously.

"Slow down. Slow down, Greg. You're going to break the line." Trey held onto the side of the boat. "Slow and steady.

Slow and steady." His grandfather had taught him that. Hell, he'd taught him everything he knew about fishing except what his dad had taught him about creek fishing. Too many people got too excited and lost their catch. Fishing was a tough thing.

Greg ignored him, his pole making a right angle towards the water. His reeling slowed, less from his effort than the fish's far below. It began to pull the small boat and Trey swiveled and toggled the trolling motor on. He maneuvered the boat to provide a steady pull against the tug of the captured fish. It had to be a catfish and a big one.

The excitement was contagious and soon, Trey, found himself shouting and encouraging Greg. He prayed that the line or the rod wouldn't snap. He prayed that his friend wouldn't get jerked in, forgetting to let go and drown in the murky depths. Trey couldn't help but remember the words of Old Man Hassle, imagining that his young friend had a God on the end of his line. He prayed to the fish themselves, begging them to let these two boys catch one.

Just as suddenly as the hit, however, came the snap, as the line gave away to the combined pressures of the fish and the reverse pull of the boat. Greg fell back hard, hitting his head against the metal rim of the canoe. Trey stopped the engine immediately and managed to catch the rod before it fell in the lake.

Greg sat up. Tears flowed from his eyes.

"Are you okay, Greg?" asked Trey, the wake of the fight still sending ripples across the still water.

"Fuck me," the little boy said, wiping his cheeks with the front of his T-shirt. "I just hurt my head is all."

Trey watched him rubbing the growing bump and knew that it was a deeper pain. He had almost caught the big one... he'd had it and it was gone. But that's what made fishing special and so unique. You always tried for that bigger fish, every moment a chance. When you lost it, it was forever lost and you had to start over, not where you left off. When you finally caught it, the glory was so fleeting, it was no time at all before you went looking for an even larger one.

"Shit. That was a big one too. Damn big," said Trey.

"Yeah. Damn big," repeated Greg, still staring at the water.

"I wonder if it has any brothers?" asked Trey. "I still got my line in the water. You better fix yours."

Greg spent a few moments staring longingly at the lake, then hurried to refit his line.

Trey returned to his own line and argued with himself over the need to check the bait. It was an important argument, one when many experienced fisherman made mistakes. If you pulled it up as the fish was contemplating the catch, your chance was forever lost. If you left it in the water with an empty hook, you were wasting the day. It was a tough choice, but Trey decided to leave it be.

It was right after they finished their egg salad sandwiches when Trey's rod buckled.

It caught Trey off guard and he almost lost the rod as it slipped and banged against the edge of the boat. It wasn't until the last moment that he managed to grip it, already half in the water. He jerked the rod back out, partly to set the hook and partly because he stumbled back, knocking over Greg in the process. He stood up and felt the thrumming tug of the line. He immediately knew it was the largest catfish he had ever latched onto.

Trey squatted by the motor and struggled to turn it on. It gave a hum, but when he glanced over the edge, he saw the blades turning excruciatingly slowly, evidencing a dying battery. He cast a glance over his shoulder and eyed the community dock, half a mile away. With only one paddle, it would take forever to reach it.

Trey decided against the motor and screamed for Greg to reel in his own line. After a momentary look of annoyance, Greg complied and pulled his line in. It took a few moments, but finally the two managed to change places. All the while, the canoe was being pulled inexorably towards the pilings. It was mere moments before the front of the boat hit the sticky wood and with his free hand, Trey grabbed hold. It was better than being drug out into the lake, or even the weeds. What he prayed for, however, is the fish wouldn't wrap the line around the pole.

Luckily, he didn't have his usual trout rig, but the heavy-duty rig he had been given last Christmas and it wasn't called the Ugly Stick for nothing. The line was twenty pound test and could handle upwards of a hundred pounds if used skillfully. The tip of the rod continued to dance and jump as he could feel a long hulk, struggling far below to get free.

Suddenly, the line went slack. Trey momentarily stopped reeling and cried out, tears filling his eyes. Almost as fast, he realized the fish could be attempting to surface. He wiped his eyes and redoubled his fight, taking line in furious and quick. He couldn't match the speed of the fish, however, and when it surfaced, Greg screamed. Its gaping maw, at least two feet across, snapped at the air on the left side of the boat as it rose out of the water. He wondered who was catching who. The head of the great fish slammed into the water with a huge splash, soaking the boys and the boat and disappearing in the murk of the water. Something rammed the bottom of the boat sending Greg into the water and Trey to the bottom of the boat. On the right side, a tail flapped the surface angrily several times.

Then chaos returned to order as the fish disappeared and the urgency of the moment subsided.

Greg, treading water, began to alternately scream and gurgle as he panicked, trying to kick the fish and swim back to the boat, simultaneously.

"Trey... Trey... gggg... Help me."

Trey, picked himself up from the cramped floor of the boat, now covered in fish guts and soaked with the bloody mixture from his earlier cutting. The rod forgotten, he grabbed the paddle and held it out towards his struggling friend. Within seconds, Greg was back in the boat, hyperventilating and crying.

"Jesus H. Christ. Did you see the size of that thing?"

"Did I see it? It almost ate me!" screamed back Greg.

Trey was about to tell him how stupid that was, then stopped. It had been the biggest fish he had ever seen. Too many times he had swum in the deep water, the 'Jaws' soundtrack playing in his mind. Even though no one had ever heard of a person being eaten in a freshwater lake by a shark or a fish and even though no one had ever been chewed up by a catfish, he couldn't help but wonder.

Trey glanced around and noticed his rod had disappeared, surely, on the bottom of the lake being drug around by his own Moby Dick. He maneuvered Greg into the seat and noticed the young boy was beginning so shiver uncontrollably. Trey jerked of his shirt and ordered his friend to remove his shoes. He massaged the boy's arms and shoulders until he could see the blood return. Both of them were crying, their chance at greatness, twice removed.

"I wanna go home," said Greg, trying real hard to stop crying. "I don't want to fish anymore."

"Okay. Okay," said Trey, wanting to stay and try again. The lure of all fishermen who had just lost the big one was upon him, but he had lost his rod. There was only Greg's and there was an unwritten rule never to fish with anyone else's pole. His grandfather had said that 'if you caught something on someone else's rig, it wouldn't really be your own.' The great fish, if it could be recaught, would belong to Greg.

Trey eyed the sky and saw a storm moving in, hard grey clouds pushing aside the day quickly. They probably had only fifteen minutes before it hit; just long enough for Greg to dry off before he became soaked again. It would take twice that to make it back across the inlet to the community dock. Trey eyed the immense TNT dock and thought about taking shelter beneath. He had no idea how long it would last however, and Greg really needed to get home and into dry clothes.

"Shit," said Trey, accepting his fate.

It was then he saw his fishing pole, about five feet under the water and wrapped around one of the pilings. It had snapped and the line appeared to be all that was holding it in place.

"Look! There's my pole," he said, pointing into the water.

Greg turned slowly to where Trey pointed, then sat straight when he saw the unmistakable lines of the rod. "Maybe you can save the reel."

"Sure," said Trey, brightening. He had thought it lost forever. Then he noticed the tip, it thrashed once, twice, then a series of hard jerks, creating bubbles that rose to the surface. "Holy Cow.

Look at that! The fish. It's still on."

Instead of being thrilled, Greg got a worried look on his face.

"Don't go in there. Don't go into the water." Greg shook his head hard and stared into the bottom of the boat. "It's just too big. Too damn big."

Trey watched his friend for a second and then glanced back at the fishing pole. He let his eyes drift along the piling and for the first time, noticed there were bars jutting out from the sides; like those on telephone poles, but previously camouflaged by bits of seaweed and moss. It was a huge fish, but 'Jaws' could never happen here. All he had to do was climb down, cut the line and then get his reel back. His dad was going to wonder where it was anyway, considering it was a Christmas present and Trey's favorite gift. If they went to the mountains next week, he would never be able to explain it away.

"Naw. It's okay. The fish is gone. I know that. I'm just going to get the pole. My father would kill me if I lost the whole rig. Anyway, if he finds out it's missing my parents will know what we did today. And my parents will tell your parents and then we'll be grounded from the lake all summer."

At the threat of grounding, Greg brought his head up sharply. The lake was their life. Trey watched as the emotions moved through his friend's face. Finally, his friend sighed and nodded his head slowly.

"Okay, but hurry up," said Greg in sotto voice. "And be careful."

'Hurry up and be careful,' thought Trey. Those were two things that shouldn't go together. He wasn't going to hurry, but he would certainly be careful.

Trey paddled the canoe back up to the piling, the shadow of the dock placing them in darkness. The smell of decay was strongest here. He noticed the eddies of black oil and multicolored gasoline slick mixed with trash and the brown bubbles of pollution. If the lake was Heaven, this was Hell. Trey leaned past Greg and used the short length of rope attached to the front of the boat to tie it firmly into place. He removed his tennis shoes and folded them, placing them on the seat. He stood up and stared at the disgusting water, not wanting to enter, but needing the big catch.

"Alright. Watch me, man. Everything is gonna be okay. I'm just going to get the rod and I'll be right back up." Trey placed a hand on Greg's shoulder. "Stay cool."

With that, he placed a foot on the metal edge of the canoe and pushed off. The water embraced him as he, feet first, sliced deeply from hot to cool water. He pushed himself back to the surface and side-armed his way over to the piling. Counting to three by thousands, hyperventilating, until his lungs were full, he descended pulling himself down using the slippery spikes. The rod was deeper than he though, probably fifteen feet, but it was only seconds before he reached it. Through the murky water, he saw the rod and the line wrapped around the piling six or seven times. It was the heaviness of the line that had saved his reel.

The tugging had stopped, but he doubted the fish was entirely gone. Maybe he still had a chance to catch it. He really didn't need to cut the line. He could deceive the fish. After all, he was human and he had superior brains. Trey depressed the reel and let out about five feet of slack. Careful, as not to tug on the line still attached to the fish, he began to unwind the rod from the piling. He was almost finished when he paused and returned to the surface.

"What the hell are you doing, Trey? I thought you were gonna cut the line."

Trey breathed heavily across the water and grinned. "I got everything under control. When I come back up, I'm gonna hand you the rod. Hold onto it tight until I get back into the boat."

"Don't do it, Trey," begged Greg, his eyes beginning to tear up again. "It's too big. It's gonna eat you."

Trey watched his friend and almost called him a crybaby, but then he laughed. "It's not gonna eat me, Greg. Don't get your panties in a wad. I got everything under control." He reached up and punched his friend in the shoulder. "Hey. Trust me."

By the look in the smaller boy's eyes, he could tell that any sense of trust was being smothered by fear. Trey cocked his head, winked hard, then, after another count of three, descended back down the piling.

In no time, he had the rod and line unattached from the piling. He was about to ascend to the surface when he was jerked impossibly hard. Trey flew through the water plunging deeper and deeper. He had gone fifty feet by the time he thought to let go of the rod. Even after he released it, the incredible momentum continued his propulsion towards the bottom. The pressure on his head was becoming incredible, feeling like a knife being thrust into the center of his brain. Something within his mind, however, kept him from screaming and releasing the precious air he needed to survive.

Finally, his descent slowed. Trey glanced upwards and like a lighter darkness, could glimpse the faraway surface. Or what he thought was the surface. He was too deep, deeper than he had ever been before. Trying hard not to panic, he began to ascend, as slowly as possible because of the immense pressure being exerted upon his body. He achieved only a few feet before he felt his ascent halt as something gripped each ankle painfully.

Trey stared down and watched in horror as the viney weeds wrapped around his ankle. In the almost darkness, he watched as two more moved for him like tentacles from some great beast, encircling his wrists and pulling his arms out hard. Many more waved below, as if beckoning him deeper. The decaying corpses of a hundred fish stared back at him, as did the skulls, picked clean and gleaming.

Trey thrashed, attempting to free himself from the living weed, realizing he was quickly running out of air. Yet as his air depleted, instead of his vision dimming, he saw the water brightening. Although he was very deep, he could now see through the water like it was near the surface and clear. A figure came into his vision, rising gradually from the depths beneath him. The only movement was the minute openings and closings of the mouth and the almost intelligent wavings of its long whiskers. When the catfish was even with his head and staring straight into his eyes, it opened its mouth wide revealing a mouthful of smallish teeth and rows of pulsating gills. Trey slammed his eyes shut, jerking at his bonds. He refused to see what was about to eat him and felt the warmth of urine seep from his water-shriveled penis. When the first of the whiskers brushed against his face, he screamed, releasing all of his air, condemning him to death.

He finally even lost enough strength to scream and his body reflexively went to suck in the brackish water of the lake, filling his lungs with what he could never breathe... but it didn't happen that way. Trey felt a warmth along his face and neck, flowing into his chest. A calmness filled him, stilling his panic and his need to breathe. Slowly, Trey opened his eyes to stare into the bottomless eyes of the catfish. His fear had left him and he watched as the whiskers, dozens of them, caressed his skin. The mouth opened and closed and he couldn't help but admire the synchronicity of the gills.

Trey hung in the water, held fast by the weeds, staring into the huge maw of a fish that he had wanted to catch. The need to breathe had departed him and he wondered if he had drowned. He wondered if he was dead.

Perhaps

The voice was in his head and filled him with the fullness of love. It was the same feeling as when Guinn had told him she loved him for the first time. Every part of his body had been filled with the heavy electric feeling of happiness. If this was death, he wanted more of it.

Love is a wonderful thing. It is life.

'Yes, it is,' he felt himself thinking. 'It transcends death. Makes life good living', as his grandfather had said. He realized, without panic and as if it was utterly sane, that the fish was speaking to him.

'Am I dead?' he asked.

Perhaps, came the same reply.

'How am I breathing?'

You are not.

'Then I am dead.' Although he said it, the thought held no terror for him.

Perhaps.

'Why do you keep saying that? Why do you keep saying *perhaps*?'

The choice is yours.

The answer confused Trey. Maybe the fish was mad for his attempts to catch him. Even with the love pervading his body, he laughed at the insanity of the concept. How could a fish be mad? How could it have feelings? Still...

'Are you angry?'

No. It is the way of the world.

'To hunt you, to kill you?'

It is the way.

'Then what is the choice you speak of?'

Would you die for me?

'For you?'

Trey was sure he didn't understand the question. Die for a fish? For a catfish? Why should he give his life up for a... but it wasn't just a fish. Could a fish do this? Trey remembered what Greg had said about the Catfish Gods. It was stupid, but he was alive and not breathing. Only a God could make that happen. He didn't know what to say. Trey thought of Billy Prescott. Had he been asked the question? Had he answered wrong?

'I don't understand.'

Would you die for me?

Trey stared hard at the fish hovering in the water before him, tender whiskers caressing his cheeks. It was easily more than a hundred pounds. Maybe ten times that. Its eyes were bottomless black pools, but held strange warmth. Trey could not deny its majesty. It was magnificent. It would be perfect above the mantle of any fireplace, eclipsing the largest swordfish. It would make a bass of any size appear to be a pathetic minnow.

Trey knew his answer was important, but he knew, as well, that the fish understood his every thought.

'Why should I die for you? I don't understand.' He stole himself for death, but pleaded desperately for an answer.

Because I would die for you.

The answer surprised him. A fish like this, powerful, magical... a Catfish God... would die for him? Truly, he was nothing special. Sure, he felt himself important, but in the greater world picture, he was nothing. What would make this catfish die for him? He knew his mother would die for him. He knew his father would as well. And his grandfather, the old man wouldn't hesitate. Till this day, as he was kneeling before the casket, Trey had never told anyone that he had begged God to take him instead; to let his grandfather live again. If he died now... if he was to perish down in the depths of Chicamaugua Reservoir... maybe then he could see his grandfather again. Maybe he could make him some more martinis as the old man lorded over the world. Maybe he would see him smile.

Trey stared deep into the eyes of the fish, alien, but mysteriously human, searching for the answer. There, among the blackness, he saw the same look that Guinn, his mother, his father, his grandfather, even Greg on occasion, had given him. It was the feeling that pervaded his being. Instead of drowning, instead of feeling the quick burning warmth of a lungful of watery death, he felt the warmth of love. Unconditional and pure, it was there for him, just for being alive. Would grandfather want him to die for him? He pictured the old man's tall John Wayne features and knew the answer.

'Yes. I would die for you.'

Then you understand. Go in peace and live long.

The firm grip of the weeds suddenly released him and Trey felt himself floating towards the surface. He watched the imperious figure of the Catfish God until it had became one with the shadowy depths. It wasn't until his head bobbed to the surface that his body contracted and jackknifed. He automatically relented and allowed his body to breathe in the sweetness of the putrid, yet life-giving air of the dock.

"Trey. Trey. Trey," came the jubilant shouts.

He glanced up and saw Greg, cheeks puffy and hair matted as if the storm had come and gone. His eyes were as red as his hair and his voice held the hoarseness of a widow.

"Trey. I thought you were dead," said the boy, tears renewing their slalom through his freckles. "It's been hours."

"Hours?" asked Trey absently as he levered himself into the boat. He examined the sky and noticed the sun setting.

"I... I couldn't leave. I... I thought you were dead. I didn't know what to tell people."

Trey stared at his friend openly with a fondness that hadn't been there before. Greg noticed it and his eyes widened. Then his face went serious and he wiped his cheeks.

"How can you be alive?"

Trey shook his head. "I have no idea, man. All I know right now is that I love you for waiting."

"Yecch," Greg said, poking his tongue between his lips and smiling. "You gay or something?"

Trey looked off toward the community dock and began to paddle. "Naw. Just happy to be here."

His grandpa used to say that.

SOME THINGS WERE BETTER OFF NOT TALKED ABOUT

BY DAVID WHITMAN

*"*They say Judgment Day is gonna be here soon," Judd said, staring at his burning marshmallow. "Jesus is coming, and he's pissed as hell. He's gonna stomp us out like a bunch of rats." With that final statement, he extinguished the fire from his marshmallow with a puff of exhaled air.

His friends stared at the smoking marshmallow for a moment as if it held deep and profound truths, the flames of the campfire flickering across their faces dramatically. They let Judd's words sink in and all sighed at what seemed to be the same time.

Judd sat back with a scholarly look of feigned intellect on his face, feeling that he had impressed his friends with his observation.

Max farted loudly. "That is the biggest crock of shit. Man, Jesus ain't coming nowhere. That hippie looking dude is probably up there surfing the clouds on some sort of rainbow colored surfboard."

Kenny Joe and Bailey Butler started laughing simultaneously in redneck stereo, their impressive bellies shaking with mirth. This really angered Judd who felt what Max had just done was sacrilegious.

"Go on, make fun," Judd hissed. "You'll see when Jesus comes down and takes your ass come Judgment Day. You won't be making jokes then-you'll be on your knees crying like a little schoolgirl. You're my best friend and all, Max, but there will be nothing I can do to save your ass."

Max snorted up some phlegm and spit it into the campfire. "It ain't my fault they paint Jesus in the pictures to look like some blue eyed guitar player rock star. Hell, if I see Jesus I'll hand him a guitar and ask His Holiness to play me a couple of rock riffs or maybe a little Spanish flavored groove."

Judd actually smiled at their laughter this time. "Go on, keep digging your hole. I can already feel the devil getting your room ready."

Max spit again. "Shit. If Jesus don't have no sense of humor, I don't want no part of him."

Kenny Joe nodded. "One only has to look at my ex-wife and see that Jesus must have a sense of humor, bro. Hell, I ain't never missed a day of church in my life. What did that get me? A big fat slut. And not only was she fat, she was evil."

Bailey nodded emphatically. "I must agree."

Judd just shook his head and tried not to laugh. Sometimes he craved a little more than these types of conversations. A talk on Judgment Day had just degenerated into the disgustingly witty observation, 'not only was she fat, she was evil.' He sighed and walked towards the tent. "I'm going to sleep. This is tiresome."

Max smirked at his friend. "Well, you have to admit, Judd. If Jesus could play the guitar, that sumbitch would be fantastic."

Judd sighed again and pulled off his jeans. *Sometimes Max just tries to bug me on purpose,* he thought as he adjusted his boxers. He heard the sound of one of the guys popping a beer can as he wiggled into his sleeping bag.

Something slid up his leg, slithered slowly around his balls, and then came to rest. He knew what it was without putting his hand in his pants as he felt the cold, scaly skin against his own warm flesh.

Trying his best to remain calm, Judd tried to shout out, "Max!" but it came out as a kitten-like squeak. After a few minutes, he managed to yell his friend's name loud enough to get his attention.

Max stepped into the tent. "I ain't your maid, Judd. If you want a damn beer get it your own goddamn self."

"Max, go get the lantern."

Max moved closer to Judd.

"Don't come any closer!" Judd hissed. "Just get the lantern. There is a snake wrapped around my balls."

"You're kidding, right?"

"Get the lantern!" Judd exclaimed, trying hard not to upset the snake, which he felt coiling around his testicles.

"Is it a big one? Can't be that big."

"Oh my fucking motherfucking god."

Max exited the tent muttering, "Okay, okay, jeez."

"Don't tell Kenny Joe and Bailey," Judd called out, knowing full well the brothers were already being told.

Five minutes later, they were standing around Judd's sleeping bag looking at him the way men looked at their dying comrade in those old war movies. There were tears going down Judd's face.

"Oh now, don't cry," Max said. "We'll figure something out."

"If that snake is poisonous, you're screwed, bro," Kenny Joe said, looking down his friend as if he was already dead.

"I must agree," Bailey said.

"You two aren't helping any!" Judd hissed, cringing as the snake tightened around his testicles, squeezing them.

"It's probably not even poisonous," Max suggested, watching his friend's ashen face in the lantern light. "Probably just some garden snake. Did it rattle?"

"I don't think so," Judd said. "But you know my hearing has been screwed all day since Kenny Joe blew off that shotgun too close to my ear."

"Sorry about that," Kenny Joe said, looking genuinely remorseful as he stared down at the crotch area of the bulky sleeping bag.

Judd's eyes widened as the snake circled around his penis and he tried to hide his embarrassment as the physical movement brought him to a semi-erection. "Oh dear Lord, I'm being punished for what you said about Jesus. I'm going to die in this tent."

"That's just stupid," Max said. "It'd be my dick that snake would be around then."

Kenny Joe stepped back a little. "The Lord, he works in mysterious ways."

"I must agree," Bailey said, poking his finger into his round belly.

Judd tried his best not to scream at the top of his lungs. "Can you two please get the hell out?"

Max stepped forward. "Ok, Judd. I'm going to try and pull the sleeping bag off of you, maybe then we can at least see the bugger and get him out."

Judd grimaced as the snake moved yet again. "Okay, but do it slow, man. This is my life we're playing with here."

Kenny Joe and Bailey stood together, their breathing held in check as they watched Max approach the sleeping bag. Max looked like a soldier entering battle, teeth clenched, his face a mask of grim determination.

Judd bit his lip as Max gently pulled the sleeping bag off his body.

A rattling sound emitted from between Judd's legs.

"Oh my god," Judd whispered. "You may as well just kill me now. It's a rattler."

Max just mouthed 'Oh God' over and over as he stared down at the sleeping bag. "You know I'm scared of snakes. Oh god. Should I keep pulling?"

Judd nodded, a bead of sweat running down his forehead. Max took a deep breath and cautiously pulled the sleeping bag from his friend.

The snake rattled again.

All the men stopped breathing, too scared to exhale. Max didn't stop though, he continued his mission bravely. A half a minute later, he had the sleeping bag down just over the crotch of Judd's undulating boxers.

"That shit wouldn't have happened had you worn briefs like a real man," Kenny Joe observed.

"It looks like his dick is taking on a mind of its own," Bailey added.

Judd didn't even hear them. Instead he looked down at his crotch in pure terror, his sweat-drenched face dripping down his neck.

The snake squirmed around in his boxers as if it was trying to get comfortable. For a brief second, the snake poked its head out of the hole and stared at the men with unblinking eyes, its forked tongue flickering around menacingly. It vanished back inside. The small rattle sack was sticking out of Judd's boxers just so.

"I'm going to try and pull it the hell out," Max said, as he heard both Kenny Joe and Bailey exhale in fear. "This is going to be downright scary. For one thing, what am I supposed to after I've pulled the damn thing out? Kenny Joe, go grab that bitch-be-quick-stick."

The bitch-be-quick-stick was Max's lucky walking cane. He brought it with him on every outdoor excursion he could, using it to make clearings and even sometimes kill snakes that scared the hell out of him by slithering in his path. Kenny Joe returned in seconds with the stick.

Max held it in his hands, feeling its power. "Okay, Judd. I'm going to pull this thing, but quick. We can only hope she don't bite you."

The only sound that could be heard was the crackling of the campfire. Max reached slowly towards the rattle that stuck out from Judd's crotch, his fingers shaking in the air.

"God, god, god, god," Judd chanted as Max's fingers came dangerously close to the snake's tail.

"Get ready, Judd," Max said, his fingers only inches from the rattle. "I'm gonna pull this bastard away from you."

With a flash of speed, Max wrenched the snake away.

Judd shrieked and curled up into a fetal position.

Max tossed the snake into the corner of the tent and whacked it with the bitch-be-quick-stick as his friend screamed. Within seconds, the small rattlesnake was nothing but a bleeding mass of bone and flesh.

"It bit me on my dick!" Judd shrieked as the men's faces instantly lost all blood and went totally white. "My dick! I'm fucking dead! I can already feel it killing me."

"Oh shit," Max exclaimed, his knees nearly buckling out from underneath him. "What the hell we gonna do? It will take at least an hour to get you to any hospital."

Kenny Joe knew what Max had to do. "You're gonna have to suck the poison out, bro."

"I must agree," Bailey said, staring down at Judd's shaking form.

"No...goddamn...way," Max said, shocked to his core at the suggestion.

"Fucking bit me in the dick!" Judd shrieked. "Fucking dying! Fucking help!"

Max shook his head. "I can't even believe I'm considering this. Sucking another man's dick. Oh Christ, I can't."

"We won't tell anyone, Max," Kenny Joe said, as his brother nodded. "You got to save Judd, that sure as hell won't make you no fag."

Max nodded, his stomach wrenching. What a night this had turned out to be. "Judd, I'm going to have to suck that poison out."

Judd stopped crying. His face seemed to drop to an even whiter shade than before. "Uh...what?"

"If I don't suck it out, you're gonna die."

Judd put his hand over his by now hugely swollen penis. "No way, man. Screw that shit."

Max looked at the enlarged member. "Look, you think I want to do this? Now don't be an asshole and let me suck your dick." He paused for a moment. "Uh...did I just say that? What I meant to say was I can't just sit here and let you die."

Judd shook his head violently. "Max, you ain't gonna suck my dick and that's final. I can't even believe we are having this conversation."

Kenny Joe coughed and pulled a buck knife from his pocket. "Well, there is one other way."

Judd nodded, sweat dribbling down his neck and into his drenched shirt. "I'd rather have the thing cut off then have it sucked by my best friend."

Max sighed heavily. "Man, you are insane."

Kenny Joe opened the knife and wiped it off on his pants. "Look, after we cut it off we can just rush him to the hospital. We can put it on ice and maybe they can get the poison out and save it."

Bailey waved his arms as if he had an idea. "Hey! Remember that Old Pete's wife? Aren't they camping about twenty minutes away? Maybe she'll suck it out! She may be an old hag, but I'm sure it's like riding a bike. She probably get the poison out, but quick. And it's gotta be a plus that she got no teeth, right?"

There was silence in the tent as they all just stood there looking at Bailey.

Kenny Joe walked over to where Judd's penis jutted out of his boxers. "Okay, Judd. Let's do this quick."

Judd screamed. "Wait! Can't I at least get some ice on this fucker? Christ, man, what the hell do you think I'm made of? This shit's going to hurt!"

Max ran out and came back in with a handful of ice. Judd winced and bit his lip as the ice began to take effect.

"I once knew this woman who did some amazing things with ice," Bailey said, curling his mustache as he studied the swollen penis. "This reminds me of that."

Once again, there was silence in the tent.

Judd held his penis out. "Okay, let's get this over with."

Kenny Joe put the knife against the penis as every man in the tent winced and unconsciously held their crotch.

Then he began to saw.

Judd screamed so loud that Max felt his eardrum had exploded. "What the are you doing, asshole! Don't fucking saw it! OH MY GOD *OW!*"

Blood ran down Judd's fingers and into the ice. Bailey walked out of the tent and vomited into the grass.

Judd snatched the knife from Kenny Joe's hand. "Give me that! I'll do it!" He put the knife to his bleeding penis and held his breath. "Oh god, I can't do it. Fuck it, Max. Suck the poison out."

Max grimaced. "You sure, man? I'm not so sure I can do this now that I been thinking about it. It will make me feel queer. Not just queer as in fag, but queer odd."

"What, and you think I want you to do this?" Judd asked, rubbing his bleeding penis with a piece of ice.

Max looked like he was about to cry. "This is a nightmare." He looked over at Kenny Joe. "Go grab me that Jack Daniels."

Kenny Joe left the tent and returned instantly with the half-full bottle of JD. Max took it and drank hungrily, bubbles shooting up in the bottle. He handed it to Judd who also took a heavy sip.

Max got down on his knees and leaned over the swollen penis, his stomach feeling as if a little fat man was disco dancing around inside. He looked for the fang holes, gritted his teeth, and closed his eyes before bringing his mouth to Judd's member.

Judd looked down at the top of his friend's head and cried. The sight of his best friend's face buried in his crotch was the most disturbing thing he had ever seen.

Kenny Joe and Bailey peeked into the tent forty-five seconds later and watched the surreal sight of one of the most macho men they knew giving a blow job. It took Bailey two weeks to stop shuddering when he thought about it.

"That's just wrong," Kenny Joe said, wanting to turn away, but watching anyway. "There ain't no way we can keep this to ourselves."

"I must agree," Bailey said, nodding his head up and down rapidly.

Two weeks later, the whole town had heard about the snake situation. Max and Judd never spoke of the incident again, although they would beat half to death anyone who brought it up. Some things were better off not talked about.

THE APPALACHIAN EASTER OUTHOUSE FEUD

BY WESTON OCHSE

"It'd been your Grandpa Jessup's idea to put the outhouse on top of the *Hell Hole*. On account of the Easter of '46, of course. After the long battle, he'd gotten sorely drunk, ramblin' on about them Nazis and them *Eye-talians*. You see, he'd hoped that after the Big War he'd be able to stop fightin'. He said he'd seen enough killin' to last him two lifetimes. Why, he was so busy walkin' from Sicily to Berlin that he'd almost forgotten about *The Feud*. And then he come home on Ash Wednesday and all the preparations was in gear — he was sure pissed. Grandpa Jessup had thought his fightin' days was over, so his goal was to make the Devil eat shit."

Jimmy Lee glanced sidelong at his Granny as she paused to take a medicinal swig from a small silver flask. Even old and shriveled with skin drawn tight against the bones, she was the toughest woman he'd ever heard of or seen. And he'd even been to the city once.

"Well, after the battle was over, even before the smoke had cleared, he ordered your uncles to go and drag the old outhouse back from behind the barn and bring it into the ravine. Them boys, your uncles, was hootin' and hollerin'. They knew what your Grandpa was up to. Even the Whitmires joined in and they passed around jugs and jugs of their *special* brew, if you know what I mean. Well, when they placed the outhouse over the hole, Grandpa made sure he was the first one to take a dump. He grunted and groaned so loud that everyone on both sides was laughing until their teeth hurt. Then he up and came out and told everyone he had been so tired of taking the Devil's shit that he felt it was only right to give a little back. It was a regular Hoot n' Annie with everyone singing and dancing and taking their turns trying to fill up the hole. Why, in as long as I can remember, it was the first time that the Whitmires and the Wheatons had gotten together for anything but a fight."

Jimmy Lee grinned and practiced his aim on the dozens of crosses the women had painted on the outhouse during the special ceremony they'd had on Ash Wednesday. Some of the crosses he didn't even recognize, but he'd heard they were ancient and never really used anymore.

"... and so to this day, we always build an outhouse after every battle and the day after Easter is nothin' but one long party. And it was all 'cause of your Grandpa, God rest his soul."

He remembered last year's party when he and Annie Whitmire had snuck up the slope with their own jug and she had showed him her titties. Even let him touch them — once. He tried to spy her out on the opposite slope, but couldn't see her anywhere. She was up there though. She had to be. Everyone was. It was the agreement. They was tellin' the same story over there, being as this was *The Tellin' Time*.

"Jimmy Lee?"

"Yeah, Granny," said the blonde boy.

"See that sassyfras down there? It's blockin' your Granny's aim a bit. Think you can scoot down there and make it go away?"

"Be too easy, Granny," said Jimmy Lee. He laid his rifle aside and readied himself for the run.

"Don't you let them Whitmire's get the best of you boy," said Granny Wheaton eyeing along the blue-metal of the old .44 caliber pistol she held in a two-handed grip.

Jimmy Lee jumped up, his machete held tightly in his left hand, and leapt over the log they were hiding behind. He skipped down the embankment screeching a rebel yell, sending even the most curious squirrel back up and into its nest in fear of being the next tail on a hat. Momentum and gravity soon sent him ass-over-tea-kettle through the sapling sassafras and hip-high ferns. He finally tumbled to a stop, upside down and grinning against the side of the wooden outhouse, somehow managing not to slice off an arm or a leg or an ear with the machete he'd managed to hold onto.

On the other side of the ravine, Granny spied young Quinten Whitmire loping down to meet her grandson, a Louisville slugger swinging in great arcs over his head as he made his way to the bottom.

"Quinten," she yelled. "You get your scrawny ass back up there and leave my grandson be or I'm gonna put a hole in you that even your Ma can't sew up."

"You harm my boy and I'm gonna do the same to you," came a shriek from the other side of the ravine.

Quinten had almost reached the bottom and even Granny could see the poor boy's too-close-together eyes dance with excitement. She knew that what he lacked in smarts, he more than made up for in size. Jimmy Lee had scrambled a third of the way back up the hill and was already hacking at the arm-sized trunk of the sassafras that was blocking his Granny's sight-picture. It was amazing it had grown up so large in a year. Must have been all that shit that made it grow so fast.

Quinten yelled and launched himself up the hill at Jimmy Lee just as the machete separated the slender trunk. Jimmy Lee grabbed the unwieldy bush and hurled it back into the face of his onrushing cousin, then turned and began scrambling back up the slope toward Granny. Quinten was faster and surer of foot, though. He planted his boot in the center of Jimmy Lee's back and lifted the Louisville Slugger above his head. He was preparing to bring it down when it exploded in a shower of nasty, sharp fragments. The sound of Granny's shot caught up to it a moment later. Quinten staggered back a few steps, giving Jimmy Lee the chance to crest the hill in a rush, slipping breathlessly beside Granny.

"Quinten!" came the shriek from across the ravine.

The big boy turned and fell to his knees, his hand going first to his throat, then his chest, before his head bounced softly on the loamy earth.

"My boy. You shot my boy!"

Over two dozen men and women popped up from behind

the bushes and trees on the other side of the ravine and fired. The thunderous cavalcade of buckshot, subsonic lead and high-powered bullets sliced through branches, bark and logs. Splinters and huge chunks of wood flew from the front of the large log Granny and Jimmy Lee were hunched behind. The fusillade lasted a full half a minute before it finally stopped. Echoes of the assault reverberated back and forth within the ravine until they finally slipped away, leaving only the sound of falling leaves and branches.

From behind a large boulder came a tall man dressed in a black turn-of-the-century priest's robe, which fit tightly from shoulders to hips, flaring like a dress to the ground.

"Stop this nonsense, you fools. Look. The boy's fine."

All eyes went to Quinten, who was dusting the leaves off his pants and picking up the fragments of his bat. They watched as he stacked the broken segments, like pieces of kindling, in the crux of an arm and headed back up his family's side of the ravine.

Granny chuckled and spit out a thin stream of tobacco spit. "If I was gonna shoot the boy, Gladys, I would have shot him. You know I don't miss."

Gladys rushed out from behind her tree and met her son as he crested the rise.

"You okay, boy?"

"Yeah," said the boy with a wide, toothless grin.

"Don't yeah me, boy. And don't you scare your ma like that again."

The smack of Gladdys's hand on Quinten's face sounded like another gunshot, bringing out every hidden cousin on both sides of the ravine — almost a hundred people aiming weapons and hateful grins at each other.

"Enough of this. Jacob, you over there?" said the priest, standing imperiously behind Granny.

"Sure am, David," said an identically dressed man from the Whitmire side.

"Then let's get this started. It's almost time anyway," David said eyeing the outhouse fearfully. He cleared his throat and climbed onto the log. Men, women and children knelt and lowered their heads solemnly. David cleared his throat one more time and eyed the kneeling figures of the families before he began.

"Our Lord God has once again brought these two families together in his time of need. By his great wisdom and divine understanding, he selected these clans for a higher purpose. A purpose that has caused them to, for a short time, lay aside their differences and their hates. A purpose that holds the fate of the world as hostage. A purpose that has brought these two mighty tribes here this day to fight evil as one family. Let us pray... "

Jacob continued from the other side, his voice carrying clearly in the crisp mountain air.

"Dear Lord, bless us as we, your humble servants, are about to embark on a mission of destruction."

"Lord hear our prayer," came the reply from every mouth.

"Dear Lord, bless us on the day of your Son's death, for the great weakness of the human spirit that has crippled the barriers between this, your holy place and the other unnameable one."

"Lord, hear our prayer."

"Dear Lord, bless us on this day of rejuvenation and give us the strength to conquer the great evil."

"May the Lord be with us."

From both sides, everyone stood and moved to their respective priest who laid hands on each person, each weapon, until even the smallest child had received the blessing. Then as one, all trained their weapons on the lonely outhouse hunched on the empty floor of the ravine and waited.

The first indication was when the birds and the bugs and even the cicadas fell silent. Then it was ten more minutes of waiting, where the loudest sound was your own heartbeat and every trigger finger quivered in anticipation.

Suddenly, the entire outhouse began rattling for what seemed a full minute, threatening to burst the boards. Then, just as suddenly as it had started, it stilled.

Jimmy Lee peered down the length of his 30-30.

He wasn't aiming at the outhouse. He had his own sector to shoot in at the base of their side of the ravine. And if any of them evil bastards entered it, he was gonna make them wish they hadn't.

The door flew off its hinges with a loud shriek and the tiny ones poured through. They were about two feet high and hard as hell to hit. When they landed on the ground, they shrieked like crows and headed in every direction. From the corner of his vision, Jimmy Lee figured there must have been at least a hundred of the little bastards. The first several shots rang out, but Jimmy Lee didn't look. Ten of the little devils were heading towards his sector and he felt his lips go dry.

The sounds of gunfire increased and Jimmy Lee added his own beat to the deadly staccato song. He worked the lever of the old rifle like a wild-west cowboy, taking the first in the head, the second in the throat and the third in the stomach. Each one threw up its tiny hands just like a real person. When the bullets passed through their tough little bodies, they were hurled back and black smelly shit bubbled out of their smoking husks. It was their blood and the thick stench was already drifting up and out of the killing ground.

Regular bullets didn't work. They'd found that out the first battle and their lack of preparation had almost killed them and sent the hordes crawling across the Earth. It was the silver that had been soaking in holy water for nearly a week that did the damage.

Preacher Man said their bodies couldn't take it.

Preacher Man said they was like werewolves that way.

Jimmy Lee missed with his next two shots, but found his aim again and brought five more down. When his sector was empty he stole a look at the rest of the battle and saw the little demons getting thrown back — twisting, dying and finally transforming into obscene piles of hell-spawned fertilizer.

Granny said it was what the white men did when they came that had started everything. She said the Injuns had been *one with the land*. And then the white men came and started killing everything and everyone. It was a Cherokee Chief that had finally gotten fed up and worked some strange magic. It was supposed to clear the white men out of the hills. And it did — but it also unleashed a demonic horde that killed everyone who had set foot in them for a hundred years. It was a long time before the land had finally been freed of Satan's Horde.

A piercing scream erupted from the depths below the outhouse and Jimmy Lee winced, his ears threatening to pop. He tightened his grip on the Winchester and tried to keep his aim on his sector.

Finally, the roof splintered and blew apart as dozens of large winged creatures surged toward the sky. Their green skin was pulled tight over human-shaped bodies and oozed pus that fell back to the earth in sizzling patches, killing everything it touched. Their immense batwings glowed as the noon sun poured through them detailing each vein, artery and delicate bone.

Granny emptied her pistol into one attempting to fly over and drop its gelatinous acid. The creature fell with a multi-octave scream and Jimmy Lee joined his Granny in a smile at the satisfying crunch the ground provided the demon's delicate, deadly structure. Granny jerked a speed loader from her cleavage and reloaded the smoking chambers. She shot a wad of tobacco spit toward the downed demon and rejoined the fray.

Across the ravine Ernie Whitmire was running in a circle, succeeding only in fanning the flames of his shirt. Beside him was a dead avian demon that had erupted into its own unholy bonfire. Jimmy Lee felt Granny's hand push him low and he heard the explosion of the one she'd shot.

He yelled his thanks, then rose and took out two more of the little ones, who had been sneaking up the hill in a low crawl. They tumbled back down, turning into rolling mounds of shit before they *squelched* to a stop at the bottom.

Jimmy Lee heard a new humming below the gunfire and demonic screams. He shuddered and realized the Super Maggots were coming — big horkin' maggots covered with ugly purple fur that were deceptively fast. "Like corn through a coon hound," his Grandpa had said. They could squirm up to you and take your leg off with their acidic mucus before you even had chance to feel the pain. Jimmy Lee's older brother, Josh, had lost an arm last year pulling one off his already-dead cousin, Odd Todd. And if you listened to their hum long enough, you were sure to become hypnotized. Preacher Man said it was like sonar — like what bats do.

The first Appalachian Cocktail arced through the air from the Whitmire side and hit the outhouse. The glass shattered and the crumbling wood was suddenly coated in a sheet of white-lightning fire. Soon the air was filled with dozens of the glistening bombs and the floor of the ravine was a lake of burning moonshine. Jimmy Lee stared as fifteen of the Super Maggots escaped and headed straight for the log he and Grandma were using as cover. He fired round after round into the hairy beasts until his chamber clicked empty. Cursing, he fumbled for his box of shells. He started reloading his last six as Granny and the rest of the clan alternated their fire from the air to the ground and back.

Without warning, Granny screamed and fell face first into the log, shattering the left side of her bifocals. Jimmy Lee swung his Winchester around and fired twice, downing the avian that had somehow made it through the barrage and dropped a handful of acid on Granny's back. The dead avian fell behind Jimmy Lee and started smoking immediately. He rolled his body over his Granny's and let the ground smother the fire on her back. He felt hope when he saw her chest move, but he had no time. He had to get Granny away before the avian exploded.

Jimmy Lee dropped his rifle, grabbed her under her arms and started pulling her backwards, wondering how the hell such a small woman weighed so damn much. He got only a few feet before he tripped and fell back hard, bouncing his head on the hard Tennessee clay. And then the humming became seriously louder.

Three worms suddenly appeared atop the log, their eyeless heads lifting as if smelling his incapacitation. Jimmy struggled to rise, but his Granny had fallen on his legs. He hunted desperately for the rifle and spied it laying by Granny's feet — too far and out of reach. The worms descended hungrily, heading straight for the two of them.

Jimmy screamed like a girl.

A long black cloak brushed past, temporarily blocking his

vision. The Preacher Man aimed from the hip and streams of holy water shot from the end of an orange and green Super Soaker. Each worm burst into a gout of purple fire as the Preacher Man screamed divine condemnation. Their savior fired until his plastic cannon was empty then paused to admire his handy work. Jimmy's mouth, still opened in an unleashed scream, closed as the Preacher Man turned, winked and headed for another part of the battlefield — just a little too wild-eyed for a man of God.

There were four more waves of demons, but Jimmy Lee hadn't seen them. Everyone was too busy and his Granny was weighing him down, so he had just lain there and prayed. He heard the Ground Pounders come, but they were such big targets that even his little six-year-old sister Suzy Lee had no trouble hitting one. She even stood on top of the log, firing her Uzi like she was a Middle Eastern-born rag-wearing terrorist. Since they couldn't aim too good, the automatic weapons were always given to the little kids. And after Jimmy Lee shot Uncle John John in the ass that time, the kids were placed up front.

The sun had set hours ago and just a few still-smoking trees were the only signs of another successful battle; not to mention the hundreds of piles of shit that covered the ground like mines.

Jimmy Lee finally found Annie Whitmire. She was already a little tipsy and he grinned in anticipation. Maybe he'd get more than just a feel this year. Maybe they could roll in the weeds.

She stood in the growing crowd of cousins surrounding the brand new outhouse that had just been placed over the hole. About a dozen banjoes and at least three dulcimers were hammering out a version of *Go Tell Aunt Rhodie.* All the cousins wore different sized smiles — winning was never a sure thing. Everyone was relieved it was finally over.

A hush fell on the crowd and a path opened near Jimmy Lee. Granny walked stoically by, pausing to give him a big hug. She stood back and smiled and he felt warm pride well up in his body. She was proud of him for saving her. Everyone loved Granny, and no one more than him. Maybe they'd write a song about him. Maybe he'd be famous.

Jimmy Lee smiled back, then doubled over in pain as she sunk a tiny, hard fist into his stomach. As he gasped for breath and fell to one knee he heard her reprimand, "Never leave your rifle, boy."

The crowd erupted with laughter and all Jimmy Lee could do was grin sheepishly. Granny continued toward the outhouse, pausing only once to hitch up her gun belt then entered the small structure. It was her due as the oldest surviving member of the clans to consecrate the victory.

Uncle John John limped to the front of the door and raised his arms. The two clans silenced and waited solemnly.

Then, like the imperious voice of Satan himself came the clear, thunderous sound of his Granny. The noise of her defecation filled the ravine and surrounded the two clans in a warm embrace. The older ones remembering Grandpa Wheaton, nodded and smiled.

Granny exited with a hitch of her jeans and a face filled with pride. She received congratulations from Whitmire and Wheaton alike. This was the true end of *The Feud*. The line formed to the right and people started pushing and jockeying for position. Many had been saving up for days and were dancing with impacted plumbing. Jimmy Lee eyed the line and guessed he had at least a two-hour wait. He headed off for a jug of the Whitmire Special.

It wasn't long before he saw Annie standing alone. She leaned against a tree trying to act innocent and vulnerable and coy. Jimmy Lee smiled a little drunkenly as he watched her twirl her long yellow pony-tails. His Granny had told him to watch out for this kind of stuff. He almost turned and left, but the memory of last year's *feel* took control of his feet. Just then, however, Quinten stepped squarely in his path. Jimmy Lee watched as the bigger boy's mouth struggled to form words.

The inbred Whitmire never got the chance. Jimmy Lee swung the empty jug and caught the boy on the side of the head. The jug cracked and broke into three large pieces as Quinten sagged to the ground. Jimmy Lee stepped around him and strode up to Annie, ready for a hero's welcome. His leer changed to a frown as he noticed her frightened stare at something over his shoulder.

Jimmy Lee spun. Quinten was on the ground jerking and shaking like he was having some kind of fit.

"What have you done to my boy now, Jimmy Lee?" came Quinten's mother's squeaky voice as she ran up to her trembling son.

A crowd began to form. Purple-tinged froth oozed out of Quinten's mouth and several people shrieked.

"Oh My Easter Hell! Get the Preacher Men. The boy's possessed!"

It wasn't half a minute before Preacher Jacob and Preacher David each arrived, a dripping Super Soaker in each hand.

"Strip him," commanded David and three men held the boy down while his mother ripped off his clothes.

Now, Jimmy Lee noticed that the purple bile was also seeping out of the shaking boy's ass. Several of the cousins crossed themselves and backed away. There was always one that got it after every Feud. *The Devil's sneaky like that,* his Grandpa had said, and it was Quinten this time. Jimmy Lee shuddered. It could have just as easily been him.

Jacob and David began shouting their prayers for exorcism and their unison voices filled the night. Quinten's scream of pain as one Super Soaker was rammed up his ass and the other into his mouth added a high-pitched edge to the eerie chanting. His scream hit critical mass when the Preacher Men began to pump the holy water in.

Jimmy turned and grabbed Annie around the waist. He'd seen enough. Quinten would be fine after a few more pints.

Or quarts.

Or gallons.

CARRYIN' ON LIKE IT WAS THE END OF THE WORLD

BY DAVID WHITMAN

"Great godawmighty," Kenny Joe whispered, wincing at the horror before him.

Judd was lying face down on a table, an ominous looking machine suspended above him. A long, thick metallic shaft ran from the machine and deeply into his ass. Blue lightning streaks were streaming from a basketball-sized metallic ball on the top. A leather-like strap was wrapped around his head and in his mouth, giving him a terrifying appearance. He looked like a reject from an amateur porn bondage video gone seriously bad. Judd looked at his three friends in a manner that could only be described as horrified, eyes pleading. To the left of the machine were dozens of buttons and controls.

It had been a fantastic evening of fishing and drinking right up until they had seen the brilliant light and heard the incredible roar of engines. Now they found themselves trapped onboard this spaceship after a brief and violent war with their captors. Max still got the shudders when he thought of Kenny Joe in that tank like a museum display, his huge plaid belly pushing up against the glass, threatening to smash it open. Luckily, those little bug-eyed bastards died easily. His heart was jumping around in his chest like an electrified frog.

"Great godawmighty," Kenny Joe repeated.

Judd squeaked in an angry monkey-like chatter.

Max jerked at the strap around Judd's head, trying hopelessly to ignore the pole suspended above and where it was going. "Can you hear me, buddy?"

More angry chatter answered the question as Max tried to remove the binding that ran around his friend's skull. Bailey handed him his fishing knife. Max cut it quickly, throwing it to the side.

"Oh my motherfucking *GOD* get me out of this thing!" Judd shrieked.

Kenny Joe moved closer to Judd. "Does that thing hurt, Judd?"

Judd's head whipped violently, spittle flying from his mouth like venom. "I HAVE A FUCKING ANAL PROBE IN MY ASS, GODDAMMIT! OF COURSE IT HURTS, YOU FUCKNUT!"

Kenny Joe moved around the other side of the machine, studying it with wide eyes of wonder. "Lordy, Lordy, Lordy," he chanted, staring at the shaft in awe. He leaned in closer and scrutinized where the pole entered the anus, wincing in the way men do when they watch a woman kick a man in the balls. "I hope they at least greased that sucker first."

Bailey nodded at the words of profound wisdom.

"MAX, GET KENNY JOE THE FUCK OUT OF HERE!" Judd screamed.

"Would you please stop shouting," Max hissed, leaning into Judd's face. "Them aliens are all over this damn ship. For all we know they're organizing a little war party right now to come and kill us."

"Max," he whispered, flipping his head, indicating his friend should come closer.

"Yeah?" Max asked, putting his hand on his friend's shoulder in a gesture of comfort.

"THERE'S AN ANAL PROBE IN MY FUCKING ASS! EXCUSE ME IF I DON'T FEEL LIKE FUCKING WHISPERING HERE!"

Max sighed and moved to the controls on the side of the machine. He looked back over at Kenny Joe and Bailey. "You guys guard that door while I figure out which one of these buttons does what. Any one of those little green fuckers come through the door, ice'em."

Max examined the controls and knew immediately things were not going to go good for poor Judd. There were at least thirty buttons, each one covered with alien hieroglyphics.

"Max!" Judd shouted. "What the hell are you doing back there?"

Max put his finger over the first button. "I'm trying to help ya, buddy." He gritted his teeth and pushed the button, turning quickly to face the machine. The metal shaft whirred around in a half-circle and then moved forward, burying itself about an inch deeper into Judd's ass.

Judd gripped the sides of the pad until it seemed his knuckles were going to explode out of his flesh. "WHAT THE HELL DID YOU DO! IT'S GOING DEEPER, GODDAMMIT!"

In panic, Max pushed the first button his fingers found. The machine hummed, the probe vibrating explosively.

Judd's face took on an expression that could only be described as sensual pleasure.

Kenny Joe and Bailey backed into the wall, their eyes wide with alarm. Judd sighed, his eyes rolling into the back of his head.

"Jumpin' Jesus, he's enjoying that shit!" Kenny Joe screamed, pulling at his red beard maniacally, still retreating even though the wall held him back from continuing any further.

"I must agree," Bailey said, his voice rising above his normal monotone. He leaned to the side to see Max. "Uh...you better do something, but quick."

Max pushed another button, almost weeping. Sparks of lightning shot out of Judd's ass in Technicolor rainbows of electricity, smoke filling the air in dense clouds.

Mercifully, Judd passed out.

Five minutes later, Max had managed to get the machine to stop, but the probe was still plunged deep into Judd's anus. Max looked over at Kenny Joe and Bailey. "I don't know what we're gonna do."

"Just pull it the hell out," Kenny Joe said, his back still to the wall as he looked at Judd with the kind of fear reserved for someone who was coming to kick his ass in a bar. "It's not like he'll feel it, the poor bastard is unconscious now." He slammed his hands over his eyes. "I can't take it."

"Well, even if he did feel it, he might like it," Bailey

commented. "Judd is seriously scaring me. He was enjoying that! His eyes were filled with zest! I'm closing my eyes too."

Max climbed on top of the table until the probe was between his legs.

Kenny Joe opened his eyes, saw the sight before him, realized he did not like the image and quickly clamped his eyes shut.

Max grabbed the probe with both hands, braced his legs around Judd, and pulled with every ounce of strength he could muster.

"FOR THE LOVE OF GOD!" Judd shrieked, his eyes exploding open into wide circles. "OW! WHAT THE HELL ARE YOU DOING?"

Max looked down, his face full of annoyance. "I'm trying to get this thing out of your ass, goddammit. You think I like doing this?" He looked over at Kenny Joe and Bailey. "You guys want to give me a hand?"

Kenny Joe held his hands over his eyes. "No way, I'm not opening my eyes until this is over."

Bailey looked up at the machine. To him it appeared as if Max had somehow become entangled into Judd's ass, pinning his friend to the table with a Terminator-style dick. It was such a nightmarish sight that he promptly fell over into unconsciousness.

Judd looked down at where the portly Bailey had fallen. "Sure, he passes out in fear and I'M THE ONE WITH A METAL POLE IN MY ASS!" He whipped his head back. "MAX, GET DOWN FROM UP THERE!"

Max ignored Judd. "Kenny Joe! Get up here and help me goddammit!"

Kenny Joe peeked out through the cracks in his hand. "No! I'm not coming near that thing."

"Goddammit, Kenny Joe!" Max shrieked, from where he was perched on the machine. "I need your help!"

"No fucking way," Kenny Joe hissed, closing the crack in his fingers again. "He enjoyed that shit, Max! He was sighing!"

Judd gasped. "I did not!"

Kenny Joe clamped his hands even tighter around his eyes.

"Did too! And if you sigh again, I'm running!"

"I did not enjoy it, you prick! How would you like to have the machine hooked into your ass!"

"Well, I wouldn't like it nearly as much as you seemed to!"

"You bastard!" Judd shrieked. "I'm gonna kill you!"

"KJ, if you don't get up here and help me pull this, I'm coming down there and beat your ass like I did on Christmas day!" Max yelled.

Kenny Joe sighed, opening his eyes as little as possible. "Okay, man, but if Judd sighs again, I swear to Jesus I'm fleeing."

"I DIDN'T SIGH, YOU BASTARD!" Judd shrieked.

Kenny Joe climbed up onto the machine, still squinting. Bailey opened his eyes, sat up groggily, looked up and saw his portly brother and Max entangled in Judd's ass and promptly fell back into unconsciousness. His head hit the floor with a dull, meaty thud.

Judd looked down at him. "Sure, you fucker! Sleep!"

Max and Kenny Joe gripped the pole firmly, muscles tense. "Okay, on the count of three, pull!" Max shouted, closing his eyes. "One...two...three!"

They braced themselves and yanked violently, their teeth gritted.

Judd shrieked. "STOP! STOP! STOP! YOU'RE FUCKING KILLING ME HERE!"

Max and Kenny Joe climbed down from the machine dejectedly. The probe had not even moved one inch and remained deeply buried, as if it had become symbiotically merged with Judd's body.

"Now what?" Max asked, staring at the massive machine with hatred Kenny Joe picked up a small pistol shaped piece of metal from one of the dead alien's hands. "Shoot it with this thing?"

Max turned the cool gun around in his palm and aimed it at the wall. "Stand back." He pushed a button and a red beam shot out, burning the metal with a sizzle. "This will do."

"No way!" Judd screamed. "You're not shooting that thing anywhere near my ass, Max!"

Max shook his head. "Be realistic, partner. Could it really be any worse?"

Judd sighed, resignation making his face look old. "Get it over quickly."

Max aimed the alien laser at the probe and pushed the button. With one clean sweep, he managed to cut the shaft in half.

Two feet of metal still jutted from Judd's ass, but he was no longer connected to the machine.

Max looked down at the protruding rod, amused at how it appeared as if his friend had a metallic, smoking tail. "We'll worry about getting the rest of that thing out of your ass later. Now, we need to find a way to get off this damn ship."

They helped Judd from the table, and awoke Bailey.

Kenny Joe stared at the shaft that stuck out of Judd's ass and said, "Man, I wouldn't fall down if I was you."

Judd looked over at his friend. "Do you seriously know how close I am to killing you right now?"

"It almost looks like someone took the bitch-be-quick-stick out and plunged it in his ass," Bailey commented.

Judd's eyes actually looked moist with tears. The metal pole wiggled back and forth as he walked.

The hallway outside the probe room, much to their relief, was empty.

"Hell, for all we know, we could be on another planet by now," Max said as they walked, guns aimed forward ready to shoot anything that moved.

Max was holding the alien laser in his hand like a fat-ass intergalactic space hero. Judd waddled slowly and painfully, taking wide steps as the jutting pole wiggled behind him. Kenny Joe watched the rod quiver back and forth and bit back a comment that he knew would cause a fight.

The corridor seemed to be an endless path of doors. They elected not to try any in favor of just following the passage to its completion. Minutes later, they found themselves before a purple door, dull humming emitting from the room.

They got ready, their guns held out in different angles. Max glanced back at them and he was reminded of a sick parody of

Charlie's Angels. Judd was in the middle, totally buck naked, a pole sticking out of his flabby ass. Kenny Joe and Bailey quite literally rounded out each side, their beer bellies pushing out proudly, their guns held in the air. Kenny Joe fingered his beard dramatically.

"Okay," Max whispered. "Let's wait for one of them to come-"

The door opened suddenly and Judd, Kenny Joe and Bailey opened fire, sending Max scurrying to the floor to avoid being killed.

The alien just stood there for a few seconds, five or six holes in its lime-colored, leathery skin, its massive eyes widening even further. It fell forward with a soft thump, a puddle of green goo pouring out of its head.

"Who's your Daddy!" Judd yelled to the corpse, not quite aware of just how ridiculous he looked standing there with the end of an anal probe vibrating happily from his ass.

They cleared out a half a dozen aliens from the bridge rather quickly, with very little effort. Soon, the bodies of smoking aliens surrounded them, green blood covering the floor where they walked.

A massive screen showed the earth below them, lonely against the twinkling black background. The moon could be seen off in the distance like a pale, cratered apple.

Max stared down at a control panel full of buttons, each of them marked with the hieroglyphics that he had seen in the probe room. "We need to figure out how to get back down with this control panel."

The rest of the men nodded and stared down at the buttons dumbly. "What about that one with the green and blue circle on it?" Kenny Joe suggested. "That's the color of the earth."

Max nodded. "Should I push it?" he asked, looking over at his friends.

"What's the worst that can happen?" Judd asked.

"Well, that's easy for you to say, Judd," Bailey said, staring down. "You got a metal rod sticking out of your ass."

Before they could start fighting again, Max pushed the button and stepped back fearfully. There was a dull rumbling underneath their feet and they braced themselves for the worst, their eyes darting around the room with growing panic.

Through the screen in front of them, they watched in awe as the biggest missile that they had ever seen floated down towards earth, spinning silently as it fell. Their mouths slowly dropped open in unison as the missile entered the planet's atmosphere with a trail of fire and smoke.

"Oh my motherfucking god, I think you just blew up the earth," Judd uttered, his eyes watching his home planet in amazement.

"My mama is on that planet!" Kenny Joe wailed, his hands stuck to the glass.

Max wondered how it was possible that he had just actually heard someone utter the line 'My mama is on that planet' in a serious tone. "You don't know that it's going to destroy the earth, fool," he muttered just as the missile detonated on the planet below. A colossal, fiery cloud could be seen from their vantage point. "There, see, it only got a part of the earth. A piece is still there."

"Looks like some part of Europe," Bailey said. "Mama don't live in Europe, thank the Lord his own bad self."

Max could see quite plainly that it was Southeast Asia, but he decided not to say anything.

"Push another," Kenny Joe said, happy that the bomb had not killed his mother. "Just don't push no green and blue ones."

Max nodded and pushed a random button. Nothing happened. "We're never going to figure out how to move this thing back to earth. This is helpless."

Judd slapped his hands down on the control panel, pushing dozens of buttons at once. "ANAL PROBE IN MY ASS! EARTH BLOWING UP! KENNY JOE'S MAMA DEAD! I CAN'T TAKE IT ANYMORE!"

The ship lurched forward, tumbling slowly towards the earth, faint tremors reverberating underneath their feet. Gravity was suddenly cut off and they found themselves floating around the room along with several alien corpses. Kenny Joe seemed to be stuck to the front of the view screen, while Judd floated around fearful that he was going to hit his backside on a wall.

Bailey grabbed the pole in Judd's ass in a vain effort to steady himself, sending the both of them hurling wildly through the room. They hit the wall on the other side with a sickening thud.

Luckily, Judd had hit the wall headfirst.

Max floated in front of the view screen and watched the earth grow larger before his stunned face. The ship hit the atmosphere and plunged toward the planet, the view screen detonating in sheet of fire. "Oh...shit," he whispered.

Kenny Joe, still stuck to the view screen like a squashed bug, had a front row seat to the whole thing. He screamed and cried as they plummeted.

The ship vibrated spastically. Showers of sparks exploded from the control panels, filling the room with sulfurous smoke.

The last thing Max heard before he fell into unconsciousness was the womanly sounds of Kenny Joe's front seat screams.

One year later:

"You'd think you'd be used to it by now," Max said to his friend as they watched the big screen TV. They could see Judd being carried from the wreckage of the UFO, the metal rod sticking out of his ass like a sundial. The spaceship had crashed into the Atlantic Ocean and, after submerging for about an hour, floated to the top. Government officials had soon swarmed the ship.

They were watching a documentary called *The Aliens Among Us!*

Judd held his hands over his face. "That's easy for you to say, you haven't been dubbed 'Assman' by the media."

"It could have been worse," Kenny Joe commented. "They could have called you Anal Probe Guy."

Bailey cackled. "That kinda sounds like a gay porn actor." He stopped laughing suddenly and coughed. "Not that I ever watched any."

On the screen before them Max was saying, "We tried and tried to get that probe out his *BEEP,* but it just wasn't *BEEP* happening. Finally, we just had to cut the rod, so now it just stuck out his *BEEP* just so, you know what I mean?"

Judd looked up. "Did you really have to do interviews, man?"

Max nodded. "Shit, for twenty thousand I woulda done that interview buck naked in a pink bow tie while sodomizing a monkey."

Judd shook his head looked at the screen, just about ready to cry. Kenny Joe was now being interviewed. "I could tell by looking at the poor *BEEP* that it *had* to hurt. Hell, if you had a metal shaft shoved straight into your *BEEP* would you not be *BEEP* hurtin'? I was wincin' just looking at him. And of course he was *BEEP* carryin' on like it was the end of the world."

"Look at it this way, Judd," Kenny Joe said, slapping him on the back. "You're a star now. Shit, they're selling 'Assman in Space' T-shirts and everything!"

At this point, Judd started to cry. He knew that shitpie would always be on the table when he came for dinner. He just couldn't catch a break.

INGREDIENTS ARE THE SECRET TO GREAT TASTE

BY WESTON OCHSE

"What the fuck do you mean, it ain't my turn?" shouted Enus into the racing wind of the speeding pickup.

They were confident the deputy sheriff had taken the last turn-off where Zebulon had left a skid of dust as a swirling temptation. The blue and red Ford pickup had swung around the bend in the road too quickly for them to see if the bastard had taken the bait, though. Zeb didn't care. He was hell bent at near seventy miles an hour — the fish-tailing back end fighting the road at each turn.

"Just what I said. I mean it ain't your turn," said Zeb, wrenching the wheel hard to the right. "Anyways, you had the last one."

"The last one? She don't count. Hell," said Enus, "you can't count her. She was near eighty years old. That gash was gray as hell, man."

"Thems the chance you take. It was your turn and you can't even start complaining. It ain't like that man I had to do last week. At least yours was a woman."

Enus chuckled at the memory of his lifetime friend embracing the hippie they found hitchhiking last week. They had both *thought* he was a woman. His legs and his butt were tight and pretty damn good looking. Then the fairy pulled his hair aside and they saw the two weeks growth of beard. By then it was too late. And Zeb had made the hippie pay for it.

"Fine then. At least I get to help," said Enus. The last was a question more than a statement. The grin Zeb gave him in return was enough to let him know that tonight would be a group effort.

Three miles later they skidded to a stop in a roadside picnic area. Zeb repositioned the truck so it faced back the way they came and grabbed up his sheep skinner. It was a six-inch, wicked-looking blade. Its grip could double as a spiked set of brass knuckles and Enus had only seen it used once. The look on the poor patrolman's face as his forehead sprouted five new holes was still funny, even after six months.

"I think we ditched the motherfucker," said Zeb grabbing a beer from the Styrofoam cooler between them. "Lucky for him," he said, taking a deep gulp.

"Yeah, lucky," said Enus.

He ignored the cooler and grabbed the earthenware jug. It was one of Daddy's specials —- *The Sweetness*, they called it, and the taste lightened his feet.

Half an hour, six beers and an empty jug later, they were cruising the highway again. They called it *rousting*. Their daddies did it and their daddy's daddies had done it. It was family tradition and besides the guarding of the still, it was all they ever did.

Their hunting ground was a road that ran between the dark forests of Ooltewah and Cleveland, Tennessee. Travelers had two choices. They could take the newer Interstate 25 or the old highway. Zeb and Enus preferred the less traveled highway and concentrated their rousting there. Besides the occasional cheerleader who dumped her date, or the young boy who ran away from home because his mommy and daddy cut his Sega-time down, the only people who traveled it were leftovers.

That's what daddy called them. Leftovers, those folks who had already wasted their chance and were merely waiting for Darwin to exert himself. Zeb and Enus were Darwin's messengers, and in the battle of survival of the fittest, they were always on top. It wasn't as if they threw the leftovers away. Leftovers were special ingredients that made everything taste better. You never knew what you were gonna find. Daddy said it was the mystery that enhanced the taste.

It had been a slow night and just as they were about to head home, the headlights illuminated a solitary figure walking along the side of the road. Zeb immediately slowed, the sheep skinner gripped in his left hand. They could tell by the walk that it was a man and Enus laughed loudly.

"Like you said, Zeb. It's your turn."

Zeb shot him a look that was meant to kill, but it only succeeded in making Enus snort white-lightning through his nose as he laughed hysterically.

"Big bad Zebulon," continued Enus. "Rouster of men and a closet homosexual."

He dodged the half-full can of beer and grinned wider as it flew through the open window.

"Hey, don't get mad at me. I offered to help, but you said, Nooooo."

The sheep skinner rose and sank between Enus' legs, impaling the seat. A little of the moonshine spilled from Enus' shaking hands, hiding any piss that may have inadvertently escaped due to the proximity of the razor sharp blade to his manliness.

The pickup pulled just ahead of the walking man and stopped on the wide shoulder. Enus opened his door and leaned out. The light had been removed several years ago, a solution to too many hitchhikers who bolted.

"Hey, Man. You wanna ride?" Yelled Enus.

Their target was dressed in a black leather duster that hung all the way to the red clay dirt on the edge of the road. His hair was likewise black and flowed halfway down the back. Enus thought of the hippie and hoped this one would scream the same way.

"I said, do you wanna ride?"

The man stopped by the back of the truck, his face and eyes cast in shadow. His hands were clasped solemnly in front of him.

"Yes," came a voice like a serpent's hiss.

Enus glanced at Zeb, who indicated the sheep skinner in his hand.

"No problem, stranger," said Enus. "You got any bags?"

Zeb cracked his door and began to slide slowly out.

"Do I look like I have any bags?" asked the dark man.

"Well, no," said Enus, letting the insult slip. He'd have plenty of time to make the fucker pay.

"Come on in then, we need to get going."

"I don't think so," said the voice.

"Then I guess I'll just have to kill your sorry ass right here," said Zeb from behind the man.

Zeb lunged, the glistening blade held in a practiced hand, falling fast towards the unprotected back of the stranger. Suddenly, his target wasn't there. Zeb almost castrated himself on the follow-through, barely correcting in time.

"Behind you," yelled Enus.

Zeb spun around to find his target and cursed as the stranger raised its head. The eyes were solid white and the mouth showed twin fangs, descending.

"Fuck. It's one of them," said Zeb.

"One of what? A faggot?"

"Worse. A fucking vampire," said Zeb with resignation.

The pickup wound through the hills and finally skidded to a stop as the road dead-ended in an unmarked cul-de-sac. Kudzu covered trees surrounded the half-circle like sentinels and cicadas sang in the darkness. Two men stood in the beams of the headlights, shotguns trained at the windows.

Zeb and Enus jumped out, the latter carrying the Styrofoam cooler.

The men lowered their weapons, but still held them at their hips, just in case.

"What you boys bring us?" asked the one in the newer looking overalls.

"Sorry Dad," said Enus. "It was a bad night."

"Whatya mean it was a bad night," asked the other, much older gun-toting man.

Zeb lowered his head and answered his Grandfather. "We killed another one."

Both men lowered their barrels to the ground and simultaneously spit out streams of ugly, brown tobacco juice.

Enus shuffled forward and opened the cooler. Within, lay a steaming black heart, their latest ingredient.

His father glanced inside and jerked his head behind him. Through the trees, Enus saw the intricate pipes and pots of the family still. The contraption hummed and rattled as heated air created the Whitmire family's special moonshine.

"That's a big one," said the boy's father, inspecting the heart.

"I'm getting sick of the taste, though. Bloodsucker Special used to be a hot seller. Now it's like that Coca-Cola crap. Everybody drinks it," said the Grandfather.

CIRCUS CLOWNS AND ELEPHANT CRACKS

BY DAVID WHITMAN

"My god do I hate fucking clowns," Judd said, sipping his Budweiser from a Styrofoam cup, already feeling quite drunk. How they had managed to get him to the circus in the first place, he had already forgotten.

"That's because you're afraid of them," Max snickered.

Judd snorted. "Yeah right. They annoy the hell out of me, that's why. Look at that one with the blue hair. He keeps looking at me and beeping his horn. He does it one more time, I'm going to go down there and stick that fucking horn up his ass."

Kenny Joe studied the clown as if imagining the scene Judd had described, a big, goofy grin brightening his chubby face as he brought the beer cup away from his lips. The foam made his van dyke mustache look gray. "That would be funny as shit if you started a clown riot, bro."

"I must agree," Bailey said, giggling like a child at the antics of the clowns.

The clown with the blue hair shot a cocky glance up at Judd, held his horn in the air, and tooted it three times.

"Oh my god, that's it," Judd said, leaping up from his seat and climbing down the bleachers, fists clenched tightly to his side.

"Go on, beat that clown's ass!" Kenny Joe screamed after him.

Max was excited. "I can't believe he's really going to do it!"

Judd got to the bottom, jumped over the small gate, and threw himself upon the clown. The other clowns, as if sensing their comrade in trouble, ran to his aid, leaping into the kaleidoscopic pile one after another.

Soon, Judd was entangled in what appeared to be some sort of clown insect, gigantic shoes and rainbow colored gloves jutting and shifting around in every direction, a cloud of dirt balled around them like an insanely drawn cartoon.

Max, Kenny Joe and Bailey might have helped had they not been literally rolling out of their seats in laughter. The sight of their good friend getting his ass beat by a gang of clowns was just too much for them to bear. Kenny Joe found it particularly delightful, his big belly shaking up and down convulsively as he roared so hard he could not breathe. Other spectators also found it amusing, judging by the barrage of hilarity erupting around the ring.

Judd felt as if every multicolored fist that slammed into his face was accompanied by a laugh track.

After a five-minute beating, the clowns heaved Judd out of the ring where he fell hard, gasping in pain. The clown with the blue hair leaned over Judd, honked his horn three times, and ran back to join his colorful comrades.

A portly security guard waddled up to Judd, leaned forward and said, "I would arrest your sorry ass, but I'd say what just happened to you was punishment enough." He shook his head and walked away.

Judd closed his eyes and wished he would die. When he opened them again, his friends were standing around him in a circle.

"Oh my fucking God, that was funny," Max said.

"I must agree," Bailey added, nodding his head.

"'I'm going to go down there and stick that horn up his fucking ass,'" Kenny Joe said, imitating Judd's voice, then falling back and erupting into giggles.

Judd struggled to his feet and pointed at each of his friends. "Fuck you, fuck you and fuck you. Get me out of this tent."

By the time they made their way back outside Judd's mood had improved considerably. They bought some more beer and walked around taking in some of the sites of the circus. The

Butler brothers lost twenty bucks each trying to toss a basketball through a hoop while Max and Judd ate corn dogs.

"Max," Judd said solemnly as they walked, his face still swollen from his beating. "Do you think things will ever turn around for me, man?"

"You take things too seriously, Judd. You just know when we're two old bastards, sitting on the porch drinking whiskey we'll be laughing at this shit."

Judd smiled, then winced as his bleeding lips cracked. "The way things are going, I ain't gonna make it to be no old man. I agree with you, though, on one thing. This shit is probably be gonna be a lot funnier after some years go by."

Max snickered. "I think it's funny now, man. You just got your ass beat by a clown posse. *Publicly*, I might add."

Judd sighed wearily and then offered a twisted smile. "I know. I swear my life is one long beating."

They came upon a large enclosed area with four elephants. Kenny Joe grunted when he got a whiff of the elephant shit and covered his nose. Bailey commented that dog shit was a much worse smell, but that elephant shit had a sweeter scent, with a touch of tang. Judd just looked at the both of them, knowing he would fall over in shock if they ever had a conversation that was above the level of a mountain cretin. Each elephant had a leather harness and was giving rides to small children from one side of the area to the next.

"Man, I'd pay money to see Judd riding an elephant," Kenny Joe said as he stared at the beast with just a hint of fear. He took a long sip of his beer to chase away his jitters.

Judd tossed his empty beer cup into the garbage. "Oh really? And how much money would you pay?"

"Twenty bucks."

Judd waited a few seconds, but barely had to think about it. "Okay, but only if Max will ride with me."

After a little bit of negotiating they walked over to purchase a ticket. The ticket seller, an acne-ridden teenager with an "It's Miller time!" hat, stared at Judd suspiciously. "Ain't you a little old to be ridin' elephants? This ride is for children."

Judd glared at the teen. "Listen, fucknut. I just got an

assbeating by a dozen clowns in front of an audience, and I'll be goddammned if I'm gonna take any lip from a zit-faced kid in a fucking Miller beer hat."

Bailey agreed. "Obviously, Budweiser would have been a better choice."

The teenager studied the men for a few seconds, swallowing apprehensively. "Okay, that'll be five bucks. I could get in trouble for this, you know. Bart don't like no adults ridin' him."

Judd stared at the obscenely large elephant, his eyes taking in the beast. The elephant met his gaze for a moment and he felt a tingle of fear tickle his stomach.

Judd and Max approached the beast warily, eyeing it up the same way they would one of the animals they hunt in the woods.

Kenny Joe shook his head. "Goddamn, but if that elephant don't have the biggest set of balls I ever seen."

Bailey nodded as if Kenny Joe had made a profound and important observation about the universe.

Judd climbed up the ladder, followed by Max. They were being led across the field by one of the animal handlers, the large beast shaking them back and forth as it walked.

"This is the way they get around in India," Max commented as the beast clomped slowly across the field.

"Are you that much of a fool?" Judd asked, still smarting from being made fun of about the clowns. "Maybe like in 1890 they got around like this, moron."

"Hey don't snap at me just because you got your ass beat by some clowns."

"Max?" "Yeah?" "I'm going to let that go, but if you ever bring that incident up again I'm going to get the bitch-be-quick-stick out and beat you until you can't breathe, you got that?"

"Not such a bad ride for twenty bucks," Max said, trying to change the subject.

They were almost near the end of the field when the elephant let out a primal shriek and charged toward an open gate, nearly unseating the both of them. Judd fell off to the side where he dangled around like a puppet, his leg caught deep within the harness.

"Oh shit, oh shit, oh shit," Judd chanted as he slapped back and forth against the animal's side.

One of the handlers tried to close the gate as the beast charged, roaring and swinging its trunk furiously. The Elephant hit the metal explosively, sending the handler into the air like a rag doll—he slid across the dirt for about twenty feet, coming to a stop against the wall of a portable bathroom. The bathroom fell over like a large bowling pin, leaving the stunned and unconscious handler lying there like a pulverized action figure.

The elephant ran over to the handler and proceeded to kick him around before kneeling over and crushing him with a sickening snap of bones.

At the same moment, the elephant seemed to sense it had riders on its back. It lashed out with its thick trunk, slapping Judd in the ass with a thunderous clap.

Judd howled, trying desperately to clamber back into the harness. Max turned around so that he was riding the elephant backwards and tried to help his dangling friend. He managed to grab the back of Judd's khakis only to have them rip off, sending Judd backwards and almost out of the harness.

Judd was now bouncing from side to side in his underwear. The elephant lashed out again, cracking him in the ass with the sound of gunfire. As Judd squealed, Max made another grab, this time only succeeding at ripping Judd's underwear off as well.

SNAP! The trunk slapped into Judd's exposed backside. By now, his ass had a blood red welt across it.

"STOP FUCKING HELPING ME!" Judd howled, as the elephant slapped its leathery trunk into his ass again. It had Judd by his left leg and was attempting to pull him from its back. One of the belts on the harness broke and Judd felt himself swing around to the backside of the animal, his face slamming into its balls.

The elephant gave up on Judd and smashed into the monkey cage, sending dozens of the small creatures scurrying into the screaming crowds. One monkey had somehow landed on the elephant's head, shrieking and slapping his hairy palm down emphatically.

Just before the Elephant crashed into the bright orange circus tent, Max thought briefly of jumping off, but found he could not leave his friend. Chaos detonated into the tent as the beast sent clowns and spectators running in different directions. With a swing of its powerful trunk, it sent one clown airborne with a blaring squawk. The clown landed in the center of the crowd, his enormous psychedelic shoes flying from his feet and into the screaming masses. Max had the disconcerting feeling that he had become a live action cartoon. He couldn't be sure, but he thought he saw a *POW!* and a *BAP!* coming from the heads of the clowns as they flew around like Technicolor angels with noisy horns. It was the first time in his life he felt he truly understood what it felt like to be Judd.

Judd had stopped screaming and just sort of dangled over the elephant's backside, his head crashing up and down dully. He did experience a certain kind of satisfaction as the trunk smacked the clown with the blue hair and sent him sailing into the bleachers, smiling a bit for a brief moment.

Max struggled to pull Judd back to the top as the beast continued to wreak havoc throughout the tent. He felt a painful slap on the back of his bald spot and turned around just in time to see the monkey scamper back to the safety of the elephant's head. He turned back around and pulled at the harness with all of his strength, praying to God he would somehow save his friend. As if a miracle had arrived, he had actually almost pulled Judd all the way back to the top.

Max felt another biting sting as the monkey smacked the back of his neck, chattered angrily, and then returned to his seat on the enormous head. The harness came loose in his hand and Judd swung back over the side, blasting face first once again into the mammoth testicles.

"You little bastard!" Max yelled, turning around to face the monkey. The Elephant, obviously feeling the pain of Judd's collision backed up into one of the tent poles, squishing Judd in an effort to rid itself of what it probably thought was a giant tick attached to its balls.

The monkey was screaming and chattering at Max in what could only be described as animal obscenities. It jumped up and down a few times and let out a string of what Max was totally convinced was the monkey version of "Eat shit!"

"Come here, you little fucker," Max hissed, crawling towards the monkey as the Elephant crashed back outside into the screaming crowd and proceeded to run down the walkway that ran between the game center. Max swung out and cracked the monkey from where it sat, sending it soaring into mass of fleeing people. It caused a small panic where it landed, but Max had little time to notice as he saw Kenny Joe come gliding out of the crowd with a pitchfork.

Kenny Joe screamed what sounded like a war cry and launched his pitchfork into the side of the beast. The elephant bellowed and turned to face its attacker. Kenny Joe dropped the pitchfork, eyes wide in terror as he let go a womanly shriek and fled back from whence he came, striking old ladies and children to the ground in his effort to get away.

The elephant was spinning around in circles attempting to find the pain in its hind leg, Judd trailing in flight behind him like he was on the Dumbo ride at Disney World gone horribly wrong. As Max held on for his life, he remembered the buck knife he kept on his belt.

The elephant headed towards the end of the field and onto the interstate. A helicopter circled above them as Max sawed his knife into the leather harness, filming the whole thing from the safety of the air. Police cars were lined up behind them as Judd swung back and forth into the elephant's ass with a dull thud.

Teeth gritted in determination, Max finally cut through the harness. Judd tumbled to the road, a tangle of leather and naked flesh. Max waved at the helicopter like an action hero and leapt away, landing in a muddy ditch just to the side of the road. The elephant destroyed two police cars before they managed to kill the poor beast.

Two months later, Judd, Max, Kenny Joe and Bailey sat on the beer-stained couch and watched the television screen in anticipation. Each of them had a beer can between their legs. All week long they had seen the commercials.

"Welcome back to *When Animals Go On A Rampage!*"

the television blared. "In this day and age, people videotape everything! Watch what happens to this poor soul as Bart the Elephant goes on a rampage after years of living a docile existence in the circus! We must warn you that some of what you will see will be disturbing!"

Judd buried his face in his hands. "I can't believe the whole world is seeing the worst moment of my entire life."

Kenny Joe shook his head. "I thought your worst moment was the time that snake-"

KJ, could you kindly shut the hell up?" Judd said from his buried hands. "I told you that was never to be spoken of."

"Ouch," Kenny Joe muttered, wincing as he watched the TV screen. "I bet that welt is *STILL* on his ass."

Bailey scrutinized the video, a scholarly look on his round bearded face. "Well at least you had the elephants balls to cushion your head, did you not?"

"Ooooh! That has to hurt!" The television host screamed. "Poor Judd Peterson, this has got to be something he doesn't want his kids to see!"

"Well, Judd," Kenny Joe continued. "At least you're a star. Everyone knows who you are now."

Judd started weeping, wondering why God had wished so much abuse on him.

A CHORUS OF EARTHLY RAGE

BY WESTON OCHSE

The hard rays of the full moon filtered green through the thick kudzu canopy illuminating the 1972 Ford LTD in a cold sweaty aura. Coleman slid from the driver's side and raised his arms above his head stretching out the kinks from the two-hour drive out of Chattanooga. He spun his red baseball cap around and wiped his forehead with a broad hand.

Davey stepped from the passenger side of the car and brushed the residue of the burger and fries off his lap. He paused to stuff the wrapper and box back into the paper bag before he joined his lifelong friend near the trunk.

"I'm sure as hell gonna miss you, Davey," came Coleman's slow drawl. "Why the fuck y'all gotta leave the country for two years. Can't you just get your converts here?"

Davey winced at his friend's choice of words.

"It's just the way we do things, is all. There's only so much we can do around here and there's so many who have yet to hear the word of God. It's our Mission to spread the word."

Coleman inserted the keys into the lock and opened the trunk. He peered at the struggling figure packed within and turned again to his friend.

"My Momma, she says y'all are gonna take over the world someday."

Davey raised his lanky arm and punched the body in the trunk. Two times. Hard. "Your Momma's right."

Coleman pulled the groaning skinhead from the trunk and let him fall to the ground. He knelt down, careful to plant his knee firmly in the man's crotch and checked the tape around the ankles, wrists and mouth. He reached into his back pocket and pulled out the bent roll of silver duct tape. The stickiness of the blood seeping from the man's nose, missing teeth and cracked lips made the tape loose. He reapplied it by adding two more glistening strips.

The skinhead's eyes were crazy with fear as he watched Davey's every movement.

Coleman stood and glanced around the clearing.

"I wished we didn't have to carry this boy all the way in."

"You can wish all you want," said Davey. "John Henry likes his privacy." He cocked his head and picked up the far sound of a howl. "Do ya really blame him?"

A savage zest of unearthly howling raged from the roaring maw of a house that appeared to grow like a tangle of wood from amidst a mound of carefully collected junk. The brown-gray boards vibrated and the black plastic garbage bags, taped over windowless frames, puffed in and out with frustrated rage.

An old man sat on the second step of the three-step porch, leaning back on elbows, feet kicked out. He stared at the approaching boys. The only movement was his left foot keeping beat to an internal song, the switch on his hearing aid turned to off.

They came dragging their burden by his arms, heels drawing snake-like furrows that surely traveled back the two miles to the car. As they approached, Coleman smiled and nodded twice. Davey patted the large swastika tattooed on the head between them.

"'Bout time you boys made it around. Vivi's getting righteous. Done scared the dogs away thinking I'd have to send them in, instead."

"You won't believe where we found this one, John Henry," said Davey, yelling over the demonic noise and making sure to look directly at the old man when he talked.

"Yeah, he was shit-kicking the hell out of this black dude right in the middle of Martin Luther King Boulevard. Old Hitler here was acting like Mike Tyson at a Beauty Pageant and he never even saw Davey get him. Ain't that right, Hitler?" asked

Coleman, wrapping hard on the man's head.

The skinhead's eyes bulged like a road-kill cat as he stared at the open door of the house, entirely unable to fathom the source of the sound. A pool of yellow began to mix with the mud below him.

"That's not fair, Coleman. It wasn't like I snuck up on him. If he'd been paying attention he could have blocked the crowbar." Davey cast a wounded glance at his friend.

"Aw shit. Looky here. Old Hitler soiled hisself"

Davey glared at the limp form between them like a mother to a child and whipped his fist into the face—five, ten times.

"Hey, Boy! This here's the home of John Henry Wordsworth and it ain't polite to take a crap without first askin'," said Davey, leaning close in so the man could hear him over the noise.

John Henry reached over and mussed Davey's thick mop of brown hair. "Remember, Son. There is nothing neither good or bad. It's thinking it that makes it so," said John Henry, standing up and digging his hands in his pockets. "I got yer money. And I swear, if you'd taken any longer I was gonna have to find where the dogs had gotten to."

"What you gonna do when I leave?" asked Davey, his face a little sad.

"Fear not, my boy. Hunting season's in two months and will provide a supply to last old Vivi through the winter. I'll miss ya, but don't you worry."

John Henry scratched his beard and leaned down to look into the skinhead's rheumy eyes. He pulled out a wickedly long knife and lifted the man's chin up with the tip to get a better view.

"Let's see who we have here. Coleman, run and get the chair."

The muscular boy let go of his burden and the skinhead immediately sagged to the ground. Davey let his side go, as well, and wiped his hands on the sides of his pants, upset about the dirt and blood that had soiled them. Coleman scampered around the side of the house and picked through a spiky pile of junk. He returned a few minutes later with a grimy chair, made from white PVC tubing.

John Henry cut the tape around the wrists and ankles and the boys levered the captive heavily into the chair. Within moments, the skinhead's wrists were retaped to the chair's arms, his ankles to its legs, and his forehead to a length of pipe that protruded two feet up from the back of the chair.

"Let's see if he can talk," said John Henry, glancing at Davey.

The gangly boy grasped the edge of the tape and jerked it free. The skinhead immediately broke out into a scream, bubbles of blood popping through the ruined mouth and floating gently down to the dusty earth. As loud as he was, it was a mere undertone to the rage blasting from the house. Still, Coleman brought his boot up and into the man's stomach, cutting off the scream in mid-terror.

John Henry leaned in, knelt down and perched an elbow on the skinhead's leg. "Cowards die many times before their deaths, the valiant never taste of death but once. So why don't you be our little Prince Valiant and just stop yer yammerin'. Stop worrying what's going on with old Vivi and pay attention to what's going on here." He locked eyes with the man and spoke to the boys. "Check his wallet?"

Davey dug deep in his back pocket and pulled out a worn brown leather wallet. Flipping it open, he said, "Lemme see. He's got eleven dollars, a few business cards. Hey. Here's a coupon for two-for-one subs." He shoved the coupon and the money into his pocket and glanced happily at Coleman. "Finder's keepers. Okay, he also has a rubber. Says, ribbed and lubricated."

"Maybe that means he's a clean one," said Coleman.

"That would be nice for a change. Sure make Vivi happy," said John Henry.

"Okay, here it is," said Davey, pulling out the driver's license. He looked from the license to the skinhead and back to the license several times. "Ha. You know I think he looks better bald. His name is Edwin James Roomer. Edwin. I think Hitler is more fitting."

"Come on, Davey. Get on with it," said Coleman, tracing his finger back and forth across the swastika design on the man's head.

"Sorry man. Says he's not an organ donor. Not very considerate of him. Also says he's AB negative." He looked excitedly at John Henry who had broken into a smile. "Hey! That's her favorite, ain't it?"

"Sure is," said Coleman, who had been looking hard at Davey as he spoke. "I think it's time to ask him a few questions. Get something to clean his mouth out, will ya, Coleman? There's too much blood for me to get a good gander at what he's saying."

Coleman scampered off again, but only went as far as the porch before he returned with a large Mason jar of clear liquid.

"Is this okay, John Henry?" he asked breathlessly. "Alcohol kills germs on contact, right?"

John Henry nodded. "So they say. So they say. It's some nasty shit anyway. Just some more of that old *Bloodsucker Special.*"

Coleman poured the white lightning over the skinhead's face, making sure to get a liberal amount into the cracked and broken mouth. A reciprocal scream erupted immediately, but it took a few moments before it crescendoed enough to be heard over the already agonizing din from the house. The skinhead tossed his head back and forth, his eyes rolling up and arms struggling to rise as if to wipe the blistering toxin clear of his wounds. His legs undulated and his entire frame rose in an arced bow that only returned to the chair after Davey's fist buried itself into the man's sternum. It took several moments before the skinhead finally swooned back into fearful reality.

His eyes had locked once again on the howling door and it wasn't until John Henry had tapped the knife on the man's forehead several times that he looked at the old man kneeling, once again, before him. A thin rivulet of blood ran the length of skinhead's nose and dripped like an hourglass.

"Listen to what I have to say, boy. It's important. Do I have your attention?"

It took two more pokes of the knife before the skinhead nodded.

"What were you doin' beating on that black man?"

The skinhead blinked twice, his bloody, cracked lips trembling.

"Come on, Son. You gotta answer the question."

The skinhead tried to struggle, but stopped after a few small attempts. His body sagged in the chair, as if it realized, finally, that it couldn't escape. He struggled to speak and it took him several tries before the words formed successfully.

"I didn't really mean to hurt him bad. I was just... "

"Now, Now. There's no reason to be making up stories. No reason at all. You don't want to meet your maker with a lie on your lips, now do ya?" asked John Henry, standing up stiffly.

He shoved the knife back in the sheath dangling from his leather belt. He stepped back and appraised his prize, huddled and small in the chair. He ran his hands through his thick mane of wild silver hair and knelt down once again.

"You have one chance. One chance in the world to save yourself. Are you ready?" asked John Henry.

The skinhead nodded, his head picking up pace until it threatened to come free from the body.

"Alright. Here it is. Tell me a riddle."

John Henry, Coleman and Davey stared at the Skinhead, expectant looks on each face. The skinhead blinked several times and tried to speak but each time stopped, as if to reconsider these words of life importance. It wasn't until the tears began to pour freely that he spoke.

"My mother... my mother, she loved me," he said simply.

Coleman and Davey glanced at each other, faces creased with sadness.

John Henry reached up and stroked the boy's cheek. "Yep. That's certainly a riddle."

He stood and craned his neck towards the house and held it there for several ponderous seconds before he turned back to the skinhead. He sighed and looked hard at each boy. "Davey, Coleman. Grab the chair, let's take it inside. Vivi's waiting."

The skinhead screamed. "You told me it was a riddle. You told me it was a riddle. You said I had a chance!"

"You did, my boy. But you see, everyone has that riddle."

The skinhead's screams merged with the roar from the house as the boys carried the chair up the porch steps, Coleman behind and guiding. The warped wood was most surely groaning beneath their feet, but the sounds went unheard. Coleman turned and shouted something to Davey, but, this close to the house, it was lost in the hurricane of screams.

Davey understood though and head-butted the struggling skinhead. The boys halted by the front door and waited for John Henry, who inched his way past, crossed himself twice and then stepped over the threshold.

The interior was a museum of peeling wallpaper, faded furniture and mustiness. As with the windows, picture frames and mirrors hung glassless along the vibrating walls. The boys could feel the tremors in the floor, now, and tightened their grips on the chair. Their steps became smaller as they edged along the hall. At the head of the basement stairs, they stopped completely. Each cast terrified looks at the darkness below, the wind of a thousand screams pushing their hair back like a hot desert wind. The corrupt stench wrapped them in a cloying grasp and began to tease Davey's dinner forth. He gulped three times, his mouth sandpaper dry. Descending the stairs was always like a descent into hell. Halfway down, the skinhead came to.

Then he fainted.

They could feel Vivi's bulk before they could see. Her presence displaced air and space, adding claustrophobia to the list of fears she induced. John Henry snapped on a heavy-duty plastic flashlight and the boys dropped the skinhead when Vivi came into view.

The chair landed upright, then flipped sideways, falling hard to the dirt floor. Out of the corner of his eye, Davey saw the skinhead awaken and his mouth open in an unheard scream. Then Davey joined him.

It took several moments, but Davey gained control of his own mouth and gazed upon Vivi. There were still vestiges of humanity — bulges of flesh where arms should be, a foot peeking out from the great press of fat and a single blue eye. But it stopped there. Her flesh flowed from the far corner in great putrid waves until they covered almost the entire basement. Her head, impossibly large, leaned against the building's foundation. Vivi's mouth hung open — a gaping maw, easily three feet wide, from which the greatest of the screaming chorus came.

As the beam of John Henry's flashlight worked its way over the body, the boys saw the hundreds of other screaming mouths, lips peeled back in agony. Each mouth set within the flesh of her immense body, part of it. Each one screamed in a different key, completing the unrelenting chorus of rage..

John Henry turned and fixed the beam of light on the skinhead. The boys turned shakily and quickly sliced the tape. Their prisoner made no move to run. His limbs were no longer his to control as they spasmed with fear. The boy's grabbed him by two limp arms and tossed him onto Vivi's flesh. The effect was instantaneous.

Silence.

Unreal, complete silence.

The skinhead began slowly to move towards Vivi's still-wide maw, each mouth gripping the body and propelling it incrementally forward. The process took several minutes until the skinhead had been moved to the head where he was able to stare into Vivi's depths. But the mouths continued their urging and first his head, then his torso, and finally his feet disappeared until the skinhead was swallowed hole.

John Henry walked back to the boys, righted the chair and sat down heavily. He flipped a cigarette into his mouth, lit it and sighed.

"Too bad really," he said. "The boy had promise."

Davey and Coleman could only stare as the mouths along the body opened and shut as if each was tasting — or chewing.

John Henry finished his cigarette and snuffed it out with two fingers. He placed the butt in his pocket and stood.

The tension in the room was mounting. It was like being in the eye of a hurricane and each boy knew the violence would continue with redoubled efforts.

The sound began as a thin whine, something far away and barely heard. It grew louder and louder. The boys stared at the waves of flesh and with a *pop* another mouth appeared, screaming its rage to the world — its singular tone, deep and new. The new mouth screamed a monotone lament for a full minute before the hundreds of other mouths joined it in an ear shattering blast of loss. A blast of sound that would continue, until the next member of the unholy choir was delivered.

THEM BATS IS SMART, THEY USE RADAR

BY DAVID WHITMAN

Judd had fallen asleep a few hours earlier, a can of Budweiser in one hand, the pussy stick clutched firmly in the other. He sat in his chair and fingered the stick, his thoughts on having a good time later that night with Max and the Butler brothers-Kenny Joe and Bailey.

Feeling the urge to pee, he got up and trudged over to the bathroom, scratching his ass as he walked. Max would arrive in about ten minutes, so it was probably a good time to get ready. He walked over to the toilet and lifted up the seat before unzipping his fly.

He reached down to grab his penis and his hand came away empty.

He stood rigid, feeling like someone had stuck a five-foot long, icy rod up his ass, eyes widening as he stopped breathing. Afraid to look, he slowly brought his hand back down into his jeans and felt around. His fingers traveled through his thick pubic hair, but where his penis should have been there was only a moist wrinkle of skin. Although he hadn't had any in a year, he knew it was a pussy.

"Hey Judd, how's it going?" Max asked from the bathroom door, causing Judd to shriek and wrench his hands from his jeans.

"You almost gave me a fucking heart attack!" Judd howled.

Max pulled at his perfectly trimmed mustache and grinned. "Jesus! You screamed just like a woman."

Judd stiffened, the words hitting a little closer to home than they were intended. "I did not!" Realizing how high his voice sounded, he repeated his words, much deeper this time. "I did not."

"Did too."

Judd remembered stealing the pussy stick from the old voodoo woman while he did yard work and he shuddered. It was supposed to guarantee pussy. How could he *not* have stolen it?

"Max, you take that shit back now, or we're gonna be wrestling right here in this bathroom," Judd said, being careful to keep his voice as manly as possible.

Max studied his friend. "What the hell is up your ass?"

Judd decided he needed help. "Max, remember when I got bit by that snake and you sucked the poison out?"

Max sighed. "Yeah. Let's not bring that shit up again, though. It's not exactly a situation I want to re-live. Although, Lord knows, I've experienced it enough times in my nightmares."

"Well, the point is I consider you a close and personal friend."

"Judd, this better not be going where it sounds like it's going." Max grinned and fluttered his eyes femininely. "You're not coming out of the closet or something on me, are you?"

"Godammit, Max!" Judd screamed. "This is serious, man! I have a problem here, a very serious one!"

"Okay, okay. Jesus. What the hell is wrong?"

"If I show you, you need to promise to keep it between us."

"Judd, you know I will."

"Yeah, uh huh, like that time you told Kenny Joe and Bailey about my Mr. T dream."

Max laughed. "Well, you couldn't hardly expect me to keep *that* secret. That was hysterical. I still think you need to go to a therapist to sort that one out. Being spanked and tickled by Mr. T while he chants 'Them bats is smart, they use radar, fool!' is just fucking scary."

Judd frowned. "The point is that Kenny Joe still makes Mr. T jokes, and that was two years ago. You need to promise to keep this secret."

"I promise."

Judd gulped, a thin bead of sweat running down his forehead. Although he wanted to show his friend, his hand refused to move. He closed his eyes and tried to bring himself under control, inhaling deeply. Finally, he unzipped his pants and pulled them down.

Max leaned down almost like he was studying the engine of his beloved Ford and nodded casually, his brain trying to come to terms with the fact that it was real. Every time he looked up at Judd's face, all he could do was shiver.

"If you fucking laugh, I will choke you until you die," Judd said, his face flushed with embarrassment. He ran his fingers through the bush of pubic hair just above the labia and shook his head, a tear in his eye. When he finally spoke, his voice was quivering. "I just woke up and my dick was gone."

"You can pull your pants up now, man," Max said, rubbing his eyes. "No need to keep it out now that I've seen it."

"Max, what the fuck am I gonna do?"

Judd told the story of the voodoo woman and how he had stolen the pussy stick, leaving nothing out. He spoke in the hushed words of one recounting a guilty memory.

Max and Judd walked into the living room as they heard Kenny Joe and Bailey's Ford pull into the driveway. "I don't know what to tell you, man. This shit is too weird. Even for us."

The Butler brothers strolled through the screen door without knocking, each of them carrying a case of Bud. "Hey all," they chanted in unison.

"You tell them and you fucking *die*," Judd whispered into Max's ear.

"What the hell you two whisperin' about?" Kenny Joe said, already grabbing a beer from the case.

"Nothing," Judd said quickly and grinned. "Toss me a beer, bitch."

Kenny Joe shook his head and looked at his rotund, bearded brother. "You hear this guy? Called me a bitch. Anyone calls me that and expects a beer has got some serious problems."

"I must agree," Bailey said, grabbing his own beer and cracking it open. He took a long sip, his eyes rolled back in a way that could only be described as ecstasy.

Judd walked over to the cabinet and grabbed a bottle of Jack Daniels. "Fuck the both of you. I'm going to be needing the harder stuff tonight, anyway."

"Good," Kenny Joe said, sitting down on the case. "More beer for me then. So where we going tonight?"

"I figured we'd just hang out here," Judd said, taking another long swig of the whiskey. "There's a good game on tonight anyway."

As the night went on, Judd continued to hit the bottle of Jack Daniels until it was nearly empty. Every time Judd would catch Max staring at him, he would glare until Max would look away. By the time the game was over, Judd had passed out against the sofa, the bottle of JD still clutched protectively in his hand.

"So then I grabbed that fat bastard by his fucking hair and demanded he sing me a good song," Kenny Joe said, crunching up his beer can. He threw it to the floor where it bounced between Judd's legs.

Max grinned and took a sip of his beer, staring at the discarded can and trying desperately not to think of Judd's pussy. "This is too rich. What song did he sing?"

Kenny Joe smirked. "I'm getting there, man." He looked over at his brother, who was fingering the belly button on his enormous gut. Bailey picked out a piece of red and blue lint and tossed it into Judd's hair. "Throw me a brew, bro."

Kenny Joe caught the beer, cracked it open with a *snap* and continued. "So this snaggle-toothed bastard looks me in the eye and goes, 'I ain't singing shit to you, you redneck, cretinous piece of white trash.'"

Max and Bailey gasped. Kenny Joe nodded, agreeing wholeheartedly with their surprise. "Yep," he continued. "The nerve of this bastard. So I pulled out my Colt .45, cocked it and stuck it to the side of his head. I gave him a big old shit-eating smile and said, 'Let's hear some of that sweet voice.'" He paused dramatically and watched with satisfaction as his two friends leaned in for the climax of the story. "His eyes sort of turned to the right side of his skull as if he was trying to look into the barrel of my Colt sideways. He pauses for a moment, and then he sings in the sweetest voice you ever did hear, 'I got sunshy-yee-ine on a cloudy day. When it's cold outside, I got the month of May.'"

They all detonated into laughter. Bailey fell to the floor, holding his jiggling belly, a sight that only made them roar all the harder.

Max was wiping a tear from his eye. "You're the man, Kenny Joe. That was fucking perfect. That fat bastard had it coming to him all year."

Kenny Joe stared down at Judd and burped. "Look at him sleeping already. Looky at the way his eyes go back and forth underneath his eyelids. That means he's dreaming."

"Dreaming of Mr. T," Bailey said as they all exploded into laughter again.

"Them bats is smart, they use radar!" they all screamed simultaneously.

Judd rolled over from his side to his back and muttered, "Fuck all of you." They stared down at him quietly until they again broke out into howling hysterics.

"Poor Judd," Kenny Joe said, gazing down at his friend affectionately. "The man just can't catch a break. Snake bites to the dick. Anal probes in the ass. Crazy ass elephants runnin' amok. The man must have pissed off Jesus or somethin'. What else could happen to the guy?"

Max was quiet for a moment and then sighed. The secret was just too big to keep to himself. He told his friends the story of Judd and the pussy stick and watched their faces. "Apparently, poor Judd thought this stick would make every woman that he wanted just throw themselves at him. The way he tells it, he just had to have this stick. Now he comes home, falls asleep, and wakes up with this hairy pussy. Fucking disgusting, man. People should not screw around with voodoo women."

Kenny Joe and Bailey watched Max for a few seconds, turned simultaneously to Judd's crotch area, and then looked back to Max's face.

"You don't hardly expect us to believe that, Max," Kenny Joe said. "We may be drunk and gullible, but we aren't *that* drunk and gullible, man."

"Go on and look for yourself, man," Max suggested. "He won't wake up."

Kenny Joe and Bailey crept up to where Judd lay on the floor, his mouth open as he mumbled something in his sleep, a line of drool streaming down the side of his face. They looked over at Max as if to seek permission and he nodded like a wise man.

"You do it," Kenny Joe said to his brother as he pulled at his thick beard nervously. "I ain't never unbuckled a man's pants, and I don't intend to start now."

"Fuck that," Bailey said, backing up. "You do it."

"I ain't doing it."

"Well, I ain't fucking doing it neither."

Max snickered. "It's not like he has a dick. If he ain't got no dick, he ain't much of a man, is he?"

"Whether he has a dick or not is still debatable, Max," Kenny Joe said. "I still don't believe your ass. You have a tendency to fuck with me a lot. I still remember that time you had me convinced they were going to bring the *Dukes of Hazard* back. That pissed me the hell off. That was totally evil on your part."

"They did do a TV movie, though, remember?"

"Yeah, but it was disappointing. They was all old and it didn't even have Boss Hog. You can't have a Hazard County without no Boss Hogg. It ain't right. It's like Crazy Horse without Neil Young, it just don't work."

Max got up and stepped over to where Judd lay. "Oh for Christ's sake, move out of the way." He undid the button of Judd's Levi's and unzipped the fly. He grabbed the jeans at the cuffs and pulled them down until they reached Judd's ankles. The area where Judd should have had a bulge in his underwear was flat and he gestured towards the crotch. "Go on and look."

Kenny Joe reached down and placed his finger under the waistband of the underwear, pulling cautiously, almost as if he was awaiting the strike of the deadly snake that had once terrorized his friend. They stared at the pussy in dumb confusion before fleeing to the furthest corner of the room.

"Holy shit, bro!" Kenny Joe howled, eyes wide. "That's fucked up!"

"I must agree," Bailey said, nodding up and down rapidly.

"No shit," Max said, frowning down at his passed out friend. "We need to go and put the fear of God into that voodoo woman for doing this to him."

Kenny Joe shook his head. "No fucking way, man! She took his dick! What if she does the same thing to us? Maybe switches our dicks around or something, gives you Bailey's dick and I get yours."

"That best not happen," Bailey said, rubbing the bulge in his jeans. "My dick is massive. The eyes widen when I bring it out."

Max sniggered. "How would you know? You can't see it with that gut.""I use a mirror. Plus I can see it in their eyes."

"He ain't lying, Max. It is pretty damn big," Kenny Joe said. "I used to be very envious until I accepted it."

Max shook his head. "Let's not go there, man. This conversation is getting uncomfortable. Let's take the pussy stick back to the voodoo woman and ask her to take off the curse."

The men reluctantly agreed, still afraid of the consequences of messing with such scary voodoo magic. It was a visit they would rather not have taken. The voodoo woman had frightened them greatly. As they drove back to Judd's, Bailey kept putting his hands to his pants to see if his penis was still there.

What they learned was something that would disturb them until the day they died. They drove back to Judd's house with haunted eyes, saying very little as the music of Hank Williams wafted through the truck. The words to *"Lost Highway"* had always meant something special to them.

"All's I know is I'm not the one who's gonna do it," Kenny Joe said, as they pulled up in front of Judd's place. "No fucking way. No fucking how."

"I must agree," Bailey said as they got out of the truck.

"We're drawing straws," Max growled. "You guys have been his friend as long as I have. Also, I'm the one who bailed him out of the snakebite incident."

Judd was sleeping peacefully on the floor, jeans still pulled down to his ankles. His hand was resting comfortably over his crotch.

They sat on the couch, each of them trying desperately to think of a way to escape. They stared down at their passed-out friend and tried to make him somehow appealing, but it just wasn't happening.

"Why can't we just forget about the whole thing?" Kenny Joe suggested.

"Because the voodoo woman said one of us has to have intercourse with him to cure him," Max said, grabbing another beer. "We can't just leave him like this. He's our friend, man. He's been our friend since grade school. If the situation were reversed, he would be helping us."

"What if we catch the pussy?" Kenny Joe asked, his voice quivering.

"What in the hell you talking about?" Max asked.

"Well, it's like a disease," he explained. "What if we have sex with him and one of us catches the pussy disease? I admit if I woke up with a pussy I would play with it a lot, but it would get old real fast, man. Real fast. Don't they have to use a douche on that thing all the time so that it don't stink? And tampons too?"

"The voodoo lady said if we do this, then Judd will get his dick back. She was very clear on this."

"Aren't you afraid this will make us gay, though?" Kenny Joe asked. "That's terrifying."

Max took a long swig of his beer before answering. "Listen, my friend. Judd has no dick. Therefore, he's not a man, right? Isn't the general definition for being a woman, having a vagina? So how can it be gay?"

Kenny Joe gaped down at his rotund and bearded friend. "Well, he sure ain't no woman, or if he is, he is the ugliest woman I've ever seen. Talk about falling down the ugly tree and hitting every branch on the way down."

"That poor bastard built himself a tree house and fucking lived up there for years before falling out," Bailey added.

"Well, I agree the man ain't pretty," Max said, finishing off his beer and grabbing another. "But the point is, that it is not homosexual to do this. Admittedly, it ain't normal, but it is not gay, nor will it make us gay. We need to help our friend." He walked into the kitchen and came back a minute later with three matchsticks clutched in his fist. "Time to draw."

"Oh my god, bro, this is the scariest thing I have ever fucking done," Kenny Joe said, staring at the three wooden sticks like they were tipped with the heads of his ex-wife.

"Who wants to go first?" Max asked, holding his hand out.

Bailey reached forward and grabbed a matchstick, his frog-like eyes bulging. He exhaled loudly when he saw his was normal. He looked up at the ceiling and blew a kiss. "Thank the Lord all mighty. I love you so damn much, Lord. You my man."

Kenny Joe said a silent prayer, held his breath, and grabbed a matchstick. He gripped it before his face in trepidation and then beamed. "Jesus loves me, yes I know. 'Cuz the Bible tells me so."

"*Fuck*," Max hissed. "This is so goddamn unfair."

Judd wheezed and then farted loudly.

Max looked down at his friend, his eyes almost in tears. "Oh man. This is disgusting. We're gonna have to do something to make him look more womanly. I can't just fuck him like this."

Kenny Joe grinned. "Want to take him out to dinner or something first? Maybe catch a flick or something?"

Bailey snickered at his brother's joke.

"Kenny Joe that wasn't even a little bit funny, man," Max growled. "I'm serious here. We need to do something to make it easier for me. He has a—I mean *SHE* has a fucking beard for Christ's sake!"

After a brief discussion, they decided it would help if they shaved Judd's beard. Ten minutes later, Judd had a smooth face, give or take a few bloody nicks. Bailey tore off little pieces of toilet paper and stuck them to the wounds where they made little dots like measles.

The men stared down at Judd and tried to think of him as a woman. Again, it just wasn't happening.

"I think he's even uglier without the beard," Kenny Joe stated. "No wonder he hasn't been clean shaven since the seventh grade."

Max nodded. "Maybe we can put makeup on him or something. A wig might help too." He grabbed Bailey's arm. "Go next store and ask Mrs. Anderson if you can borrow one of her wigs."

"What if she asks why?"

"Just tell her we're going to a costume party."

"But all her wigs are gray. You wanna fuck an old lady?"

"Bailey...""Okay, okay," he muttered and walked out the front door.

Max studied Judd. "Okay, we're gonna need makeup too."

"Max, this is getting ridiculous! Just fuck him and get over with!"

"*HER*! Don't say him! Semantics are important here, man."

Kenny Joe shook his head and frowned. "Just fuck *HER*, then, and get it over with."

"Do you want to do it instead?" Max asked, glaring at his friend. "I thought not." He snapped his fingers and ran into the kitchen. "I got it!" He came back carrying a plastic cup full of magic markers.

Max pulled out a red marker and colored Judd's lips. He stepped back and studied his friend's crimson mouth like an artist. He narrowed his eyes, nodded to himself, and grabbed a blue one. His face lined with concentration, Max applied the wet tip to Judd's thick eyelids. He looked over to Kenny Joe for approval. "What do you think?"

"He's still fucking ugly. Maybe even uglier."

A teardrop fell down Max's face. "I know. Maybe the wig will help."

As if on cue, Bailey walked in with a gray beehive wig. "This was all she had." He saw what they had done with the magic marker. "Oh, man. That is just scary."

"Just shut the hell up," Max said, grabbing the wig from his hand. He placed it on Judd's head and frowned. "Fucking frightening."

Kenny Joe painted large circles on each of Judd's cheeks with the magic marker. He grabbed two of the sofa pillows and stuffed them into Judd's shirt in a vain effort to make breasts. "The finishing touch."

Judd looked obscene. The blue "eye shadow" made him looked like Tammy Faye Bakker's ugly sister. Red ink was smeared all over his lips, giving him the appearance of a one-dollar whore. His rouge, two large, red dots painted on his cheeks, made him look like a frightening fuck doll. The beehive wig made it look like he was wearing a giant melting ice cream cone on his scalp. Tiny dots of toilet paper stuck to his face like freckles. One pillow fell to Judd's side like a huge, sagging breast.

"So how you gonna do it?" Kenny Joe asked.

"What do you mean?" Max asked, staring down at his painted friend morosely.

"Well, you gonna do him-"

"HER GODDAMMIT!"

"Okay, *HER*! Are you gonna do her missionary style or doggie style?"

Max frowned. "You better not be fucking joking, man, because I am *so* close to choking you."

"I'm serious," Kenny Joe said, his face devoid of a smile. "It's something you need to consider."

"I would do it missionary," Bailey suggested.

"Of course, I'm going to do it missionary. I'm a self-respecting Baptist."

Kenny Joe and Bailey nodded in unison, agreeing wholeheartedly with the profound truth in his words. Judd muttered in his sleep and they watched him quietly.

"Well, I guess we better leave now," Kenny Joe said, patting Max on the shoulder.

Max sighed. "Judd better appreciate the hell out of this." He exhaled sharply. "Shit! No condoms."

Kenny Joe went into the kitchen and came back with a box of plastic wrap. "There you go, bro. I remember fitting my dick into a zip-lock bag once, but that's a tale for another time."

After the Butler brothers left, Max had a brief moment of panic. He thought of all the times Judd had bailed him out of one ass-burning frying pan or another and he couldn't help but break out into a grin. Any time he had ever needed anything, Judd was there with a smile and a six pack.

Max gazed down at his painted friend and shook his head sadly, a ghost of a smile on his face. The only magazine he was able to find to get himself aroused was a *National Geographic*, but he was quite surprised at how fast he achieved an erection.

He found a nice picture of a group of beautiful Pygmy

women in the magazine, nestled it deep into Judd's beehive wig, and tried not to weep. He grabbed a thick wad of plastic wrap and put it to use, his heart beating in trepidation. When Max entered his friend, he whined.

Every time he thrust himself deep into the warm pussy, a wave of foul, whiskey-tainted air would blast into his face. At one point, Judd moaned quietly, a sound he found terrifying. Max closed his eyes and tried to pretend it was a woman, but Judd's hairy legs kept tickling his thighs.

He ejaculated five minutes later and rushed into the shower. He scrubbed himself in the hot water for an hour, nearly using up a bar of soap.

The next morning, the penis had grown back. Everybody thought things had gone as well as possible considering the circumstances.

It wasn't until Judd started gaining weight that things got complicated.

HUMANITARIANS

BY WESTON OCHSE

The Lincoln Town Car pulled into the yard, dust and leaves crunching beneath its tires. Adam stepped out, briefcase in hand, wondering for the third time why he was here. What had brought him to this point? The sad thing was that if it weren't for this sad family, he would have been fired on Monday.

The dogs launched from the porch and stampeded towards him. He'd learned to keep completely still after Monday's episode and since he only had one good suit left, he followed the lesson closely.

There were eight of them, and never had the AKC even fathomed that such color and body combinations existed. He'd run from them on Monday, and when the owners of the house had finally called the dogs off, his clothes had hung in strips. They'd loaned him an old pair of jeans and a stained flannel shirt, and when he'd returned to the office, everyone had laughed — that is until he'd plopped the contract on his boss's desk.

And then all the bastard had said was, "We'll wait until the check clears before we start celebrating."

This time the mongrels recognized him and after a few minutes of spastic sniffing, they shuffled back to their places on the stoop. Adam sighed and headed across the dirt yard to the house. He wove around several rusting hulks of trucks that had seen their best days when his father was still in canvas hi-tops and black and white television was the height of technology. The house was a miracle of clapboard and tarpaper architecture. He imagined the builders blindfolded, drunk and in the midst of acid experimentation as they hammered and stapled the incredibly rambling structure into crazed existence.

More unbelievably, the Wheaton's had purchased homeowners insurance.

"Hey Momma, it's that insurance guy again," said the thin girl who opened the screen door.

Adam waved and smiled his *trust me* smile at Enid. She was a sweet girl and he felt sad for her physical problems. Her left arm was six inches shorter than her right and her eyes were slightly off-center, so that staring into them made one queasy. He fixed his gaze on her mouth, a slightly less disturbing vision with the orange tint of never-brushed teeth.

"Good Morning, Enid," he said. "Is your Momma around?"

She stared at him with cross-eyed befuddlement. "Of course she is, Mister. Didn'tcha hear me callin' her?"

Adam grinned and stepped carefully over the step that he had fallen through on Tuesday. "No, I didn't," he said. "Will you tell her I'm here, young lady?"

"You need to get your ears checked, Mister. I done told her and she said she was comin' as soon as she finishes up with the turkey."

Adam smiled and decided if he mentioned that Enid only had one ear and shouldn't be talking about ear problems, he wouldn't make his fourth sale this week to this seriously strange family.

"Let Mr. Connors in, Enid. Don't make him stand there at the door," came the husky voice of the mother from deep inside the shadowy depths of the kitchen.

Enid opened the screen halfway and stepped aside so Adam could enter. He sucked in the fresh Tennessee air before he accepted the invitation, then crossed the threshold. If this had been two years ago, he never would have stepped foot inside the place. The recession had hit him hard, however. With his company going belly-up, and the divorce, and his present boss on his ass to make his quota, he had little choice.

It wasn't so much that everything was dirty. It was just that a film seemed to be coating the furniture, the walls and the floor.

To his left were the two boys, who sat watching Goldberg slam The Blue Flame again and again on the wrestling ring mat. Not boys, really. They were thirty-three year old twins, who in their simple-minded enthusiasm grinned toothlessly at their favorite sport. The remnants of homemade pork rinds lay scattered along their three hundred pound, overall-covered frames, and littered the carpet at their booted feet.

Enid indicated he should sit in a low-backed chair by the plastic covered window. He sat and sank deeply into the old cushions. On his first visit, he'd discovered it was the Grandmother's Chair, but the old woman spent most of her time in bed. The exception was Wednesday, when she'd come shuffling out in an old robe.

She reminded him of a gnarled tree — thin, but tough enough to have weathered innumerable seasons. She'd touched him and felt his muscles, commenting on how poorly fed he was. He guessed that since she'd lived through the Depression, being well fed was an important thing in her life. He'd always felt a little on the scrawny side though, and her clucking had made him feel like the one hundred and fifty-pound man he was.

But this family seemed determined to change it. He could have sworn he'd gained thirty pounds in the last few days. They were forever feeding him and offering him drinks. He'd even eaten the pickled pig's feet and chicken beaks offered up in an un-appetizing bowl of brine. After all, he needed the commission more than his pride. The pecan pie was the best, though. Yesterday, to the extreme happiness of the mother, he'd eaten an entire pie.

"Mr. Connors. It's so nice that you found the time to come back to us."

"Mrs. Wheaton, of course I returned. You told me your husband was returning today and how keen you both were on the Term Life policies for your family. If there is anything that's important, it's providing for the survivors in the event of unfortunate death. I can't tell you the times where folks felt everything was going okay and they had too many credit cards and... "

"We don't own any credit cards, Mr. Connors."

"Still," he continued without hesitation, "It would certainly help finances if... "

"What the fuck is goin' on here and who the hell is this man!"

The figure that stood the door was not the patriarchal presence he expected. The intimidating shadow and deep voice revealed a man that had to tip-toe to reach five feet, but wore his machismo upon his tanned and wrinkled face like a matador.

Adam stood quickly, his briefcase slipping to the floor. The twins jumped up and ran over to their father. They surrounded him, hopping from foot to foot in childish glee.

"Da, you bring us presents? Did ya, huh?"

The father glared at his two sons momentarily, then smiled.

"In the truck boys. Bring in Da's things and there's something special for ya in the cage." When the boys scampered out the door, Mr. Wheaton returned his attention to Adam and his face reverted to what appeared to be a comfortable sneer. "Now you! What the fuck are ya doin' here? If it's my Mable you're after, you're gonna have a fight on your hands." The last he punctuated by drawing a long fish knife from his hip.

The smaller man went into a crouch, the tip of the knife steady — deadly.

"Sir! Sir! I am not after your Mable, I'm here to... "

"What do ya mean you're not after my Mable? Ain't she good enough for ya!"

"Well, yes. Of course. I mean no. I mean, I'm here for insurance, Sir."

"You're gonna need insurance after I'm done with ya," screamed the smaller man launching himself across the living room.

"Henry! Stop this now. Poor Mr. Connor is here for dinner."

Henry sat on the insurance man's chest, the tip of the knife quivering at the pale throat. He turned to see his wife in the kitchen door, her hands covered with brown and white feathers. His mask of rage smoothed into a broad smile.

"Why didn't you say so before?" he asked, standing up and sheathing the knife. He reached down and helped up the insurance man. "Sorry about that, Mister. Welcome to our home."

Adam stood shakily and tried to catch his breath. His hands went absently to straighten his mussed suit, but his eyes were still locked on the knife at Henry Wheaton's hip. Adam's brain screamed for him to run, but his legs refused the commands. The dire need for a commission still held him in a tight grip.

"Pleased to meet ya, Mister," said Henry proffering a small strong hand.

Adam felt himself accepting and squeezed a weak reply to the iron grip of the smaller man. With the handshake, however, his fear seeped away and he smiled. It was just a misunderstanding. Maybe he could still unload the insurance — and if he did, he'd shove it down his boss's throat.

"Pleased to meet you too, Mr. Wheaton," he said, trying hard to control the quavering in his voice.

"So Mable says you're here for dinner," said Henry, looking Adam up and down. "You're a little thin, though." He turned to his wife. "You been feedin' him, Honey?"

Mable smiled proudly. "Sure have. He's been here everyday sellin' us insurance. But I've been makin' sure he's been eatin'. It's all that unhealthy big city livin' I say."

Henry nodded once. "Good. Good. Bring me the jug and get on back to the kitchen."

Henry sat on the couch. Picking up a few loose pork rinds, he shoved them into his mouth. His gaze went to the television and he grinned as Goldberg threw The Blue Flame into the second row of the screaming crowd. When Goldberg shot his victory sign, Henry joined in, the middle fingers of his hands rising toward the ceiling. As the man laughed, rind residue shot out and onto the coffee table where they landed among magazines and spit cups.

The boys exploded through the door, whooping and hollering. Each carried a metal Coleman cooler and the stench of fish swirled into the room. Sitting atop each cooler was a small metal birdcage containing a beautiful multi-colored parrot.

"Ma, Ma," said the one on the left. "Looky what Da got us. We got us parrots."

Henry watched his boys run into the kitchen, the look of fatherly pride unmistakable. He glanced over at Adam and winked.

"Gonna teach them them to talk," he said.

Adam wondered who was going to teach whom. He took a moment to collect his thoughts and cleared his throat. He grabbed the briefcase where it had slipped to the floor and propped it on his knees. He dialed the combination, flipped it open, grabbed several documents and closed it. Placing the documents on the top of his laptop desk, he began his spiel.

"Now, as you know, Mr. Wheaton, I have been concerned with your family. Your wife and I," said Adam, gulping, "have developed a comprehensive plan in the event of virtually any untimely disaster."

He paused to make sure he had the man's attention and waited while Enid handed her father an earthenware jug. The man uncorked it with his teeth and took a long swig. When he finished, he whistled long and slow.

"They call this concoction *The Sweetness*. My cousin makes it and it's the best, damned shine you'll ever taste. Here," he said proffering the jug, "Try some."

"Maybe later, Sir. As I was saying, your house is insured and covered in the event of fire, flood, earthquake, tornado and of course the special consideration your wife insisted on... er... demonic possession. And I can guarantee that we have provided your family with the best rates available in today's tumultuous market."

Henry nodded for Adam to continue.

"Tuesday, I returned and we initiated a comprehensive plan for your truck and the John Deere out back. So if anything happens to them, all you need to do is call me and I will take care of everything. I pride myself on individual service and... "

"Okay. Okay," said Henry, his eyes glazing over a bit with the words. "Tell ya what, Mr. Connor. Let's talk about that after dinner. I'm hungry as a bear after a winter snooze and I need something to fill my gut."

Adam stared blankly for a few seconds then nodded slowly. It appeared he was going to get fed again.

They had been eating for three hours. Well, he'd really done the eating. The rest of the Wheaton's had merely picked a bit, seeming more concerned with his health. Henry had just returned from a fishing trip down to the Florida panhandle and had brought back four hundred pounds of amberjack. Mable had begun to pickle it right away and offered a bowl for Adam to taste. He had to admit, it was very good and contained some unique seasoning. He'd also forced himself to eat some of the pork rinds they were so proud of, as well as half a pecan pie and four boysenberry muffins.

His stomach felt distended and all he really wanted to do was lie down and take a nap. They must have noticed and had made him a pot of coffee. The bitter dark taste of chicory made it an exotic counterpart to his usual early morning vanilla java. The caffeine also spiked his brain awake. He was looking forward to concluding the deal.

The aroma of turkey was making its rounds through the house, and even though he was full to bursting, it teased his taste buds until his mouth watered. It took little effort for them to entice him to the dinner table. The spread was incredible. It was everything one would expect at a Thanksgiving and more: Mashed potatoes and gravy, fried okra, pickled fish and pig's feet, boysenberry jelly, pickles, corn on the cob, plates of butter, dressing, cornbread and an immense turkey.

The boys gnawed on their roasted parrots, holding them daintily with pinkies extended. They'd explained to Adam that their Da liked them to eat them because it made the boys talk better. Adam had nodded, somehow knowing that that would be the reason.

Around the table sat Enid, the twins, Henry, Mable, Granny and Adam. But the only two that were seriously eating was Enid and Adam. Henry had expertly carved several huge slabs of juicy white breast meat and laid them on Adam's plate. The turkey had been carefully basted in honey and the meat fell apart in his mouth. He didn't even need to chew it was so perfect. It wasn't until the second plate that he voiced the question that had been bothering him.

"Why aren't you eating? I'm feeling more than a little guilty sitting here and devouring your excellent food."

"Don't you worry, Mr. Connor," said Mable. "This food is for you and Enid. The rest of us are humanitarians and we don't like to eat animals."

"Humanitarians?" asked Adam. The political term seemed out of place in the kitchen and he'd never heard it mentioned with food before.

"But as you see, Enid's joining ya," added Henry. "We could never get her to stop. Even though she's thin as a sassyfras tree, she never turns down a meal."

"Enough of this shit, Henry. I'm tired of waiting and getting hungry as hell," said Granny in a reedy voice.

Henry cast a glance at his mother and then locked eyes with his wife who nodded in return.

"As soon as you're finished, Mr. Connor, we'll get down to business and finish this once and for all."

Adam gulped down his mouthful of food and nodded sharply. He wiped his mouth with his napkin and pushed the plate aside.

"Let me just go and grab my briefcase," he said, pushing away from the table.

"Not yet, Mr. Connor. We got something special to show you first," said Henry.

Adam paused and glanced around. If it was more food, there was no way he'd ever be able to eat it. As it was, he felt what could only be what a woman pregnant with sextuplets must feel like on delivery day.

"Well, I don't know, Mr. Wheaton," he said. "I really can't imagine eating another bite."

"Then it's perfect timing. Come on and lemme show you what I mean."

Henry stood and gestured for Adam to follow. Adam pushed away from the table and ambled across the wooden floor of the kitchen and into a room he'd previously mistaken for a closet. Instead, it was a large room dominated by an immense stove set against the outside wall. Henry tugged open the door which opened downwards. The small man pulled out a six-foot metal tray. Deep grooves had been cut along the edges to catch juices as they bubbled out of the meat. Five bands of metal were arrayed along the stainless steel.

"Take off your clothes Mr. Connors," Henry said, as if he said it to men all the time.

"What? Take of my clothes? But... "

"Come on. Either you do it, or I'll have my boys do it for you," Henry said, his voice hardening.

"But why do I need... my... clothes... off?" his voice trailed away as he spun around to see the smiling faces of the family and realized that the oven wasn't made for pigs, or cows, or horses.

He spun and ran toward the door and hit the Mongoloid brothers at full speed. He bounced off and hit the floor hard. They grinned stupidly, picked him up and held him fast. Enid slid next to him and with a long knife, began to cut away his last good suit. He soon stood naked. He struggled the best he could, but the iron-like grips of the twins made it virtually impossible to move.

They threw him on the metal tray. Carefully, they secured his arms, legs, and neck with the metal bands.

He screamed for them to stop, but they ignored him.

They left him momentarily and he found himself offering them his car, his savings account, his house, his condo in Jamaica and his first born child if only they'd let him go.

They reentered. Granny carried a large twenty-gallon pot of breadcrumbs, parsley and celery. A garden shovel stuck out from the top of the mixture. It took his panicked mind but a few seconds to realize that it was stuffing and it was meant for him.

"Go on ahead and chop off that, pecker, Mable," said Henry. "We'll make jerky out of it. You know how much Momma loves to chew on her jerky."

Four things happened at once:

Granny approached his ass with a garden shovel full of dressing.

Mable approached his manhood with a paring knife.

Henry approached his stomach with his fish knife, apparently ready for the gutting.

And Adam realized that being a humanitarian had absolutely nothing to do with politics.

I SAW RENNY SHOOTING SANTA CLAUS

BY DAVID WHITMAN

Casey stared down at the corpse, a big smile erupting underneath his mustache. "I can't fucking believe you killed Santa Claus."

Renny was poking the fat man with his boot, his face pale. "You made me do it. You told me it was a prowler."

"No, my friend. I told you it *might* be a prowler. You're the one that got all gung-ho and shot the fat fucker."

Renny leaned down and studied the dead man. Santa's mouth was open, showing off white teeth in an even whiter beard. His blue eyes still registered the shock of being shot. Blood was pouring out of the Santa suit from the side.

Renny jumped when the camera flashed.

Casey pulled the picture out of the instant Polaroid camera and shook it back and forth in the air. "Well, that was a Norman Rockwell Christmas moment if I ever saw one. Who you going to get next? The Easter Bunny?"

Renny threw the shotgun to the carpet in front of the Christmas tree. "This shit isn't funny. He can't be the real Santa Claus. There ain't no such thing, man."

Casey looked at the developing picture and smiled. "Well, there ain't no such thing anymore." He sang in an off key voice. "I saw Renny shooting San-tee Claus. Underneath the mistletoe last night."

Renny frowned. "I'm glad you think this is so fucking funny. There is a dead man on my living room floor in a goddamn Santa suit, and you're cracking jokes."

Casey handed Renny the picture. "You need to learn to appreciate the absurdity of life, my friend. This is too ludicrous to not laugh at."

Renny stared at the picture, shaking his head. He was leaning over Santa, his face a mask of horror. He handed the photo back to Casey who stuck it in his back pocket. "We have to get rid of this body."

Casey was pulling at the dead man's beard. "Yep, it's real. This is *so* fucking bizarre. Why don't you just call the police?"

"Well, number one, we have enough drug paraphernalia in this house to start a commune. Number two, this gun is unregistered. And number three, once they find out I have a gun, I'm going right back to prison."

Casey smiled. "As opposed to killing Santa Claus and then trying to dispose of his body?"

"Would you cut it out with the Santa Claus shit? This is serious. I can get sent to prison for a very long time. It's like this: we either dispose of the corpse, or get rid of the drugs. You choose."

Casey looked down at the red and white body. "I guess it's the corpse then. We can't afford to get rid of the drugs." He searched through the deep pockets of the Santa suit and pulled out about five tightly rolled joints of marijuana. "Looks like Santa likes to partake of a fat blunt or two now and then."

Renny stared down at the joints. "That bastard. He *was* a prowler. Those blunts were on my dresser. The Butler brothers gave them to me for Christmas."

Casey laughed. "Well, see? I was right. He was a prowler."

Renny grabbed the joints from his friend, pocketing them quickly. "Let's get this corpse the hell out of here. There's a wheelbarrow in the garage."

After about ten minutes of struggling with the amazingly heavy corpse, they managed to get it inside the trunk. Renny tried to close it, but realized the man was too fat for it to shut all the way.

Casey burst into laughter. "Oh this is too fucking much. Now what you gonna do?"

Renny moaned. "We're gonna have to tie the trunk closed."

"Yeah, but then he'll be sticking out. Then everyone will see what you did to poor Santa."

Renny growled. "I'll throw a sheet over him, godammit! Stop it with the fucking jokes!"

"It's hard, man!"

Renny looked around the garage for some rope, but only found some cheap fishing line. "This is gonna have to do." He tied the trunk closed.

"You forgot to put a sheet on him," Casey said, snickering. He could see the Santa suit peeking out from the half open trunk.

Renny picked up an old blanket and shoved it through the crack of the trunk. "Happy now?" He waited until his friend nodded and then muttered, "Asshole."

Renny opened the garage door and they got into the car. He pulled out into the snow-covered road and watched the white flurries bounce across the windshield as they drove. Many of the houses on the streets flashed with festively colored lights.

"Dashing through the snow, with a one corpse we did slay," Casey sang in a surprisingly good Sinatra-like voice. "To a field we go, laughing all the way."

Renny turned to his friend, saying nothing, his face reddening.

Casey looked over and tried his best to hide his smile. "I'm really trying. But it's too ridiculous. Look, it's Christmas, you shot Santa Claus and now you have him stuffed in your trunk. Not to mention he had five fat blunts in his pocket. Five of YOUR fat blunts. All of this and you expect me not to laugh?"

Renny actually smirked. "It is kind of funny I guess."

"Kind of funny? It's hysterical. I can't wait to answer the inevitable question, 'How was your Christmas, man?' I'll be like, well, Renny killed Santa in front of the Christmas tree and I helped him get rid of the body." Casey noticed a glowing 7-11 off in the distance. "Hey, can you stop there? I need to grab some smokes."

"Uh...are you sure that's a good idea considering what we have in the trunk?"

"Oh please. Who the hell is going to look in the trunk? It's fucking Christmas, for Christ's sake!"

Renny turned into the parking lot of the 7-11. He waited impatiently and watched the snowflakes as they danced around the windshield.

As he watched in pure, unadulterated horror, a police car pulled into the parking lot. Renny stared straight ahead and tried to act as normal as possible. Out of his peripheral vision he noticed the cop get out of the car and walk directly towards him. At the same time, Casey came out of the 7-11, nodded at the cop, and got back into the car.

Renny kept a passive face as the officer knocked on the glass. He rolled the window down and tried his best to smile. "Hello, officer."

"Merry Christmas, guys. Remember me?"

Renny squinted. It was the same cop who arrested him last year on a misdemeanor charge of marijuana possession at his Daddy's hoedown.

The cop smiled. "I can tell by your face you recognize me. Staying out of trouble on this fine Christmas night?"

"Actually, we killed Santa Claus and stuffed him in the trunk," Casey said, his face keeping a deadpan expression as he lit his Kool cigarette. Renny imagined himself wrapping his fingers around Casey's throat and squeezing until the veins popped.

"Cute," the cop said, looking towards the back of the car. "You know, that trunk can't be sticking open like that. It's a hazard and may distract you. What the hell you got in there anyways?"

Renny swallowed heavily, his smile growing weaker. "Just some presents I'm taking home to my kid. I haven't seen him in six months. I'm hoping this Christmas will give us a chance to get together."

The officer nodded. "I hear ya there. I got the same problem." He pulled his pants up over his beer belly and straightened his shirt. "Well, have a Merry Christmas guys."

Renny nodded, hoping desperately the cop didn't notice he was starting to sweat. "You too, officer."

When they pulled out of the parking lot Casey howled in

laughter. "Oh my god was that fucking funny. You should have seen your face when I said that about the Santa in the trunk! That was priceless!"

"Are you a goddamn retard!" Renny screamed. "Do you want us to go to prison?"

"Calm down, man," Casey said, a giggle escaping his lips. "Like he was going to believe me when I said that."

"That's not the point, dumbfuck! You made him take notice of the trunk. That was stupid."

"You're going to make me laugh even harder, stop. Think of it as a funny story you can tell your kids."

Renny turned off on a barely plowed side road. "Man, you need help. What kind of story would this be to tell a freaking kid? And then, little Jimmy, we couldn't fit Santa in the trunk."

Casey chuckled. "That's the spirit, man! See, you're even starting to find humor in this."

Renny sighed. "Yeah, I am. It's just too messed up of a situation for it not to be a little funny." He pulled off to the side of the road. "Okay, this should be good enough. We can bury the body out here and hope they don't find him until spring sometime."

They exited the car and untied the fishing wire. Santa's eyes were open and he groaned.

"Oh shit!" Renny hissed. "Now what?"

"Oh no," Casey said, backing away from the car like it was wired with explosives. "I thought you said he was dead."

"He looked dead to me. Didn't he look dead to you?"

Casey pulled a wool hat from his pocket and stuck it on his head. "We're going to have to leave him here."

"Are you kidding me? No way. It's Christmas, man!"

"He tried to steal your blunts. Did he not?"

"Yeah, but that doesn't mean I can murder Santa Claus. No way, no how." Renny stared down at the corpulent man. Santa was watching them fearfully, his eyes white in the darkness of the trunk.

"It's not Santa Claus," Casey said, leaning forward. "It's some fat bastard who broke into your apartment and tried to steal your blunts. Think of it that way, and it's not so hard to leave him out here, is it?"

"I'm not leaving him out here. I can't. Especially not on Christmas night. And don't you think I *KNOW* it's not goddamn Santa Claus for real, whipdick?" He looked up into the sky and squinted. The snow was starting to fall heavily.

"Are you forgetting you already shot the fat bastard?"

"Uh...no, asshole, but shooting him before was shooting a prowler. Shooting him now makes it murder. Screw that."

"Well, we can't take him to the hospital," Casey said, pulling his cap down over his head tightly. "Someone will see us and then find out that you shot him. So where does that leave us?"

"We'll have to take him home and hope we can make him better."

"Oh man. I should have gone over my girlfriend's house tonight. This night is fucked."

They tied the trunk closed as best they could, but it was definitely weaker as they had destroyed some string while untying it. Renny started the car and headed back into the opposite direction. The mood had darkened as both of them were a little nervous as to what they were going to do.

"Stop here again," Casey said as they passed the 7-11.

"What the hell for!" Renny shouted, his patience running out.

"I need some coffee, man. You don't have any at home."

Renny tried not to scream and pulled back into the parking lot, slamming on the brakes at the front of the store. "Hurry the hell up!"

Casey opened the car door. "Okay, okay. Jeez. Take a chill pill, man."

Renny watched as Casey ran into the store and rubbed his temples in a vain effort to rid himself of his massive headache. He gasped as the trunk lid shot up in his rearview mirror. In his side mirror, he watched in horror as Santa climbed out of the trunk and started to walk drunkenly towards the road.

"Uh...uh...uh," Renny muttered, struggling to find the proper word.

Casey walked out of the 7-11, the cup of coffee to his lips. He froze when he saw the portly man staggering out to the road. "What the hell?" he mouthed at Renny.

Renny opened the car door and jumped out. "Shit, shit, shit. Help me get him!"

"Just let him go," he said turning around and looking inside the building nervously. "Someone is going to see us."

"We can't just let him go, fucknut!" Renny shouted, taking off after the old man who by now had made it to the main road where he was crossing tipsily. "I shot him! He saw our faces! He heard us talking from the trunk! If this shit gets back to the cops, I'm going right back to prison! He knows where I live, man!"

Casey watched as his chubby partner ran through the snow-covered parking lot. He sighed, threw his coffee down onto the ground, and took off after his friend.

Renny tackled Santa just as he reached the other side of the road. They went down in an explosion of wet snow, wrestling around madly.

Santa managed to get his boots into the center of Renny's chest and launched him airborne.

Renny went squealing into the road, sliding through the snow, his mouth wide open. Casey jumped up just in time as his howling friend went sailing past and he turned to watch almost curiously.

"Get him!" Renny shrieked, still sliding backward.

Casey shouted out a war cry and launched himself on Santa, his face filled with macho anger. Two seconds later, he was trying to crawl away from the plump man, screaming in pain, his eyes wide as snowballs. Santa bit down ferociously onto his calf and he screamed.

The rabid Santa pulled Casey back as he struggled to crawl away, his fingers making lines in the snow as he went backward.

"FOR THE LOVE OF FUCKING GOD! HE'S GOING TO KILL ME, MAN, HE'S—" Casey screamed, abruptly cut off as the old man launched a fist into his face.

Renny got up from the road and ran full force towards the fighting men. He tripped at the curb and fell clumsily into them, shrieking as he hit.

Santa kicked and bit savagely.

Finally, in a move that was more luck than skill, Renny

managed to slam the chubby head into the curb, knocking him back into unconsciousness.

The squad car from earlier in the evening pulled up next to the curb. The cop rolled the window down. "Evening, fellas."

"Evening, officer," Renny and Casey said in unison. They were lying on top of the unconscious Santa, big fake smiles plastered on their faces. Casey dabbed his sleeve on his bloody lip.

"Ah, Christmas," the cop said, staring at them with a crooked smile. "This looks like a picture right out of *Currier and Ives*. Always lay an assbeat into Santa on Christmas, do ya's?"

"It's my girlfriend's father," Renny said. "He's drunk. We were taking him home to sleep it off when he leapt from the car. We had to stop him or he would have froze to death, officer."

"Uh huh," the cop said. "You know, I'm almost inclined to believe this story, as I find it hard to believe anyone would have the audacity to beat Santa's ass on Christmas. Need any help getting him back to the car?"

"Nah," Renny said. "We'll be okay. Thanks anyways."

"Okay," the cop said, rolling his window back up. "Oh, and fellas…"

"Yes, officer?" they said again simultaneously, practically holding their breath.

"Merry Christmas."

"Merry Christmas!"

"Get that poor drunk bastard home before he freezes to death," the cop said and pulled away.

Renny watched the squad car drive leisurely down the street. "Shoot me. Shoot me now."

Casey got to his feet, rubbing his bleeding lip. "Let's get this fat fuck back into the car."

After lots of struggling, they managed to get Santa back inside. This time they threw him into the back seat. The ride home was uneventful.

With great effort, they dragged the old man into the house and placed him on the couch. They sat down heavily on the floor, exhaling big sighs of relief at being back in the warmth.

Casey lay backwards all the way, sprawling himself. "I can't believe we got our asses beat by Santa Claus."

Renny laughed, his sore body shaking. Seconds later, they were both in hysterics.

"Oh man," Renny said between giggles. "Imagine how funny we must have looked to that cop."

After they had rested a bit, they decided to see if they could help the old man. They managed to get the top of the Santa suit off.

To their astonishment, the wound was gone.

"What...the...fuck," Renny whispered. "He was bleeding all over the floor." He picked up the Santa suit. There was a huge hole where the shell of the shotgun had ripped through. Blood still caked the hole. "How in the *hell* did he heal himself?"

"I don't even want to think about the implications of this," Casey said, his face turning white as he studied the Santa's huge belly. The old man was breathing quite normally. "I only have one suggestion in a situation like this."

Renny turned to his friend. "What's that?"

"You pull one of those blunts out of your pocket and we get so high that cannabis smoke drifts out of our ass."

Renny smiled, pulling one of the joints from his pocket. "Oh...how high they got, pa rum-pum pum pum."

Casey snickered, lighting the end of the joint for his friend. Renny inhaled of the smoke deeply and passed it back to his partner.

Ten minutes later, they were completely stoned. They sat back on the floor and studied the sleeping Santa.

"So," Renny said, blowing a ring of smoke into the air. "Do you think it's really Santa Claus?"

"Well, if it is, it's a good thing we didn't leave him out in the snow like that. That would have been just wrong."

Renny dug deep into his pocket. "I have two more, want to smoke them?"

Casey fell back, exhausted. "Nah, save them for tomorrow."

When Renny awoke the next morning, Santa was no longer on the couch. There were two neatly wrapped presents in his place. He shook Casey awake and pointed at the lavishly decorated boxes.

"You've gotta be kidding me," Casey said, rubbing the sleep from his eyes.

Renny picked up the presents cautiously. He threw one to Casey and shook the other before putting it up to his ear for a listen.

"You go first," Casey said, swallowing nervously.

Renny tore upon the box as carefully as if he were opening up a ticking bomb. He gently ripped off the top, peered inside and then closed his eyes, a wide smile on his face. He tried to hold it back, but he started to giggle. When he held the open box up to Casey's face, he too started to laugh.

Inside was a big lump of coal.

Casey's box held the same thing. What had happened last night now seemed surreal and dream-like in the morning.

"Merry Christmas, man," Casey said, holding his coal up at his friend.

Renny picked his own lump out of the box and held it up. They knocked the coal together like wineglasses. "Lord knows we deserve it, man. Merry Christmas, my friend." He put his hands in his pocket and then frowned. "Oh, that jolly, fat thieving fuck."

"What?" Casey asked, rubbing his coal with a big smile.

"My last two blunts are gone."

THE STERILITY OF EARTHLY RAGE

BY WESTON OCHSE

The angry explosion died — disparate sounds of violence sliding softly to the ground along with the mottled pieces of flesh, leaving the scene silent and lonely. There was no blood. There never was. Only the way the body had fallen, arms and legs slightly askew as if it had merely tripped and fallen backwards, reminded Greta of its former humanity. The 12-gauge hole in the stomach reminded her of its current deadness.

Greta worked the pump hard and the quick *snick* of the ejected shell was followed by its small, hollow bounces along the wet asphalt of the alley. She aimed from the hip at the still form and cautiously approached, stepping over white pumps, a flowered handbag and the few surviving beads of the white faux-pearl necklace that had disintegrated in the blast. Wary of hands reaching out and gripping her ankles, she pinned a wrist to the earth with a booted foot and stared into the wound.

The movement was imperceptible at first, and she would have missed it had she not been staring so intently. What could have been mistaken for tiny pieces of exploded flesh began moving. At first minutely, they picked up speed until faster and faster the maggots became an undulating mass of writhing bodies as they tasted the purer air of the alley. They rubbed and slithered in an intertwining knot of protection around and against each other as if they knew her intentions.

The bile rose in her throat and threatened to add the Technicolor ingredients of a pepperoni-and-cheese pizza across the length of the dead body. She fought it back, determined to stay long enough to finish her work. Greta curled her nose at the putrid stench. She gritted hard, keeping her meal in and the taste of deadness out, and invaded the mass of maggots with the still smoking end of the barrel. Its touch sizzled the sightless beasts and sent them pushing away until what lay beneath was revealed in all its bleak, ugly truth — an unborn, disfigured fetus staring at her with wide, intelligent eyes.

The hellish creation reached up with tiny clawed fists as if it knew her next intention, begging, pleading for her not to do what her conscience insisted. It opened its mouth revealing needle-sharp teeth and emitted a tiny peal of terror. Its scream went unheard as she blasted it apart.

Greta jerked a tin of turpentine from the cargo pocket of her pants and doused both the host and the thing she'd never think of as a baby, concentrating the toxic liquid into the wound. She tossed aside the empty container, lit a wooden safety match, dropped it and stepped back. With a *whoosh*, the body caught fire and thick oily smoke poured into the clean mountain air. The cheap dress caught quickly, flames racing along the nylon seams.

Greta stepped around the inferno and, with the toe of her boot, flipped the blonde wig that had fallen off into the greedy flames. Resting the barrel on her shoulder, she strode down the alley in search of more prey.

She couldn't help but feel the irony of the situation. She'd seen specialists in several different states and each, in their own condescending way, had told her that she'd never be able to conceive, yet this was the third pregnant man she'd killed this week.

The world was certainly on its ass. Greta had first noticed *them* about a month ago. The first indication was the general absence of men in the town. Then the businesses along Main Street had started closing their doors for good.

Tellico Plains had never been a bustling metropolis of financial activity, but it had its share of tourists. As the last stop before the Tellico, Citico and Hiawasee Rivers, the small town afforded fisherman their last chance for food, beer and the necessary bait before they attempted to conquer the diminishing population of Tennessee trout. No one was getting rich, but as long as the rivers survived, there'd always be decent business.

Posy, the bartender over at the Silly Goose, said the town was dying because of the new highway they'd put in over by Sweetwater. Still, the Tellico River ran through Tellico Plains, so folks still had to travel through.

No, Greta had a different theory.

A few weeks back she'd been making a midnight run to the Golden Gallon for a pint of ice cream and a twelve-pack of beer when her headlights had illuminated a figure staggering drunkenly along the side of the road. She'd figured it was just another drunk redneck, but as she'd passed, she'd noticed the dress and the plump pregnant stomach of a woman in the third trimester.

She'd pulled over, stopping some twenty yards in front of the woman. She's grabbed a blanket from behind the seat, the flashlight from under the dash and then hurried from the pick-up back towards the woman. She'd hoped all the television doctors and medical documentaries she'd watched had prepared her for the impending delivery.

But when the beam of the flashlight had shone on the woman, they'd both stopped. She'd noticed the bloody stockinged feet, the hopelessly out-of-style flower-print dress, broad shoulders and a week's growth of beard on the square jaw. The long, red wig hung askew, revealing a graying crew cut beneath.

They'd stared at each other for some thirty seconds. Then the man had shrieked and bolted, disappearing into the darkness of the kudzu-covered trees, arms wrapped carefully around his pregnancy.

Then leaving the town's lone fast-food restaurant a week later, she'd accidentally bumped into another pregnant woman, almost knocking the poor lady ass-over-teakettle. Greta had kept her from falling and stood aside to let her in. It wasn't until Greta had pulled into traffic, eating a handful of curly fries, that she'd realized the *excuse me* she'd heard had been deeper than her father's.

Then in the doctor's office a few days ago, everything had clicked into place. She'd just put her jacket back on and was leaving with her prescription of allergy medicine, when she'd passed by the door to the other examination room. Greta wasn't nosy by nature, but her eyes had found their own way and the image of the man stopped her cold. He sat in support hose held up by lacy black garters. The blue veins of his pregnant stomach were stark against his pale skin. He held a wig in his hands as the doctor peeked into his ears.

She'd stayed, riveted on the anachronism, until she'd heard the sharp cough of a nurse behind her. Unwilling to confront the strangeness, Greta had lowered her head and left as fast as she could.

Chaotic thoughts of Jerry Springer, Oprah, Geraldo, the front page of the *Enquirer*, N.A.S.A., and the Center for Disease Control had spun through her mind. There was no mistaking what she'd seen. No way was the man's pregnancy any kind of special effects. It had definitely been the real thing.

Worst of all, the pregnant man had been Henry Jenkins — lifetime friend of her father and Tellico Plains' Chief of Police.

The only person she felt safe enough to talk about it with was her father, but it had been his death that had brought her back home two months ago. She'd come for the funeral and to clear up some loose ends. She'd only planned on staying a week, but the amount of loose ends surprised her.

She'd tried to sell the old house, yet in the recessive market no one was buying any edifice whose primary color was tarpaper black. He also had many debts and, faithful to her upbringing, Greta had been determined to pay them off. It wasn't like she'd anything better to do. After leaving the army two years ago, she'd worked at a series of meaningless minimum wage jobs and hadn't been looking forward to working her way up to the esteemed position of Senior Fry Chef.

The funeral had been a closed casket affair. Not the way she'd wanted it, but the coroner had thought it best due to the condition of the body. The Chief of Police had told her on the phone that her father had been found by fisherman, his body burned almost beyond recognition. "He'd been camping," they said. And like he was a whale-bellied tourist from Yankee Land, they said he must have rolled into the campfire in his sleep, his nylon sleeping bag going up like a match.

Her father would have never been so stupid.

To make matters sadder, even with all the friends he'd had, only three other people had attended the funeral. In retrospect, it was probably because the rest were having a Mary Kay party.

When the funeral ended, she'd finally some time to think. With all the weirdness in Tellico Plains and seeing Henry in garters and ready to pop, a nagging feeling grew within her.

The feeling started at midnight two days ago when she'd finally confirmed her fears with a shovel and a lantern. Not a single burn marred her father's body. With trembling fingers, she'd unbuttoned his suit and shirt, revealing a long ragged incision the length of his stomach. It was nothing that any skilled doctor would make. Even a veterinarian could have done a better job.

It was as if her father had made the cut himself — a self-made abortion.

And her perplexity had turned to rage.

The hunter had become the prey.

Greta had just left Leroy's Bait and Ammo, a bag of assorted ammunition gripped in her arms, when she'd noticed her stalkers. At first she'd chuckled. She could pick them out of a crowd, now. She knew what to look for. And the three men dressed in 1950s women's clothes, criss-crossing the street behind her like poorly trained spies, fit her mental profile perfectly.

But it was daylight and she missed the comfortable feeling of the Mossberg shotgun that had become her nighttime companion. Under her leather jacket hung the .357 colt python, snug in a quick-draw shoulder holster, but that only held six rounds. Granted, they were six rounds that could turn a rampaging bear on crack and intent on tasting her long juicy legs into upholstery, but it wasn't her Mossberg.

She finally managed to give them the slip near the back door of the Silly Goose. She was safe for now, but what then. The fact that she'd been followed meant that they knew about her. She couldn't return to the house. They'd probably be waiting.

The image of Henry Jenkins sitting on her father's living

room couch and aiming his police special at the front door sent her in the other direction. She needed time to plan. She needed to quell her rage and remember the lessons she'd learned in the Army.

Two hours later, she sat in a hotel room in Sweetwater sipping on a Coors Light, forming a plan.

She'd counted thirteen pregnant men. Henry, George from the shoe store, Alvin from the garage, Jimbo, Steve, Rick —- the rest she'd recognized but really didn't know. On her third beer, she'd made the connection. All had been members of the Benevolent and Protective Brotherhood of Elks: a group of men who got drunk, played bingo and in some miracle of modern medicine had gotten themselves pregnant. And, if they hadn't changed their schedule for some reason, they had a meeting tomorrow night.

It wasn't until all twelve beers were scattered around the bed like discarded large-caliber bullets that she fell into a deep and drunken slumber.

She was in a forest, the tall long-leaf pines of Fort Bragg surrounding her, penning her in. She was in her battle rattle: a belt with two canteens and ammo pouches stuffed with magazines of 5.56 mm blanks, a rucksack filled with enough food and sundries to keep her alive for days, a Kevlar helmet, and an M16A2—deadly except for the clunky, red blank adapter that tipped the barrel.

And she was alone.

She'd been kneeling deep within an azalea bush for over an hour and many of the super stud soldiers trying to complete the last week of their special forces training had blundered by. She could have taken any of them, at any time, but she had a specific target in mind.

Fifteen minutes later, an A-Team slipped into view. Of all those who'd passed by her, these were the quietest. They made the forest a part of them — each tree and bush an extension of their limbs. Five men functioning as one. The very best of the United States Army.

When they finally crept within the kill zone, she smiled. "Don't fucking move," she'd whispered.

The A-Team halted. Greta felt them tense, especially the leader, Sgt. Henderson. He'd been caught by a woman and he'd never live it down. Sgt. Henderson was of the old school where women had no place in the Army and no place in combat.

And Greta had made it her personal goal to prove him wrong.

"I got two claymores in a V-shape ambush and you're dead fucking center. Throw your weapons down. And do it now, Old School."

It was just a game. War games to make the soldiers better. Hone and sharpern their skill. Too many people cheated, however. That's why the special forces had invented their own unique claymore mines. Instead of firing enough ball bearings to kill everyone within a forty-five degree arc and out to thirty meters, these sprayed red paint pellets. She held the clackers in her left hand, ready to paint the men red if they decided to cheat.

She heard their cursing and counted as five rifles hit the ground. Greta stood and left the protection of the bush. She couldn't help but laugh. As Sgt. Henderson turned around with the other men and she caught the agonized look in his eyes, she'd laughed harder.

Her only mistake.

He'd launched himself across the five feet that separated them and she'd squeezed the clackers. The rest of the A Team was suddenly covered in the violent propulsion of plastic and red dripping paint. But Sgt Henderson was outside the arc. She saw the fist as it hit the side of her face, and then she saw blackness.

When she'd awoken, she'd simultaneously felt the throbbing from her cheek and the minute breeze that teased her naked skin. She'd felt the roughness of pine bark against her back and buttocks and the rope, impossibly tight against her wrists and ankles. She'd opening her eyes, but realized that they already were open.

She'd been blindfolded.

And tied naked to a tree..

She began to pray.

"You can't do this," she'd cried. "This isn't fair."

"War isn't fair, bitch. Did you think you could kill us?"

"But the rest of the team's dead. You killed them," she said, reasoning and happy that the instructors would discover the deaths and the man's incompetence as a leader.

"Those uniforms are trash. We changed them. Now, it's your word against ours," he said, his voice changing from confidence to speculation. "I wonder what we should do to you?"

She felt hands move along her legs and wanted to scream. She wouldn't give them the satisfaction. More hands grasped and pulled painfully at her breasts she bit back a scream. Fingers wound through her thick mound of pubic hair and she still refused to scream. It wasn't until the end of the M16 entered her private place that she'd finally screamed and felt her soul withdraw to a safe dark place.

She'd swirled in the blackness of pain.

Misery was in her every breath.

She couldn't feel her body.

She couldn't feel the men.

She was in a different place.

A safe place.

"Why do you care," came a voice, silky and warm.

"They raped me," she heard herself mutter, rage and pain shuddering against her soul. "I want them to die."

"Why do you care," repeated the same voice. The words were a salve to her pain.

"It isn't fair. I won," she whimpered. "I'm a soldier."

"You aren't a soldier," said the voice, the sound changing to nails. "You're a woman. And women are meant for one thing."

"No!" she heard herself scream.

"You're nothing more than a baby-maker. You recycle sperm."

"No!"

"You aren't strong enough. You are weak. You are a woman," the words scraped her like broken shards of glass.

"No!"

"Then what do you want?" it asked, soft and warm again.

"I want... I want them to feel what I feel. Let them be what I am," she heard herself say.

"All of them?" asked the voice.

"Every fucking one of them," she heard herself say. "Every fucking one of them."

Her last words trailed off and the darkness left her. The ropes disappeared. The men disappeared. When she opened her eyes, she saw the cheap wallpaper of the hotel room and the beer cans scattered across the floor.

A memory of the warm metal of the barrel of the M16 still teased her insides, and as always after the dream, she wept.

Greta huddled in the bush. She was going to finish what she had started. Inside, the meeting had already begun. She heard them, laughing and drinking. Their very frivolity made her throb with anger.

She wore her battle rattle again, one of the only things she'd kept from her four-year stay in the Army. This time, there were no blanks. She carried enough ammo to kill a hundred pregnant men.

Greta slid from the bush and followed the shadows along the side of the clubhouse. She reached the corner and peaked around. When she saw that it was all clear, she sprinted around the back. With bolt cutters, she removed the lock from the basement door. She slipped the bolt cutters back into her rucksack and opened the door upward. She stared onto the depths of the basement and trained the Mossberg into the darkness.

After a few seconds of listening, she descended the stairs and tugged the door shut behind her. From atop her head, she pulled down the AN-PVS 7 night vision goggles. Flicking the switch, she was greeted with a small whine. She blinked twice to get used to the eerie sensation and the darkness of the basement came to life in green and white. She stepped quickly to the fuse box.

It was less than a minute from when she shut off the power until she burst into the upstairs room.

While she'd been waiting, she'd counted twenty-seven pregnant men and three who appeared normal. She scanned the room quickly. White shaped figures milled in confusion.

When her vision reached the small stage at the other end of the room she stopped. Atop the stage were three white shapes. Two stood, and one knelt, his head bobbing in a familiar rhythm.

Concentrating, She finally made out, not a white figure, but a figure made of complete darkness standing in front of the kneeling figure. Even the technology of the goggles could not illuminate the form, and that fact told her much.

A man bumped into her and she spun, catching him on the side of the head with the butt of the shotgun. He screamed as he went down and the sound stilled the milling men. A moment later, they were running blindly, adding their screams to the increasing din.

Greta fired mechanically. Although each flash of the barrel temporarily blinded her enhanced sight, with so many targets, she hardly needed to aim. When the shotgun was empty, she let it clatter to the floor rather than reloading. She snatched up her Colt AR-15 that a Good Old Boy over in Sweetwater had modified to automatic for her. The staccato sounds of supersonic death thundered over the screams as she raked the barrel from side to side. She reloaded five times, sending one hundred and eighty rounds of 5.56 millimeter murder into the crazy harem that had been an Elks Lodge.

She dropped the smoking rifle and drew two nine-millimeter pistols. Greta stalked among the bodies. Where she saw movement, she placed a round into a head. She was like a rancher culling a herd.

Chest heaving and sweat dripping from her body, she found herself at the foot of the small raised stage. She saw three illuminated forms sprawled along the wooden floor, unmoving. The darker figure was nowhere to be seen.

Greta cursed and ripped off the goggles, becoming as blind as her prey. She reached into her cargo pocket and removed a flare. Closing her eyes, she removed an end and lit the phosphorous. The initial spark blinded her even through closed lids, but it was nothing like it would have done had her eyes been open. Greta tossed the flare onto the stage and grabbed her last shotgun—this one had a pistol grip and hung from a strap from over her shoulder and held special ammo.

She heard laughter. "Why did you come?"

Greta spun toward the source of the question and blinked her eyes trying furiously to clear her ruined vision. She recognized the voice and felt the ghosts of hands along her camouflage-covered skin as it returned the memories of the rape.

"You know why!" she screamed.

Her vision began to clear. The immense figure, that had been mere darkness with the goggles, appeared in all its frightening reality. The figure in front of her stood nearly eight feet tall. Spines protruded along its naked body at odd, uneven angles. Broad feet displayed seven wicked claws. A mane of hair flowed down its back in a parody of a punkish mohawk. Two red eyes sat above a mouthful of dagger-like teeth. From between muscular legs hung a great dangling penis, easily two feet long, covered with purple slickness.

Greta gagged as the reality of the form struck her.

"Not what you expected?" came the warm voice.

"I... I didn't know what to expect."

"What form did you expect your rage to take, Greta?"

"My rage... ?"

"It was you who made me. Who called me forth." The demon laughed harshly. "I am what you wanted."

"No," Greta screamed. "It was you!"

"Ah, my dear Greta. My poor misunderstood sperm-recycler. You begged me to do this. You are the one who proposed this," he said indicating the carnage with a taloned hand.

"Did you know that your father was the first?"

She screamed and fired the shotgun at the laughing demon. Five rounds exploded in the flesh, creating huge divots of purple wounds. When the priest had seen her soaking the buckshot in the church's baptismal, she'd told him to fuck off. He wouldn't have understood, anyway.

The demon fell backwards, the sounds of its multi-octave pain like an airplane engine in the confined space of the lodge. Greta staggered forward, the discordancy threatening her consciousness. She fired the remaining two rounds into the ugly penis and reveled as it disappeared in an explosion of purple flesh and blood.

She stood over the thing that had been part of her for the last two years. Powerful eyes stared back into her soul and visions of her father on his knees shot through her like a bullet.

"You have gotten the best of me, child," came the wheezing voice. "I feel the tug. I am not long here."

Whatever Greta expected to feel at this point, sadness wasn't it. Empathy poured from the demon in waves and as it washed over her, her rage was sublimated with melancholy grief and the senseless deaths of the men.

The thing smiled as its skin began to slough off and its eyes collapsed inwards.

"I will return, Greta," it said as several teeth fell blackened to the ground. "Until then, my progeny shall rule."

All firmness left the demon and she watched as it slid into a pool of flesh and bone. The liquid reflected the white light of the flare and as she stared into it, she could see a swirling of faces: her father, Henry, Fred, Alvin and dozens more she didn't recognize, each agonized and screaming somewhere far away. Laughter echoed in her head as the pool shrank upon itself and disappeared in a pop that sent her to her knees with the pressure.

"Progeny," she said, the word echoing in the dead room. And they were her children.

IT'S A SICK WORLD

BY DAVID WHITMAN

"This grave better not be the same as the last one," Brooks said, gazing down at the coffin and brushing the dirt away from the lid. He pulled at his goatee as he stared at the casket.

The full moon shone down on us, granting more light than we wanted while doing such an illegal task. The night air was unnaturally cool, giving me the unsettling impression that I could feel the physical presence of the dead. Every time the wind would blow through the trees, sending shadows moving about in dream-like dances, I would jump.

City boys like me don't function well in the south. Being a black man didn't help matters any, either. I was more paranoid this far down south than I was in any big city area, but so far, everywhere I went stereotypes were being broken. I hadn't heard the word "nigger" uttered one time, nor had I felt any racism. Being in a graveyard at night, though, dug up all my fears of cartoony redneck motherfuckers with red plaid shirts and memberships in the local Ku Klux Klan. It wasn't too hard to imagine a brother hanging from one of the thick-limbed trees dotting the graveyard, a circle of white sheeted Klansman standing around with flickering torches.

I had a bad feeling about tonight. The whole atmosphere reminded me of a horror movie. I don't think I've ever seen a brother survive a horror movie. That shit always pissed me off. Even when they were heroes, like in *Night of the Living Dead*, the brother got his ass killed.

We had spent the last few months trying to make a living at our various cons and scams and not doing a very good job of it. It was Brooks' idea to get out of New Orleans and go out here in the Deep South to make some money. He figured the city folk were just too smart anymore, and that we would have a much easier time pulling a con on the country bumpkins. Shit didn't work out that way, though. If anything, they were even wiser-more suspicious to anything we tried to pull. The pickings were damn scarce. It was Brooks' idea to rob the dead, not mine. I figured that most people who had expensive jewelry willed it to their relatives.

"No, Rudy," Brooks had said as I tried to shoot down his dumbass idea. "The dead are fucking rich. I had a buddy that used to do it and he made a shitload of money. Not only that, but this kind of jewelry could never be traced back to us. Who would think of tracing it back to the dead?"

The only problem was that things got a little strange when we dug up our first grave. We shrugged that off and moved on to the second, only to have the same damn problem. This was our fourth night in Greyson's Cemetery and our fourth freshly dug grave. Shit just wasn't working out.

See, I've always believed in karma. This is why my life is so fucked up. My granddaddy always used to say, "It always comes back to bite you in the ass." I can't tell you how many times that came true. I spent my whole damn life getting bit in the ass. I just can't help myself. I keep damning myself no matter how much I try to see straight. I used to be in college. Look at me now. Shit, to think I was going to be a writer at one time in my sorry life.

I hate cemeteries to begin with. They scare the living shit outta me. Robbing graves was probably fucking up my karma in a real big way. Sometimes, I tried to rationalize our scams. I felt that if they were stupid enough to fall for our little tricks, then they deserved the loss of their money. To Brooks and I, it was like a game—a game which we lost more than we won. Robbing the dead was different—it was invading a place that should not be entered. Taking what was not meant to be ours. I just knew it was going to blow the hell up in our faces.

"Shit," Brooks muttered, as he began to pry at the coffin lid, his round belly shaking up and down. "If it happens again, I think I'm gonna cry."

I nodded and held my breath. This grave was a relatively old one belonging to a corpse by the name of Bannen Wilde. "I think it is," I said. "It looks tampered with."

The coffin opened, sending up a vague scent of dirt and mildew. We leaned over and peered in.

It was empty.

"Shit!" I shouted, falling back into the soft dirt. "Another five hours lost. Screw this shit, Brooks."

"How the hell could the whole cemetery be empty?" Brooks asked.

He knew I sure as hell didn't know the answer. Just thinking about it gave me the chills, big time.

Brooks slammed the coffin lid down, sending the stale and musty air into my face. "Fuck this," he said. "Let's not even bother putting the dirt back. Some sick bastard is beating us to it."

I threw him a smile. "Sick bastard? As opposed to our grave robbing asses?"

He nodded and rubbed his shaven head. "Well, yeah. We only want the damn jewelry. Whatever sick fuck-"

"Fucks," I added. "Sick fucks as in plural. I doubt one person would rob a grave by himself. Too much work."

Brooks paused and looked at me, thinking about what I said. His face registered his annoyance. "Whatever sick *fucks* did this are different. They are stealing the bodies. What would anyone want with a corpse?"

"I don't even wanna think about that," I said, offering the handle of my shovel to Brooks as he climbed out.

Brooks sat down on a tombstone and lit a cigarette, the glow of the match making his pale face look eerie. He held the pack out to me and I grabbed one hungrily. I watched as he blew smoke into the black night, wondering what we were going to do.

I gazed around the place with my writer's eye. Greyson's Cemetery had a mix of graves, both old and new—some of the graves dated back all the way to the colonial period. Thick trees reached out to the moonlight like mottled arms. The tombstones dotted the landscape like crooked teeth, a light breeze blowing through them. After spending the last four nights in here, I had begun to hate it.

"You know, there is a way to make money out of this," Brooks said, inhaling deeply on his cigarette.

I knew exactly where he was going. "Yeah. The kind of people that rob graves would hardly want the police to find about it."

It was decided that easily. We spent the rest of the evening putting the dirt back in the hole. The plan was to catch the sick motherfuckers in the act of stealing the bodies. We would ask for a nice sum of money and then disappear with the loot.

There was only one dark road that led to Greyson's Cemetery, so we parked just outside, hiding the Cadillac carefully in a thick clearing of trees and shrubbery. Any car that passed by in the darkness would have no choice but to ride right by us.

They didn't show up until four nights later.

A truck cruised by, its headlights off. It drove about a hundred yards past where we were hidden and stopped. It pulled inside the trees, not unlike the way we had done. We didn't see them again, they had probably just entered the graveyard from the woods.

We waited about ten minutes and then quietly crept up to where they had parked. We both had our guns out, not taking any chances.

We moved as silently as possible through the darkness. Although we didn't see anyone, I still held my gun out in front of my face like a talisman. No one was in the front seat. The back of the truck was empty as well and smelled vaguely of rotting meat.

"Should we wait for them here, or go get them inside the graveyard?" I asked, studying the trees for any kind of movement.

"Let's wait here," Brooks said, just as the world exploded into noise.

Brooks' fat body was sent airborne. He landed on me

heavily, crushing me into the ground like a pinned bug. Brooks was gasping as if he couldn't breathe.

A boot stomped down onto my wrist, sending waves of exploding pain spidering up my arm.

"Let go of the gun," a deep, cold voice said in an odd accent that I couldn't quite place. He kicked the gun out of my hand and stepped back.

I couldn't see his features. His body was unnaturally thin and his arms and legs jutted out in spider-like sticks. The glare of the flashlight hit me in the face, blinding me.

Brooks was still coughing to my left. The flashlight moved over to him, revealing a huge gaping wound in his stomach.

The flashlight stabbed back into my face. "Who the hell are you, nigger?" the man asked. "You sure as hell don't look like no cops."

"We were just curious," I said, squinting in the light.

The man laughed, a sound like glass being ground together between two cinderblocks. "You just entered into a fucking nightmare, kitty cat."

"What in the hell is going on, Caleb?" a voice said from behind the truck.

"Looks like you won't need to dig tonight, Jobe," the man answered. "I got your corpse right here."

Two more shadowy figures walked down and stopped a few feet from me. Although I couldn't tell in the darkness, one appeared to be a child.

"Don't go too close, Hezekiah," Jobe said. "We gonna take them both?"

"Yeah," Caleb said. "Daddy will be happy. Hold this flashlight into the nigger's eyes." He moved forward and stuck the barrel of the shotgun into my forehead. "Roll the hell over and put your hands behind your back. Hezekiah, go grab that wire that's under the seat."

A few minutes later and I was hog-tied, my hands attached to my ankles. They lifted me up and tossed me in the back of the truck like a bag of garbage.

"Oh shit, this is a fat one," Jobe said and I felt Brooks' body land heavily on my leg in a flash of bone cracking pain. Warm blood spilled out onto my thigh from Brook's wound.

The truck lurched forward as I struggled, the wire digging excruciatingly into my skin. We drove on for about forty-five minutes. I had given up trying to get out, because every time I pulled, the wire sunk deeper into my flesh. Every time we hit a bump, Brooks' heavy body would bounce up and down painfully on my ankle.

When the truck came to a stop, I was almost weeping. My imagination was beginning to taunt me with all sorts of heavy shit. Every redneck movie I ever saw was beginning to creep up on me. I half expected that retarded boy from *Deliverance* to jump out and start plucking away on his banjo.

A family that needed corpses would do anything.

"Hezekiah, go tell Daddy we got a surprise for him," Caleb said, pulling the back of the truck open. "The nightmare is only beginning, kitty cat."

Jobe laughed, sounding like a man who was being choked and was enjoying it sexually. "Why do you keep calling him kitty cat?"

"The poor nigger told me he was just curious. Curiosity killed the cat, get it?"

"That's just ripe," Jobe said in between fits of giggling.

They pulled Brooks' corpse from the back of the truck and left me alone for a few moments. I was surprised by what I had glimpsed of their house. Judging by the way these sick dudes were acting, I expected to be taken to a trailer or something, but it was a large two-story Victorian that appeared to be well maintained. The porch light was on, diminishing the darkness considerably.

An old man was watching at me from the end of the truck.

He studied me quietly, cocking his head to the side as if he heard something that my ears could not pick up. His eyes, in the dim light, looked like those of an insect-no pupils, impossibly large and expressionless. His neck was wrinkled, leading up to an unnaturally smooth face. White hair stuck out of his head in dirty and greasy tufts.

"Oh, Maria," the old man rasped. "I will bring you back to me, I promise."

He walked away, leaving me to puzzle out what he had meant. For some reason his sentence scared the hell out of me. It sounded so bizarre—so insane.

Caleb appeared at the end of the truck. His hair was shoulder length, protruding out of his skull like thin spider webs. His skin clung to his face in the same way rotting skin clings to a decomposing skull. He smiled widely, his cheekbones jutting out as they threatened to break through his frail skin like knives. "Hello, Kitty cat."

Jobe came up from behind him, his eyes narrowing under a thick bushy eyebrow. He had one of those brows that my daddy used to call a unibrow—one solid line of hair from eye to eye. A smile appeared in the confines of his wooly beard. "Here, kitty kitty."

They untied my hands from my ankles, but tightened the wire into my wrists. I could feel the blood dripping down into my fingers as the wire dug deep into my flesh.

They led me onto the porch of the Victorian house and through the freshly painted front door. The smell hit me like a brick, smashing into my nose in a way that could only be called intrusive. The word that came to mind was *rancid*. It smelled like someone had opened up a mass grave.

To my left was a living room. The tow-headed boy, Hezekiah, sat mesmerized by a television. He glanced at me as we walked by but showed little emotion. Family photographs dotted the wall. They led me down damp stairway and into a brightly-lit basement.

As soon as I saw the room, I started shrieking. Caleb slapped me across the face so hard that I felt my jaw come loose momentarily. I studied the place, trying to remind myself to breathe.

It looked like the room of a morgue. Brooks' body was laid out on a metal table, dozens of wires running into his opened chest. His eyes stared up blankly, his mouth still open in the shock of being shot. The wires ran into some contraption that looked like something out of an old horror movie, all projecting parts and protruding electrical lines.

The corpse of a woman sat in a wheelchair. It looked

older, the skin already pulling back and unmasking a leathery skeleton. It wore a blue sundress, the hands laid out on its legs as if it was simply relaxing. The eyes had not yet rotted completely, but they were pulled back into the sockets exposing the hard whites.

The old man studied me with his black eyes, worm-like lips pulling back over brown teeth. He followed my line of site to the shriveled corpse in the wheelchair and then he moved towards it, lovingly kissing it on the forehead.

"Oh, my God. You sick fucks," I heard myself say, almost like an out of body experience. My sanity wanted to flee, threatening to leave me and watch the whole drama from the ceiling.

"Don't talk like that in front of Maria," the old man said menacingly. "She doesn't like bad language."

At this point I didn't care what I said. I knew I was dead anyway. "She's a goddamn corpse, you fucking lunatic!"

Caleb growled dangerously. "Want me to kill the nigger, Daddy?"

The old man studied me. "She's coming back. I'm bringing Maria back!" He pulled a photograph out of his shirt pocket and thrust it into my face. A smiling old woman peered at me from the picture. She wore a blonde wig in a desperate attempt to cover her wrinkled head. "Isn't she beautiful? She's coming back and we'll dance again."

I glanced at the corpse and back to the photograph. I tried to speak but only a desperate squeak came out.

"I'm working on a way to bring her back," the old man continued as he watched me with his unblinking dark eyes. "We're almost there. The machine will bring her back."

Caleb was nodding as his father spoke, tears running down his face. "You'll do it, Daddy. I know it."

The old man moved back to Brooks, grabbed a pair of protective glasses, and put them around his head. He picked up a circular saw and then brought it buzzing down into Brooks' skull. Blood splattered up onto the old man's glasses and he brought his hand up and wiped it away with his sleeve.

I closed my eyes, feeling my sanity slipping away ever so

slowly. The sound of the drill screamed in my ears. I counted for two minutes, telling myself it was all a dream.

When I opened my eyes, the top of Brooks' head was removed. His eyes were still open and the old man was attaching little wires into the insides of the skull.

The old man had the bloody glasses pulled over the top of his head like an obscene, crimson-splattered party hat. He walked over to a badly wired control panel and pushed a button.

As Brooks' mouth began opening and closing rapidly, I started to scream, pulling away from Caleb roughly. The very thought that Brooks was being resurrected scared me so badly that I felt as if my skeleton was trying to leap from my skin.

Caleb pulled me to the floor as I kicked out, my teeth clenched together. I felt the soles of my feet connect with something solid and my ankle detonated with bone shattering pain.

The wheelchair sailed into the old man.

Maria's corpse flew out of the chair like a mannequin and landed on the floor stiffly, her head ripping off with the sound of torn paper. It rolled off under the table.

"Daddy!" Caleb screeched as his father howled in grief.

The old man was already crawling around in search of the head as I struggled to my feet. I pulled at my hands, the adrenaline howling through my veins. To my astonishment, the wire actually came loose. My ankle was shrieking at me as I limped towards the stairs. Brooks' mouth was still flapping open and shut as if he was urging me to run.

I was halfway up the stairs when I ran into Jobe. I sent my bloody fist into his face, connecting in a wet explosion of teeth and blood. I spun him around and sent him down the stairs where he collided with his brother.

I limped into the kitchen, grabbing a large knife from a holder. I fought the pain in my ankle as I moved through the hallway and into the living room. The boy glanced up at me, eyes wide. I grabbed the little bastard and pulled him on top of me, knife to his throat.

Caleb and Jobe dashed into the living room as the television flashed around us like a strobe light. They froze, not knowing what to do.

"Don't think I won't cut his throat," I threatened, pulling the boy to me fiercely. I felt the boy go rigid and hot blood poured into my hand. In my recklessness, I had pulled the sharp knife too far into his throat. The blade had gone in just like cheese.

The brothers gasped as I let go of the boy. He dropped to the floor with a thud, the nerves in his legs twitching spastically.

"For the love of God, that nigger killed Hezekiah," Caleb whispered.

For a brief moment we all stood there. The light of the television flashed around us as time stood still.

Then I leapt for the window, landing on the porch in an eruption of glass. Despite the pain, I threw myself over the porch and ran off into the woods.

I ran desperately into the darkness of the trees, ignoring my splintered ankle. If they followed me, I don't know. I didn't stop running for hours.

Sometime in the night, I came to a road and flagged down a passing truck.

Here I sit, three days later in a roach-infested hotel room. I didn't call the police. As soon as my ankle heals I'm going back to that nightmare house with a gun and some gasoline. I'm going to burn it to the ground and send those sick redneck motherfuckers to hell where they belong. I won't leave until the house is nothing but a pile of cinders. I'll do it for Brooks. Hell, I'll do it for the world. It's a sick world, and I want to make it better.

MORTY'S APPALACHIAN AMUSEMENT PARK

BY WESTON OCHSE

"What a Rush!" cried Morty.

I tried to ignore him. I concentrated on the blur of gold and green vegetation as we sped into the Cherokee National Forest.

Morty had just gone into the store for a case of beer. When the bastard had run out dripping money from an overstuffed shopping bag, I'd known that we were in trouble. Like so many times before, I tried to remember exactly why we were best friends.

I shifted in the cramped front seat of the Barracuda and gave him my patented *I got laser beams shooting out of my eyes right at your head so you better fucking look at me stare.*

But it was no good. Morty acted like a dog that had finally caught the rabbit. I could almost imagine him hanging his head out the window, tongue lolling from the side of his mouth and drool sailing in the wind. It was as if he didn't even know he had done anything wrong. Like it was okay or something. He started whistling and banging his hand against the steering wheel in accompaniment.

Finally, I couldn't contain myself any longer.

"So he says to me," I began, *"You paid for it last time, Dan. Let me do it. It's my turn.* So I says back to him, *Okay, Thanks Morty.* Of course I should have added, *and by the way, don't rob the store Morty. We sure need the money, but we already have plans for this afternoon. So robbing the store would kind of cramp our style."*

I could see a twitch beginning near the corner of his left eye as his whistling slowed.

"So, Morty? What do you think? Can we go back to our homes in maybe ten—fifty—a hundred years?"

Morty closed his eyes for a second. I thought I was getting through and smiled in anticipation. I couldn't wait to hear his brilliant excuse for ruining my life.

He sighed, opened his pale blue eyes, calmly reached down into the front of his pants and pulled out his gun. The barrel stopped about three inches from my face and as I gazed down its length, I had the distinct impression that if I leaned forward just a little bit, I could fall right into the quickly expanding black hole and never be seen again. I sat very still, my only movement to carefully change my smile into a frown. This I did slowly, as not to startle him.

I was the brains of the team, which left Morty the expert on violence, robbery, sleaze and, of course, guns. What he was pointing at me is what he called his *Magnum Baby*. I'd always thought it a silly name, but he'd said it fired large pieces of lead capable of making fist size holes in a body. I tried to imagine the damage a fist-sized hole could make to my face. I quit when I succeeded. At this range he didn't even need to aim.

I gulped down my pride and tried to keep my courage from doing anything stupid. I shouldn't have worried. That old friend fear had already thrown a wet blanket over my courage and was efficiently smothering it.

I should have known Morty would eventually do this to me. He had been my best friend since we were in high school and was always getting into trouble. And I was always being blamed for it.

Like drinking for example. The man was diabetic. His doctor continually told him that drinking was going to kill him. So of course he drinks like a wino at a wine tasting party. Usually the night would end with a trip to the hospital — the alcohol eventually causing a reaction resulting in shock. I'd call his dad to let him know his son's condition and be judged, convicted and executed because *I* am the responsible one and *I* should have stopped him.

Trying to stop Morty was like trying to stop a runaway train with a paper mache' wall. The best thing to do is let him run his course and hope he runs out of fuel before plowing into the station or derailing along the way.

It seemed that while I had been growing up, Morty had been acting like we always had when we were kids. Most of my friends at work were married and had families and I was kind of looking forward to settling down. Most of all, I was getting too old for this shit.

Morty seemed satisfied that I understood his point and replaced the Magnum back into his pants. There was no going back, either. Morty's spur of the moment thrill was probably being played on every station. Where we were going could only be better. Maybe when we reached North Carolina, I'd find a way to settle him down.

"You know what steams me about the whole thing?" he asked.

I rewarded him with a shrug.

"What steams me," he continued, "is that after all the robbing and money and shooting and car chasing, I forgot the beer."

A sheepish smile slowly crept up the length of his face. One of those special smiles only shared between best friends. This was his way of apologizing. He looked over at me and burst out in deep throaty laughter. It was contagious. Pretty soon I joined him, but one side of my brain was trying to tell me something.

I hadn't been in the Cherokee National Forest since I was a kid. My father and I used to go fishing and rafting down the rivers. Even in those happier days, the woods were remote enough that if a car were to break down we wouldn't have been found for hours, if not days.

I was consulting a map from the glove box and trying to find a back road through the mountains. The police would be looking for us pretty soon and it would be suicide to stay on the highway. I plotted a way and gestured for Morty to make the turn. It was an unimproved road, but should be easy to make in the dryness of the summer. It wasn't long, however, before we encountered a fence blocking our way and stretching off into the trees on either side of the road. What a fence was doing in the middle of nowhere, I had no idea.

Morty seemed to agree. He looked at it as if it was a girl with three heads.

"What do you make of this?"

"It looks like a fence," I responded only realizing the stupidity of my words a few seconds after I spoke.

We looked at the chain mesh and antique lock wondering who would have put up a fence. Well, I was wondering that. Evidently, Morty was wondering whether the car could make it through without sustaining much damage, because a split second later we were at full power and heading towards it.

We crashed through with a squeal of protesting metal and the fence soon folded up and lay on the ground behind us. Morty let up on the accelerator and the car coasted around a turn. About twenty wooden shacks lined both sides of the road. Several people paused momentarily to glance in our direction, then continued on their way.

Morty slammed on the brakes and skidded to a stop. The people were dressed in an odd assortment of mismatched, bright colorful clothing. Not a single outfit looked like it had even seen the inside of a K-Mart—definitely homemade.

Morty glanced my way and I looked back at him. After we were tired of that, we looked at the road again. The experience was like walking into a twisted Wild West movie where all the townspeople dressed like hippies.

I couldn't stand it any longer. I unbuckled, opened the door and stepped onto the street. Red clay dust eddied around my black work boots coating them in a fine powder. I stretched the kinks out of my shoulders and glanced back in the car. Morty patted the Magnum in his lap and grinned.

An ancient woman sat behind a wooden table covered with a delectable assortment of fruit. She was perched on a rickety stool, her raison eyes almost lost in the wrinkled confines of her face.

"Ma'am," I said, inclining my head slightly.

She picked up an impossibly large red apple, rubbed it on the hem of her blue and white dress several times and presented it to me with a smile.

I took it from her liver-spotted hands and examined it suspiciously. After assuring myself it was truly an apple, I took an enormous bite. A burst of intense taste filled my mouth and I chewed quickly. She saw my appreciation, smiled and leaned back on her stool.

Morty and I sat around a large bonfire at the entrance to a cave that the villagers used for cold storage and meetings. The rough walls, coated with a thin layer of light green moss, provided an eerie luminescence.

Brother John, a rather tall emaciated man, had invited us to sup with him, his family and a good portion of the village. Morty was a bit reticent, but once I had given him a taste of the apple, he grumbled and parked the car at the edge of the small village.

An immense communal pot rested on a slab of gray slate, heated by the wood from the fire beneath it. In addition to the fresh vegetables, tiny pieces of moss floated on the bubbly surface. I was on my second bowl. The moss was slightly tangy, reminding me of the grapefruits I used to eat in the mornings.

"This stuff is fucking great," said Morty.

Morty always had a problem in mixed company.

"The soil is very good, here," replied the Brother.

"Don't you eat any meat?" I asked, remembering the farm animals I'd seen on the way in. I couldn't help but imagine how a good steak would go with these vegetables.

"We live off the land. We don't abuse it," he said. "On rare occasions, we do have some fish."

"It was lucky we arrived before dinner," I said. "We..er.. accidentally left our cooler on the kitchen table. Didn't discover we had left it until right before we met." I tried to catch Morty's eye. "Isn't that right, Morty?"

Morty nodded and helped himself to another bowl. I could see his eyes scanning the people around the fire.

"Brother, that's religious, ain't it?" I asked.

"We belong to the Church of Divine Determination," said Brother John. "I lead the people in their prayers."

"Are you Christian, Muslim, what?"

Brother John considered me for a moment with his calm hollow eyes. "We're Christians, of course. But I'm afraid that the *mainstream* church doesn't readily agree to that concept." He paused for a moment and smiled. "Let us just say they don't approve of us."

The spoon halted midway between the bowl and my mouth. I wondered if we were entirely safe. Visions of flesh-eating religious nuts and Sam Raimi zombies lurched through my brain. I glanced at Morty who had cocked his head to one side, listening. Good, he was paying attention. If there was going to be trouble, having Morty on your side was as good as a howitzer.

"What do you mean they don't approve?" I asked, trying not to sound interested.

"We believe," Brother John began with a reassuring smile, "that God has set us on a predetermined path. There is nothing that man can do to change it. This belief isn't appreciated by most. People like to believe they have control of their lives." He laughed and was joined by several of the villagers sitting within earshot.

"So the future is already settled?" I asked.

"Just so," replied Brother John. He sated proudly at the people around the fire. Where he made eye contact, he received warm reverent smiles in return.

Morty leaned in. "What about when something bad happens? Like when someone gets sick? Or if someone dies?"

"Of course, when someone gets sick, or if any one of our animals die, we're saddened. Emotion is a human trait. It's what sets us apart from the animals. It's also, however, one of the imperfections we're striving to eradicate. We realize deep down, that God has a purpose for these things. It is not for us to challenge those purposes with human emotion."

"What about when someone you know dies, like a relative? What then?" persisted Morty.

I was happy to see he had almost returned to his old self. I was looking forward to having a little more sanity in our lives.

Brother John fixed Morty with a smile. "Like I said, we would feel sad. But you must realize, there are no accidents. If someone dies, it is God's will. We all belong to a greater purpose. Our time here on earth is but a way station, a place for us to pause and contemplate God."

"What if someone is murdered?"

Suddenly, I wished that Morty would change the subject.

"Just the same," said Brother John. "If someone is murdered, it's part of God's plan. The murderer is merely a tool of the Lord used to carry out the plan."

"Isn't that kind of unreasonable," I asked. I really wanted to say, *are you fucking out of your mind?* But my momma raised me to a modicum of politeness.

"You must realize, friend," he said, "human freedom has nothing to do with reason. Reason is an invention of man, therefore it cannot apply to God."

Morty studied Brother John with veiled eyes. I finished my bowl and set it down. All this talk about religion was making my skin crawl. I was about to stand up, proclaim our thanks and bid everyone good-bye, when Morty continued.

"Sounds okay to me," he finally said, voice tight and reasonable. "Why don't those fuckers in the mainstream like you, then?"

It sounds okay? What the hell was he thinking? It sounds okay?

"They're afraid, rightfully so, I might add, that our beliefs would lead to universal anarchy. If everyone believed in our *truths* there would be no problem. It is those few who would try and take advantage of these beliefs that make it a problem."

Morty placed his wooden bowl on the ground like it was the finest porcelain. He stood up slowly and dusted off his pants. His eyes gleamed as he gave me *The Look.* I groaned inwardly. I knew *The Look.* He was going to do something stupid. I wanted to scream out and tell him to stop. Tell him to leave it alone. Tell him we needed to be on our way.

"What do you mean take advantage?" I asked, trying to get the Brother's attention and dissuade Morty from doing something stupid at the same time.

On cue, Morty stepped casually over to Brother John, pulled out his *Magnum Baby* and placed it snug against the Brother's forehead. The Brother merely stared gently back at his would be murderer.

"Follow thy path," said the Brother.

The thundering blast startled everyone. As the Brother toppled backward, Morty spun around and began tracking the smoking barrel back and forth across the crowd.

"Okay you sicko hippie dumbfucks, who else wants to dance with *Magnum Baby*? She'll set you upon God's path just fine." He yelled. His mad eyes glittered in the firelight. The eerie green luminescence basked the side of his face with an unearthly glow.

Several people jumped up in confusion and stared at the prone figure of the Brother. After a few tense moments, however, they sat down and resumed eating.

Morty winked gleefully at me and shoved the gun back into his pants. He swaggered, kicked the dead Brother's legs out of the way and sat down.

"Just as I thought," he said getting himself another bowl of stew.

He was certifiable. I couldn't believe this psychopath was my best friend.

"Morty," I asked slowly, struggling to control my voice. "What the Hell did you just do, Morty? Are you on crack?" I knew that my eyes were about as wide as they could get.

He smiled like a patient parent. "You don't get it. You don't fucking get it, do you, Dan?" He gestured at the people around the fire with his spoon. "I'm the wolf and they're the sheep. Their only shepherd is a God that doesn't exist. This place is a freaking amusement park. You can do whatever you want. Murder, rape, whatever. You know why? Cause it's God's will. And cause it's God's will, none of these religious motherfuckers will do anything to stop me!"

"Morty," I said trying to reason with him. I wanted to reach out and grab him by his thin neck and shake him until he either understood or it snapped. "Not everyone wants to murder and rape."

He shook his head. "Don't give me that *holier than thou* crap. You're as big a criminal as me. The only difference is that I'm a doer. You're not a doer, Daniel. You never have been.

You're a watcher. You're just along for the ride." Morty paused and stood up. He held his arms wide as if to embrace the world. "And here at Morty's Appalachian Amusement Park, we got many kinds of rides."

He jumped up and stalked over to a scrawny young man, barely out of his teens. Morty reached down and picked him up, one hand on the legs and one balancing the chest. The young man went slack, refusing to struggle. He lay at the mercy of my psychotic friend.

"We got the *Oh My God I'm On Fire Ride*," Morty said as he threw the young man into the fire. The young man's screams shook me and I felt myself jump. I watched as hair and the clothes caught fire. Almost too soon, the skin began to sizzle and pop. With wide happy eyes, Morty watched the man burn from the other side of the fire.

I sprang forward to see if I could help the boy, but I was too late. His clothes were already engulfed in flames. I grabbed a smoking ankle and heaved him free. The sickly sweet odor of burned flesh invaded my senses and I felt the stew begin an upward climb. I bit it back and rushed toward the communal pot. His clothes were still on fire. His face was a charred and blistered mass. Scorched bone protruded in several places. I reached out with my bare hands and grabbed the scalding pot. I bit back a scream, but somehow held on and poured the remains of the stew over the still burning body of the young man. It was only when I smelled the burns on my own hands, that my stomach turned traitor. Then the stench of burned flesh mixed with the vegetable stew reached into my gut and jerked out my dinner.

Morty cackled, shook his head and moved to his next victim. He began kicking a middle-aged woman in the mouth. The people sitting next to her watched like it was only a made-for-TV movie instead of their friend being kicked to death in bright Technicolor reality. Whenever Morty's blood-smeared boot connected with the poor woman's face, a squishy thud echoed in the now silent cave.

"Or if you're afraid of fire, Dan," continued Morty, "You can try the *Watch Them Get Kicked In The Face Ride*."

His laugh was shrill and rising to an impossibly high pitch.

I had to stop him. My hands were beginning to ache as the adrenaline left my blood and the pain from my burns set in. I glanced down and saw that the skin had begun to peel back in places and felt woozy. I needed medical attention badly.

Morty stepped over to the next person and screamed, "Hey Old Man, you can't stop me, can you? It's God's will isn't it?"

The man returned Morty's stare with a look of calm compassion, ignoring the strings of Morty's spittle that dripped from his nose. Morty lunged twice, trying to get a reaction. He grunted and barked and laughed, but his target remained impassive.

It was at that moment that I knew Morty had to be stopped. These people didn't deserve him. No one deserved him. My mother's words returned to me from the many years and miles where I stood on the deck of our house overlooking the beautiful blue and green waters of Chicamauga Reservoir: *One day, that boy is gonna snap. When that day comes, you make sure you're a thousand miles away, ya hear?'*

Morty howled in anger at the old man's resolute immobility. "You feel sorry for me, Old Man? How come you feel sorry for me? I've been chosen by God. Don't feel sorry for me, feel sorry for yourself." Morty reached around and snapped the old man's brittle neck in one swift movement.

"Hey, Dan," Morty said, making sure I was watching, "you missed the ride. Pay attention, boy. Queue up and have another one." Morty craned his head to the ceiling and howled, "Tickets please. Keep your arms inside the vehicle at all times."

I couldn't take it any longer. He had to be stopped. I launched myself across the small space separating us. He must have seen the intentions in my eyes and drew his gun. I sped up as the gun came level with my body. Morty raised it a few inches higher and crashed it down on my head. I felt an intense brief pain before I sank into darkness.

When I cracked my eyelids and let a little light in, I discovered I wasn't dead. It hurt too fucking much to be dead. My skull pounded. My hands felt like they were still burning. I opened my eyes a little wider and saw the fire in front of me. Through the swirling smoke I could just make out glittering stars.

"How ya doing, sleepy head?" asked a voice from behind me. "I didn't think you were going to wake up. Thought I might have hit you a little too hard. Sorry about that."

I rolled over, grunting at the pain. Morty reclined on a log, drinking from an earthenware jug.

"When I was looking for bandages, I found the Brother's stash. Must keep it for communion. And you know what? These folks made some pretty good stuff." He breathed heavily and smiled at me as he took a long deep draught. Green liquid seeped from the imperfect seal of his mouth and slid down his chin.

"Looks like they make it from this green stuff on the walls. Never heard of Moss Brandy before, but it sure hits the spot."

I peeked at my hands and saw that they'd been bandaged. Morty reached over and grabbed an overturned cup. He shook the dirt out and, holding the jug in the crook of an arm, poured it half full. He knelt down beside me and gently cradled my head in his left arm.

"Here, try some of this. It'll make you feel better." He put the cup to my lips and poured liquid fire down my throat.

The cobwebs disappeared in a storm of electric agony. I remembered the mayhem. I remembered the madness. I remembered the murders.

Or had I?

I shook off his hand and peered around, afraid of what I might see. And there they were— bodies piled against the back wall of the cave like so much cordwood. I struggled to my feet, but before I could make it, dizziness grabbed me and threw me back to the ground where I embraced the darkness.

I felt someone gently stroking my hands. I opened my eyes and squinted at the brightness. I was surprised to find the aching in my hands had all but disappeared. The old woman, who had given me the apple, applied some kind of greasy substance to my burns. It felt cool and soothing. When she saw that I was awake, she smiled gently.

"There, there, young man. Just hold still and let old Grandma take care of these nasty burns." Her voice was soft and sweet, belying her age.

When she finished, I glanced towards the back wall where the bodies had been piled. Every one of them was gone. I tried to picture the old woman moving them, but couldn't.

Perhaps it had all been a dream.

Perhaps it had never happened.

Out past the entrance to the cave, people were going about their business—acting as if nothing had happened. A few of them I recognized. I'd seen them murdered.

"Good Morning, Daniel. Want some coffee?"

I spun around violently and stared. I scooted back on my hands and heels until my back touched the rough wall of the cave. I pushed myself up to a standing position and stared at Brother John holding a steaming metal cup out to me.

"Come on, take a drink before it gets cold," he said.

It must have been a nightmare.

No one comes back from the dead.

I calmed myself and argued with my feet until they agreed to move me over to the Brother. I reached out with a tentative hand and grabbed the handle of the cup. I could see a neat little scab in the center of his forehead. Funny I didn't notice it before. It couldn't possibly be from the gunshot wound.

I chuckled to myself a little more crazily than I wished and sat down beside the Brother.

The coffee tasted excellent. I already felt better. The bandages on my hands had been expertly done.

The bandages!

If what I thought happened last night didn't happen, then why are my hands burned? I glanced over at Brother John and there was a twinkle in his eye.

"It seems that God saw fit to let us live another day. Perhaps our work is not yet done, no?"

I threw down the coffee cup and jumped to my feet. I searched for something to defend myself with. Anything to keep me from the vengeance these people were only right in unleashing.

"Have no fear, friend Daniel, we have no ill will against you... or even your friend there." The Brother gestured over by the cold dead fire where Morty lay, curled around the jug, sleeping soundly. I could see the rise and fall of his stomach.

"Why— I mean how are you— not dead?"

"As I said, Friend Daniel. God must have a greater purpose for us. It's just as you think. We were truly dead. But come morning, we awoke as if from a sound sleep." The Brother rubbed the center of his forehead. "A little worse for wear, mind you, but alive none the less. It is truly a miracle."

I reached out a trembling hand and felt his forehead. It was true. The wound had almost entirely healed. I didn't know what to make of it. I wasn't a very religious person. I'd been to church a few times, but only to meet girls. This manifestation of power, though, was a little too much.

"You must be hungry. You slept right through breakfast, but give me a second and I'll get some fruit."

He walked to the back of the cave and reached inside a large light blue drum. He brought back two large ruby red apples. After brushing off a couple pieces of the insidious green moss, I mumbled my thanks and started to devour them. I had finished one and started on the other when I saw the end of the gun protruding from Morty's pants.

I took it.

Morty woke about dusk.

I'd considered leaving him, but quickly rejected the idea. One thing was for sure, I needed to get him as far away from these people as I could. To Morty's credit, he was appropriately shocked when he noticed Brother John and the rest of the village walking and talking as if last night's Amusement Park had never happened. One by one, each walked over and spoke with him. I wasn't close enough to hear, but it appeared they were consoling him. Trying to make him feel better or some similarly insane thing. They left him trembling all over.

It took some convincing, but Morty finally came around to the realization that they were still alive. But like a kid denied dessert, he sat there silent and sullen for over an hour, staring out from beneath a roiling cloud of anger. All the way through dinner, he refused to speak. A young man approached me. I recognized him as the one who'd been burned. He thanked me for trying to help him. And in these people's inimical manner, proceeded to scold me for interfering with God's will. I was mad enough to hit him, but his injuries were so extensive that they hadn't quite healed yet. Whatever mystical force controlled these people was healing the poor kid slowly.

Morty finally spoke as the last of the people went off to bed. There was a strangeness in his voice that I had never heard before.

"Better get a good sleep, Dan. We're leaving tomorrow."

I couldn't tell what was running through his mind, but I was glad we were leaving. This whole scene was too spooky. My friend had become an uncontrollable mass murderer. But then again, he wasn't. All of his victims were alive. I had no doubt that it happened, but couldn't explain the resurrections. All I knew was that God had somehow given us a second chance. I promised myself that as soon as we arrived in Raleigh, I was going my separate way.

I woke up sometime around midnight after a bad dream of *flesh-eating religious-groupie zombies.* My mouth was as dry as a Grandma's ass and when I reached over for some water, I noticed Morty was missing. With a curse, I jumped up and went searching for the asshole.

Off to the left of the cave's entrance was a row of huts. I tip-toed to the first one and peeked inside. There were two beds, each containing a softly snoring figure.

I nudged the door silently closed and slipped to the next hut. Morty stood three huts down. He'd just exited a hut, the knife in his hand dripping the blood of his efforts. He must have started at the other end.

He saw me at the same time I saw him.

He smiled weakly. "I don't know what these people are, but I'm not leaving them behind to chase me down," he whispered. "Jesus, talk about born again Christians. These folks bring new meaning to the word."

"That's not even funny."

"I don't give a damn. These folks have screwed with my head. I don't know anything anymore. All I know is with them dead, we're safer."

"They're just going to come back in the morning. Leave the poor folks alone. Don't you think you've caused them enough pain?"

I said it and it made sense, but it was so ridiculous.

Morty smiled. "I'm one step ahead of you, pal. Once they're all dead, I'm gonna burn them. Burn them until nothing's left. If need be, I'll spread the ashes from here to Raleigh. Let them try and come back from that."

"Don't do it Morty," I pleaded. "We don't know anything about these people. We're lucky they didn't kill us. We don't know what they're capable of."

"Exactly," he said. "We don't know what they're capable of. So I'm gonna make sure there is nothing left."

I shook my head slowly. There seemed to be no way that I could keep being a watcher. It was time to be a doer.

I pulled out the gun and pointed it at Morty's chest.

"No, you're not, Morty. Let's get in the car and leave now," I said as forcefully as I knew how.

He looked at me sadly, "What are you gonna do, Dan. Shoot your best friend?"

"If I have to," I replied. I pulled the hammer back like I had seen him do with Brother John. It was harder than I expected and I had to use both my thumbs. His eyes widened appreciably. His smile turned into a malicious sneer. He began walking toward me.

"You better put that down, before you hurt yourself."

I saw the tip of the knife pointed at my heart. I looked into his eyes and saw nothing there I recognized. He was a complete stranger to me. I pulled the trigger and felt the gun buck in my hands. The bullet hit him in the center of the chest and I watched mutely as he was hurled backwards. He stared down at the blood pumping from the impossibly large fist-sized hole and died.

I pulled his body over to the fire. I was exhausted—spiritually and emotionally. I didn't need any more crap. If I wanted to survive the road, however, I needed to get some sleep before I started out in the morning. Also, I didn't want to leave like a thief in the night.

I didn't want these people to think that I was the one who killed them.

Again.

The next morning, I explained to Brother John what had happened. He shook his head sadly when he looked over at Morty. I wasn't sure if it was because Morty was a psychopath or if it was because I had interfered with God's will.

They talked me into staying until noon, with the promise that they'd load my car with fruit and water for the trip. They could tell my sanity was precariously perched and they spent every opportunity counseling me in an attempt at lightening my spiritual baggage.

I sat and listened, letting it come in one ear and mentally shoving it out the other before any of the insane ideas had a chance to take root.

The lunch bell gonged and we returned to the communal cave to eat and say our good buys.

"Hello, Dan," said Morty, standing by the blackened logs of the fire pit and holding the bell.

My legs trembled and threatened to fail. The villagers seemed equally shocked. I found that a little strange, knowing their own propensity for returning from the dead.

"You know, that really hurt," he chuckled as he rubbed his chest. The blood had dried and the hole had disappeared, but the shirt still proved the event. "But what a rush!"

"Morty," I said, unable to keep the quaver out of my voice. "You're supposed to be dead."

"I guess God has a special purpose for me too," he said with a wink and a grin.

At the mention of God, the villagers began to murmur among themselves. The Brother was gesticulating wildly towards Morty. Their voices became louder. I finally understood what they were saying.

"The Christ. He is the Christ," they were saying.

Morty's smile grew from ear to ear. He had never seemed so happy. "They think *I* am the Son of God, Dan." He began laughing uncontrollably.

I rushed over and tugged at Brother John's arm. "This isn't the Christ," I said. "It's only Morty. He came back just like the rest of you."

His eyes rested on mine. "Our holy book says *'And one shall*

come among you with the sins of the world on his shoulders...
although he is not of the chosen, He will die and rise again. He
will provide for you and succor you in your times of need. He is
the Christ, so love him.'"

"Do ya hear that," shouted Morty over the din. "I'm the
Christ." He raised his arms skyward. "I am the Christ." The
final word echoed throughout the cave along with his laughter.

Brother John and the villagers knelt before him and bowed
their heads in reverence. Morty took on an imperious demeanor
and strode over to Brother John's kneeling figure.

He winked at me, placed his hand atop the Brother's head
and spoke in a commanding voice, "Arise, Brother John. Arise.
I am the Christ. Love me."

Brother John rose and bade the kneeling multitude rise, also.
They placed Morty atop their shoulders and headed towards the
huts in a grand processional. A solitary voice floated up from
within the group. The rest soon joined in and accompanied the
procession with a hymn.

I was completely and utterly amazed by the turn of events.
All I could do was followed at a distance, mindful of the gun
still tucked in my waistband. The procession passed the huts
and entered a small clearing. In the center was an immense
cross, sunk firmly into the ground. They stood Morty before it.
He turned, smiled beatifically at his worshippers and jokingly
placed his arms along the length of the cross which were
immediately seized from behind. Four large men secured his
wrists to the arms of the cross with lengths of rope. Two women
wrapped another rope quickly around his feet, securing them
to the shaft of the cross.

Morty's shouts of confusion were lost amidst the singing. A
man in the rear of the group produced a curved, single-edged
knife and passed it forward. The blade glittered wickedly in the
sunlight. I began to edge backwards. A large wooden bowl was
also making its way forward. Brother John soon held the items
in either hand. He brought his arms up. The singing stopped
and the congregation knelt in the wildflowers of the field.

Brother John turned and kissed Morty passionately upon
the lips. Then, in a quick sure movement, he drew the blade

across Morty's neck. Morty tried to cry out, but couldn't get enough air for a scream. The blood gushed forth in a bubbly rush. Before any could hit the ground, Brother John deftly moved the bowl into position and the torrent quickly filled it.

He held the bowl high. "This is the blood of Christ. Blood he sheds to wash away our sins."

Before I turned and left, I saw the agonized look in Morty's eyes. He had become their permanent fountain of redemption. He knew he wouldn't die. And I am sure he wished he could.

PEACHES

BY DAVID WHITMAN

The old man ruffled his leathery hands through the child's blonde hair. "You know something, Davy," he said. "You're the only one who has ever done good for me. The only one that I have faith in."

He looked up at the peach tree, enjoying the way the wind blew into his wrinkled face. The newly ripened fruit waved invitingly in the warm breeze.

The old man and his grandson sat on the hill under the tree, the sweet scents moving enticingly through the air. Flowers dotted the landscape around them, the colors swaying back and forth like a beautiful dream.

The old man watched patiently as the rest of his family ambled slowly up the hill, his eyes narrowing.

"I like you too, Grandpa Pete," Davy said, looking up at the old man.

Pete returned his adoring look and smiled, exposing his white dentures to the summer air. "I want you to remember that, Davy." He turned back towards his family and there was an odd glint in his eye. "Your Grandpa is leaving soon. Going to join that woman, uh your grandmother, in the afterlife. I'm going to be saying some things to these buffoons that you see walking up the hill, things that aren't going to be too pleasant. I thought it would be best if you heard it firsthand. I'd rather that you'd have your own memory of what's going to go on here, rather than some biased second hand information from one of those clowns." He said the last sentence with a smile as he waved at the group nearing the top of the flower-dotted hill.

The first son to make it up was Steve. Pete actually had to fight to keep his smile glued to his face—a fight he won much to his amazement. He was getting much too impatient for such niceties. Steve was his oldest son, a piece of shit, the very definition of redneck. Steve hadn't held a job longer than a month in his entire forty-five years. A man who would rather spend his father's vast amount of wealth than to go out into the world and provide for himself. Steve took off his John Deere cap respectfully and held it to its side, but not before putting a dip of wintergreen chewing tobacco behind his bottom lip.

Steve's wife, Mary, followed behind. She was a woman who reminded Pete far too much of his long dead wife—a woman who felt the world owed her something for nothing.

Pete's second son, Samuel, was followed by his wife, Lia. *The only good thing that those two have done,* he thought, *is bring such a perfect boy as Davy into the world. Other than that, they did nothing more than have sex, sleep, eat and shit. Might as well get a dog. At least a dog shits outside and has the decency to die after about fifteen years of freeloading. There are no bigger parasites in all of Georgia.*

"Daddy." Both sons said their greeting simultaneously and Pete winced.

Pete looked up at the peach tree, putting his hand over his eyes to block the sun and thought to himself just how much he and the old peach tree were alike. His whole freeloading family took fruit from that tree, with the exception of Davy. The boy, like Pete, had developed an aversion of peaches.

The rest of the family took the peaches gluttonously, never giving anything back, not once offering to help take care of the tree. *That's my job,* he said, chuckling to himself. *I take care of the tree, and they eat its fruit. My family scavenges from me, never even leaving home to cut their own paths. They depend upon me totally. I take care of myself, increasing my fortune every year in real estate, and they eat from me. My money might as well have peaches on the front of the bill instead of the face of some old president. Like the tree, I wince every time one of my hard-earned fruits is taken. The fruits of my labor.*

Pete hid his thought well. "Everybody grab a peach and sit down," he said, gesturing to the tree. "I have something to tell all of you." He grinned and this time it was genuine.

They all pulled a peach from the tree and sat down. Steve took three in his typically greedy fashion.

They bit hungrily into the sweet, luscious peaches as they waited for Pete to speak. Steve did not even bother to wipe the juice that ran messily down his chin. Lia took short baby bites, chewing carefully to get maximum enjoyment.

"I'm glad to see everyone here," Pete said, turning his gaze at each of them as he spoke. "The first thing that I want to tell you is that I'm dying." He saw that they tried to hide their elation, but failed miserably. They actually seemed to drool like hungry dogs, the peach juice on Steve's chin emphasizing the metaphor colorfully.

"Oh Pete, I'm so sorry," Mary said sorrowfully, although to Pete it sounded like, "Good-Goddamn, Pete, that's fantastic!"

Pete finally put aside the mask of the friendly old man he had worn for years, letting it slide from his face with smooth and satisfying precision. "Please. Spare me your fake sympathy. You're the most apathetic woman that I've ever met. You couldn't empathize with a dying child, you cold bitch."

"Dad!" Steve shouted in shock. "Don't listen to him, Mary. He must be going senile."

"Senile!" Pete shot back, sending them all into frozen positions of amazement, each of them riveted to his words. "Boy, my mind is sharper than that knife you used to whittle with when you were Davy's age. Although you did most of your whittlin' without the knife, I should add, judging by the amount of times I caught you in the barn with your pants down to your ankles!"

"Dad!"

"Don't Dad me, boy! Let me finish! I got some things to say and I want you to hear me out! The least you can do for me, after all I've done, is shut your hole and listen!" He glared at them one by one, daring them to open their mouths. "I have a confession to make. Many years ago your mother didn't run off on me. She didn't just disappear. I killed her. I killed the cheating bitch. I found her with Ned Roberts and I shot the both of them. Your mother took a bullet in the face, dead instantly. For the first time in her life, she didn't get the last word in."

With a true sense of the moment, Pete watched their reactions, locking eyes with each of them as they sat in stunned silence. The summer breeze rustling through the peach tree was the only sound. Davy looked frightened, his eyes wide on his chubby face, his mouth open in an 'o' of amazement.

No one moved. The kind old man that they had known their whole life was gone, disappearing in the smoke of murderous memories. The old man sitting before them, his back to the peach tree, was so unlike their father that he was almost alien.

Pete continued his speech. "Now, the first thing that I want you to do is to thank your mother, for she provided your nutrients."

Samuel, the brighter of the two brothers, was the first to catch on. He was looking at his half eaten peach with horror and revulsion.

Pete saw his enlightenment and smiled. "Yes, indeed. That woman made sure that you got all your vitamins in a way that's pretty literal." He knocked his wrinkled fist into the grass. "Ain't that right, Marian?" he asked, looking down at the grave. "I shot them in my very own bed and then I dragged them up here and buried them under this here peach tree. And goddamn, if the peaches didn't look livelier when they blossomed that year. Tastier too, said many. If you look really close within the fuzz of the peach, you can see the ghostly outline of your mama's face, her mouth open in a silent scream. That's entertaining stuff, I tell ya. Figures she would haunt me, the miserable bitch."

Steve studied the peach, his breathing firing out in nervous blasts. Pete could tell by the way that his son's face looked that he saw the ghostly visage of his mother on the peach. Years ago, when Pete had first seen the image of his dead wife on the skin of the fruit, he had damn near panicked. Fortunately, no one seemed to notice. Sometimes, he would watch her lips moving and he would just laugh with glee before pulling away the skin. One time, a peach was filled with a bloody, milky substance.

"And you know what else?" Pete continued. "You know how I take a walk every night ten o'clock sharp?" He paused while they nodded like zombies, their faces whiter than the puffy clouds above their heads. "I walk up to this here tree and I piss on it every night. I piss right on the cheatin' bitch's grave. Why a few times I even buried a shit or two. Another neat little twist is if you stab the tree between the midnight hour, the hour your Mama died, she will moan a little. It's kinda cute."

Steve stood up angrily and dropped his peaches. "You're crazy, old man. Mom's not really under this tree. She ran off because she couldn't stand you."

Pete snickered. "I notice you stopped eating the peaches real quick for an unbeliever, Stevie."

"Dad, why are you doing this?" Samuel asked, pulling Davy away from his grandfather.

"Because all of you are good for nothing. You came from a bad seed." He pounded the dirt to emphasize his point. "You boys ain't never done nothing for me. You take my money and give me nothing in return. I don't even get a birthday card. Every year you give me the same Christmas present that all of you pitch in for. Goddamn *English Leather* cologne. I'd rather wear skunk piss. Don't any of you notice that I don't even wear the shit? I wouldn't even put it on the dog."

"Well, it's not like we go around smelling you, Dad," Samuel said, trying to lighten up a situation that he felt his father had made up to make a point. "Now, this joke that you made up is funny. Ha Ha. We get your point. Now stop this nonsense. You're scaring Davy."

Pete got up from the ground and clenched his fists, his face red with anger. "The boy should be scared with a low-life like you for a father."

"That's it!" Lia screamed. "I've had enough! I'm not going to sit here and listen to the ramblings of a crazy old man!"

Pete stopped her with a demonstrative gesture of his hand, a sharp hatchet-like chop. "Before everybody goes running off, I got one more thing left to say. I put all my money, my entire estate, in a trust fund that goes to Davy when he's twenty-five years old. That will goes into effect today." He looked at his sons. "As for you two, I left you with one thing, and if you want to get me back, you can start by kicking me off your property. This acre of land, your Mama, and the peach tree are yours. Do what you will with them. Now, if you'll excuse me, I'm going to leave you in peace. I seem to be trespassing on your property."

As Pete walked down the hill, enjoying the smell of the fragrant flowers, he was rewarded by his good-for-nothing sons for the first time in his long life. The sounds of their whining in his ears was like sweet music. *And music,* he thought, *is good for the soul.*

SWEET LITTLE PIGGY

BY WESTON OCHSE

"Stick men, stick men, my little stick men," came the lispy singing from the shadowy corner of the living room.

"She ain't violent, is she?" asked the small woman, pointing toward the figure hunched on the carpet.

"No, my dear. Sweet Little Piggy is as placid and nice as a cool spring day," the old black woman said looking fondly on her granddaughter.

"I don't know... " said the woman, waffling like they all did the first time.

"Come over here and meet the nice lady, Sweet Little Piggy."

The hunched figure stopped its soft singing and froze.

"Grandma says come here," she repeated sternly.

Sweet Little Piggy clambered up and shambled over in a side-to-side sway. She wore a floor-length smock. Once pink, it was now covered with paint smears and pastel marks, proof of her crayon artistry. Her hands and head were the only pieces of skin visible, pure whiteness against the mosaic of childish color. In her arms, she held a large wicker basket of broken crayons, gripped lovingly, like a trophy. The young woman drew back, a hand to her mouth as she saw the figure's face. Paper-white skin was the canvas for a pug nose, two tiny triangular eyes containing tinier red orbs and a poorly corrected cleft lip. Tight red curls topped her head like a cherry on a whipped cream desert. The woman stepped back involuntarily, causing Sweet Little Piggy to snort several times.

"Now, now. Don't tease the nice lady. Say hello, my dear.

This is Miss Rosie and her daughter, Jenny Mae."

Close now, the woman could see the child stood nearly five feet tall and weighed almost 200 pounds.

Sweet Little Piggy stood smiling back at the woman, a look of childish pleasure on the deformed face. Rosie inhaled sharply as Piggy snorted again.

"There you go. Now, go on back and play some more," said Grandma Fletcher, apparently satisfied at the greeting. To the woman, "My granddaughter is an albino, so she doesn't get out in the sun very much. In fact, if it wasn't for me watchin' these children, she wouldn't have anyone to play with. She may look older, but my Sweet Little Piggy is about as smart as your sweet little daughter. Poor Piggy was shaken too much as a baby."

"But she's so big," said the woman, startling herself.

"Listen, honey," said the old woman changing the subject. "The Women's Center sent you to me. They wouldn't have done that if there'd been any real trouble at my place. Your daughter is gonna do fine here. Granted, this isn't one of those franchise places with fresh paint and them *learnin' toys*, but there's a lot of love in these walls. Put your trust in Grandma Fletcher."

The old woman's sad eyes embraced the younger in a clutch of warmth as Rosie once again studied the tenement's main room. Faded yellow velvet wallpaper hung in tatters high above the level of inquisitive hands. Below, the wall had been stripped and scrubbed clean, revealing a smooth off-white surface. The furniture was old and worn with decades of use, but appeared sturdy enough for even Grandma Fletcher's large frame. An oval carpet covered the greater part of the wooden floor. Once many colors, the fabric was now a washed-out gray. A pale yellow light came from the far corner, making shadows jump around the edges of its weak nimbus. The overhead light was dark, as were the windows, spray-painted black and draped with dark blue curtains. The only other light was a small table lamp with long maroon tassels dangling from a small brown shade sitting by the end of the couch.

Two other children, a black boy and a white girl, both near her daughter's age, sat semi-transfixed in front of a flickering console television that had seen its best days when disco was new. The children were quiet now, a far cry from their original clamor at Jenny Mae's appearance, but Grandma Fletcher had warned them away, giving her daughter a bit of space to adjust. In the corner, the object of Rosie's earlier concern, sat Sweet Little Piggy, adult sized, but child-like in her sing-song patter as she played with the large basket of broken crayons and stared longingly at the blank wall. Her legs moved frenetically beneath the smock to a private rhythm.

"And you're real sure everything is gonna be alright?" Rosie could barely control the trembling in her voice.

Tears had already moistened her eyes and threatened to burst upon darkly bruised cheeks.

"There, there. Listen to Grandma Fletcher," said the old woman resting a heavy arm around the young lady's shoulders. "I deal with many women from the Center. You ladies have had enough trouble and my job is to make the *getting' back to livin'* a little easier. You go find yourself a job and before no time, you'll be back on your feet and in charge of yourself. All this stuff that's been happenin'... well, it'll soon be just a bad memory."

"I don't know as to when I'm gonna be able to pay you." The entreating look from the woman's eyes begged not to be hit.

Grandma Fletcher's face softened. "You let me worry about that. Pay me what you can, when you can. The Lord will provide."

Within a minute, young Jenny Mae had been introduced to the two by the TV and joined them watching the adventures of a puppet and a train. Before the Rosie retreated, she left a knapsack containing a red blanket, a small battered box of crayons, some coloring books and a soiled white, stuffed kitten with a lonely glass blue eye.

Sweet Little Piggy glanced over to the couch where her grandma snored softly. The other children were likewise asleep, each curled around their own stuffed creature. All the lamps were off except the one in the far corner, making the room a comfortable gloom for her tiny, pinched eyes. On the coffee table were three plates, each had pieces of crust and smears of dark brown peanut butter left over from lunch. Sweet Little Piggy stared longingly for a moment, but remembrances of Grandma's complaints about eating too much directed her attention away.

Carrying her basket, she waddled over to the new girl who was sleeping fitfully with small jerks and tight hugs of her one-eyed cat. Sweet Little Piggy squatted and sat the basket down at her side. Her hand reached out, long slender fingers of an artist, and touched the forehead of the sleeping girl. She hummed to herself as images of violence and pain and sex strobed through her mind, each image vivid and real.

Grandma told her it was like TV, but Piggy couldn't watch real TV anymore. Grandma said it was the flickering that made Piggy fall down and do the trembles. But that was okay, because Sweet Little Piggy liked the new kids. They gave her a private TV that only she could watch—even if it was mostly the bad stuff.

She continued humming, greedily accepted the evil flashes from the sleeping child, cataloging them in her mind. Finally, Sweet Little Piggy stood and carried the basket of broken crayons back to the wall. She looked critically at the wallpaper-free surface, studying it like an artist would a canvas. She sunk her hand deep into the basket, came out with a broken red crayon and began to draw. As her hands moved hurriedly across the broad surface, exchanging colors at a frenzied pace, she began to sing, "Stick men, stick men, my little stick men."

A muffled sound brought Grandma Fletcher from her nap. She glared irritably at her Sweet Little Piggy, thinking it was she who had made the noise, but found her granddaughter sleeping in her corner, an arm curled lovingly around the basket. She sighed and felt her eyes drawn to the wall, and by the multicolored markings and broad swatches of pastel hues, she could tell her granddaughter had been drawing on the walls again.

She couldn't make out the blurry details and silently cursed her eyes, knowing blindness would come too soon. She reminded herself to get some more pine-oil at the store, tomorrow, and lay back hoping to return to her dreams of young men and better times.

The sound came again, this time more insistent. It was knocking from the front door. Grandma Fletcher levered herself up to a sitting position and took inventory of her flock. Her three wards were deep in sleepy land, but Jenny Mae was beginning to stir. The old woman's eyes embraced the figure lovingly. With new ones, she found herself both sad and happy. It was a shame that they had to travel through Hell to get to Grandma Fletcher, but once here, it was God and her that would make everything right again.

"All Right. All Right. I'm coming," she mumbled towards the intrusive knocking.

Grandma Fletcher, with several grunts and a long groan, brought her large frame up and into a standing position. She smoothed the rumpled front of her pale blue housecoat and stepped into her furry slippers, her bulbous knees cracking with age. She shuffled over to the door, a hand on her lower back in an effort to entreat a lifetime of pain away.

"I'm here, just a minute." She glanced through the peephole and then began to disengage the three shiny deadbolts and the heavy chain that secured the stout oaken door. "Back already, dear?" She asked when she saw Rosie."

"Yes, ma'am," said the woman trying to hide an embarrassed grin.

"I thought... I thought somethin' may have happened. No one answered, you know?"

"Happened? What could possibly happen with Grandma Fletcher around? I told you not to worry. We were just nappin' is all. Now tell me, did you find anythin'?"

The woman's face brightened into a beautiful smile that did much to camouflage the bruises. "Yes I did! The hotel the Center sent me too had an opening in their laundry room. They asked me if I had any experience. Ha. All I ever did was wash and iron Dicky's clothes. What's with doing a bunch of strangers' clothes too?" A sparkle danced in her eyes as she finished.

Grandma Fletcher stood back, arms crossed atop huge pillow-sized bosoms, beaming a dentured smile. She enjoyed watching the transformations in her mothers when the women discovered self-esteem again. The simple knowledge that they had skills was, enough sometimes, to get them back on track. The poor woman was so happy, she didn't even realize she had invoked her husband's name.

"Why that's absolutely wonderful, honey," she was going to continue, but paradoxical tears had begun to well up in the woman's eyes. Grandma Fletcher's face softened and she reached out and drew the woman to her. Rosie struggled slightly, but was no match for the older woman's maternal strength. "There, there, what else could possibly be the matter?"

Rosie greedily returned the hug. It had probably been years since she had received one with no expectations, but the small joy was short-lived. Rosie struggled for a moment, then succeeded in pushing herself away as Grandma Fletcher released her. Her face became serious.

"They wouldn't give me any advance. I ain't gonna be able to afford any child-care for two weeks, then maybe me and Jenny Mae can find someone." Her eyes had moved to the floor and she chewed her lip, leaving the unasked plea between them.

"Ahhh, but that's no problem. I'll take care of her for a little while longer. I do it all the time."

It was important for her to make the offer, otherwise all the good of a new job would be swept away. She had expected it, anyway. Nobody would ever give a woman like Rosie an advance. Backwoods. Bruised. They probably thought the woman had done something to deserve the abuse.

Rosie glanced up and began wiping away her tears with the backs of her hands. "God Bless You, Grandma Fletcher."

"He already has, my dear. He already has."

With bolstered confidence, Rosie swept into the room, her blue-flowered skirt catching air. She swung her handbag as if it was lighter somehow.

Grandma Fletcher leaned out into the hall and checked both ways. She thought she saw someone down at the far end, but it was just another dark blur with her old vision. She was on the fifth floor and the security system had stopped working twenty years ago making the place a refuge for junkies so she shut the door hurriedly and with stiff old hands slid the locks into place.

As she turned around to hear more about the woman's

new job, she heard the first of Rosie's ear-shattering screams. Grandma Fletcher pressed her back against the door and brought a hand up to her mouth as Rosie let loose scream after scream. The young mother had fallen to her knees facing the wall, both hands to her head, fingers pushing and pulling at her tumble of thick black hair.

The children in front of the television awoke with a start. Two of them sat hugging each other, tears and sobs beginning to rack their bodies as they relived a Mommy in pain, again. Jenny Mae stood transfixed, her thumb firmly planted between tight lips. Her eyes stared blankly towards the wall as rivulets of urine darkened the front of her pink pants and made a path down the inside of her legs.

Sweet Little Piggy struggled to her feet and waddled over to the terrified woman. She began patting Rosie on the shoulder, a kind smile, repeating, "It's okay. It's okay," an eerie metronomic undertone to the high-pitched shrieks.

Grandma Fletcher followed Rosie's eyes and saw the blurry markings on the wall she'd dismissed earlier. She stumbled forward grudgingly, the images coming into focus with each painful step until finally they were seen in all their demented clarity. A montage of apparently inter-linked vignettes assaulted her from the child-like drawings of her granddaughter, each scene framed by zigzag multicolored ovals. Two stick-like figures starred in each.

One scarlet, large and looming.

The other pink, small and fragile.

In one, the larger held the smaller by its hair, legs far above the ground. Even though it was only a stick figure, Grandma Fletcher could make out the struggling pain experienced by the smaller pink figure with the impossible angles of the stick arms and stick legs.

In another, the scarlet figure stood hands empirically on hips. A dark colored three-dimensional square contained the pink one with knees drawn up. The head was lowered pitifully as the body, even in its cramped position, was too big for the confines.

In another, the pink figure was prone, while the larger figure kneeled above holding what must have been a cigar, the orange tip hovering menacingly above the smaller stick figure. Thin tendrils of smoky gray color curled from the tip of the cigar and the dozen orange colored spots on the pink figure's flattened back.

In yet another, the larger figure struck the smaller with a long supple-looking red strap, as the pink figure kneeled on all fours, head down, back pinstriped with thin red bands. To Grandma Fletcher, it was as if she could see the stick figure's shoulders shake with the pain and desperation of the moment.

In the last, and the one that fixated Rosie's entire attention, the small stick figure's head was buried deep in the broad crotch of the large scarlet figure whose arms were outstretched, head lolling back on a thin neck.

With a final agonizing peel, Rosie collapsed to the carpet, the vestiges of her scream tapering into nothing. Sweet Little Piggy stopped her patting and looked at her Grandma.

"Amama, lady sleep," came the lispy voice, confusion and concern both coloring her tone.

Grandma Fletcher shook herself out of her momentary shock and went into motion, a look of loving irritation towards her granddaughter. This had happened before. She didn't know why she hadn't been ready for it. She just prayed that the damage could still be repaired.

The other children had been picked up half-an-hour ago—explanations and promises exchanged with the concerned mothers. Jenny Mae sat in front of the television, her arms wrapped tightly around the stuffed kitten, the girl's eyes as glassy as the cat's. She seemed to be staring through the screen—seeing something else. Her clothes had been changed into some cast-offs that Grandma Fletcher had collected in case of accidents. Some of the children came to her with nothing but what they wore. They always left with more, thanks to the charity of a kind young woman at the St. Vincent De Paul store, who, once a month, dropped an overflowing box by the apartment.

Sweet Little Piggy knelt over a piece of paper on the long oak coffee table, carefully drawing an intricate flower, her tongue stuck firmly in the corner of her mouth. She was oblivious to her Grandma who sat on the side of the couch, dabbing a wet washcloth along Rosie's forehead. The room smelled of pine oil, the wall scrubbed clean of the offending images.

Rosie moaned, her head moving slowly from side-to-side as she came to. Grandma Fletcher lifted her hand up quickly as Rosie rose up, startled, a scream poised on her lips. The washcloth fell across her face and onto her lap. Her eyes, momentarily unfocused, sharpened and went straight for the wall. She searched for several seconds then fell back, a sigh escaping her lips. She turned her head sideways and looked at Sweet Little Piggy who stared back at her with her triangular pink eyes.

"It's okay," said Sweet Little Piggy. "It's okay."

Piggy returned to her coloring. The creature's ugliness ignored, she concentrated on the paper. Rosie watched as the girl's steady hands finished drawing an orange-hued flower. With a pig-like snort, the girl finished and handed the paper to Rosie, who automatically held out a hand to receive it.

A timid smile crept across Rosie's face. She was amazed by the picture's intricate beauty. Each petal and stamen were exquisite in every detail. It could have been a photo, so complete was it in its perfection.

"For you," said Sweet Little Piggy forming the words slowly.

She glanced at her Grandma quickly who responded with a smile.

Sweet Little Piggy immediately began drawing another, her hand moving the violet crayon in the swift, sure strokes of a master. As Rosie watched, Grandma Fletcher spoke.

"Sweet Little Piggy is very special. The doctors say she has a perfect memory. She can see somethin' once and it's in her head forever, they say. Her drawin's are perfect and sometimes, we send them into contests. They always win. It helps with the rent, you know. Now, what you saw when you came in was another thing altogether. A gift of sorts."

Rosie jerked her attention to Grandma Fletcher, the previous fear returning in a flushed rush.

"Now, Now. Shush with that. There's nothin' to be a afraid

of," she said, cupping Rosie's cheek in her large black hand.

Rosie's gaze returned to Sweet Little Piggy's artwork, which was already halfway complete. The girl now drew the inner surface of the flower, creating tiny delicate veins, each a complex study in flawlessness. The small African flower almost seemed to move to the fictional wind of the image, petals quivering with their ambition.

"Now, I can't explain what she does when she draws them other things. It's like she's someone else. The doctors say it's on account of what she went through when she was a child...when her mother died. And her father," she paused, "... died. But them doctors don't know that these things Sweet Little Piggy does is true things. And they'll never find out, either. They'd just as sure lock her up and study her."

Grandma Fletcher stared a moment at Jenny Mae. "Poor, poor girl. You were right to leave, to get her away from him."

Sweet Little Piggy handed Rosie the picture she'd been working on. This one was a violet, as perfect as the other. Beautiful.

"For you," she said again, quicker this time, her mouth remembering the form.

Rosie accepted the picture, her eyes finally clear of fear. Her face had lost its tension. The trembling of her lower jaw had stilled. She looked into Grandma Fletcher's eyes, pleading.

"I never knew. I really didn't. I thought he just did them to me," she wiped her nose with a sleeve causing Grandma Fletcher to hand her a tissue she plucked from the right front pocket of her housecoat. "I mean, I knew. Just not all of it. Not..."

"There, there," said Grandma Fletcher. "I see no reason to get into that again. It's over. All over, now. You take Jenny Mae back to the Center and get yourself somethin' to eat. I expect her here every day for awhile, right. And on Wednesdays we go to see the special doctor at the University. It's free and we will take Jenny Mae with us. The sooner we get her some help, the better she will be. Right?" It wasn't a question.

Rosie accepted another picture from Sweet Little Piggy, this one a Black-Eyed Susan. She stared into the hard, determined eyes of Grandma Fletcher and nodded.

A few moments later, they were at the door.

"Tomorrow then, Right? And you, Jenny Mae, we will see tomorrow," said Grandma Fletcher holding a thick old hand out to the girl.

The child looked at the old woman, eyes still glassy, but a ghost of a smile hidden behind tight lips.

Grandma Fletcher unlocked the deadbolts and removed the chain. She turned, winked at Jenny Mae then turned the knob.

The door rebounded viciously, striking her on the side of the head. Blood erupted as she grunted in pain. The old woman sagged to the floor, unconscious, her glasses crushed under the black military boots of the attacker. A looming figure propelled the door inwards.

The man kicked her roughly out of the way and slammed the door shut. Then he spun and brought a hand across Rosie's face, propelling her into her daughter, both sprawled to the ground.

"Bitch. Did you think you could get away? I told you I'd track you down."

He was tall, a dark plaid wool coat over wide shoulders. His long hair was pulled tight into a ponytail that poked out from under the back of a cap that said *Dicky's Auto*. His starched white T-shirt was tucked into well fitting blue jeans. Although clean shaven, his face was scarred with pits of old acne. He spit the words from thick ugly lips.

Rosie struggled to stand, but reeled back as another punch landed and sent her once again, into her daughter.

Her husband launched another booted foot, this one glancing off her back.

"Leave me alone, you bastard!" she screamed, pushing Jenny Mae protectively into the center of the room.

Dicky reached down and picked her up by the hair, jerking her head backwards, arching her back impossibly.

"I'm done with you. You hear that, Bitch. You and me are quits, but you will not have my daughter." He laughed. "You are so stupid. It was so easy. I knew your bitch-friend Christina had told you about that place. Hell, she threatened me she would take you there often enough." He hurled her against the TV. "Come here, sweetheart," he said switching his voice to syrup, a hand out to Jenny Mae.

A mewling noise began down deep in her throat rapidly erupting into a long drawn-out *no*.

"It's okay, mister," came a voice from his left.

He turned and saw Sweet Little Piggy, who approached smiling, staring up into his face.

"Fuck me. What den of freaks did you bring my daughter into?" he asked, disgust replacing anger.

He swung a hard right hand at Sweet Little Piggy, but was stunned as her arm came up and caught his, just below the wrist. He tugged, but found his arm firmly trapped in the girl's powerful grip. He watched as the fat albino girl reached up with her other hand and touched his chest and closed her eyes. She began to sing, "Stick men, stick men, my little stick men."

He screamed with the impossibility of it all as he lashed out with his free hand and hit her once, twice, in the center of the face. Crimson blood erupted from the wounds and flowed down her white skin. The last blow freed him and sent Sweet Little Piggy tumbling back against the wall. He wiped the blood from his fist on the side of his jeans and advanced on his daughter. He picked her up by the waist and turned to his wife.

"Don't even think about following, cunt."

He kicked her again, this time in the leg with the steel toe of his boot. She squealed in pain. He turned, only to meet Grandma Fletcher who brought a tasseled lamp down on the top of his head, a scream of rage fueling its descent. He grunted and sagged to his knees. She brought it down again, but he managed to bat it aside with an arm as blood cascaded into his eyes blinding him.

"Bitch," he screamed. He struggled to his feet, unsteady for a few seconds, falling once more to his knees before he turned on Grandma Fletcher. She glared at him, her face strange without the permanent glasses. Her blue-white wig had fallen off, revealing a closely cropped gray scalp. She scuttled sideways, faster than she'd moved in decades, heading for the kitchen, for a knife. He lunged and caught her in a linebacker tackle. They both hit the couch and rolled onto the floor knocking over the coffee table. She ended up on top of him, but was too stunned to take advantage. He grunted several times before he managed to push her off.

"Fucking Hell," Dicky said to no one in particular as he stood shakily. He was gasping, blood dripping from his forehead to his chin. He grabbed a doily from the debris of the table and wiped his eyes clear of blood. He staggered into the middle of the room and stopped.

The albino girl drew rapidly on the wall. Her hands moved in quick, sure motions. So far, she'd drawn a two-foot high figure, perfect in every detail right down to the doily held firmly to its head.

It was him, absolutely clear and precise. Dicky reached up to feel his eye and found its puffiness matching that of the picture's.

"Stick men, stick men, my little stick men," came the voice—squeaky, lispy, crazy.

"I gotta get the fuck outta here."

He spun to leave, but almost fell as his feet refused to budge. He looked down and saw three hands tightly gripping each ankle, arms melding seamlessly into the floor. He jerked his right leg up and felt it give two inches before it was slammed back down by the strength of the impossible grip of the improbable hands. His eyes went wild and he turned left and right rapidly, looking for anything. A searing pain erupted along his back, slicing through his jacket, his shirt and his skin. He turned and saw himself, raising a lash, grinning with glee. He saw the lash fall striking his back again, the tip cutting fabric and skin.

"Fucking Hell?"

Through teary eyes, he looked at the wall again and saw the girl's hands move in an impossible blur as she transformed the whiteness into a pallet of perfect insanity. He saw a picture of himself behind him, a long lash poised to strike again. He watched as, in seconds, she drew two more versions of himself on either side of him.

He spun his head to the left as his arms were jerked out to the sides, almost dislocating by the forces upon them. He spun his head to the right and again, saw himself— evil, malignant and laughing as both of his other selves leaned back, using their weight to keep his arms immobile.

He stared forward, intent on screaming but felt it lodge in his throat like a ball of thick vomit. In front of him was another him— leering, a cigar in the corner of his mouth, arms crossed. He watched himself chuckle and puff hungrily on the cigar, the gray smoke swirling around his head like an evil halo. He watched as the cigar came out, up and down. The sizzle and pop of his left eye freed the vomit and released the tension in his bowels. When it entered his right eye, it killed him. He fell to the ground, his face bouncing twice on the carpet.

Sweet Little Piggy panted. Her chest heaved. Her smock was plastered to her body in dark sweaty patches. She had no need to draw anymore. Still, with a hoarse voice she still sung her song, "stick men, stick men, my little stick men."

She turned, her eyes slowly clearing from their previous emptiness and saw the man on the carpet, a small tendril of smoke rising from his hidden face. She saw her Grandma, Rosie and Jenny Mae all getting to their feet. She turned to the man again, her face crinkling as if to cry and approached the prone figure. She kneeled down by his head and patted him on the shoulder.

"It's okay, Mister. It's okay."

SILENCE

BY DAVID WHITMAN

"Wouldn't it be cool if there was really something on the tape?" Craig asked, his face still flushed pink from their impromptu run from the police. He ran his hands through his long, sweat-drenched hair and coughed up phlegm. "Man, I gotta quit smoking."

Dylan was not out of breath, but beads of sweat ran down his back and into his T-shirt. His shaven head gleamed in the moonlight, the sweat providing an unnatural sheen in the milky glow. The shadows on his face made his cheekbones jut out sharply.

They stared over at Silence and the tiny boy nodded, holding up the tape recorder above his skinny body like a prize, a beaming grin on his dimpled face.

"Man, I didn't even see that cop until he was right on us," Craig said, breaking out into another violent cough.

Dylan smiled, white teeth shining as he emitted a creepy little giggle. "All I saw was Silence come running up through the darkness, leaping over tombstones like he was running some kind of horror movie race track, demons biting at his ass. His eyes were so wide I started laughing. I could tell he was trying to scream the way his mouth was open so wide like that. I figure he must have thought he saw a ghost or some shit. He looked like one of them kids in the *Little Rascals* when they got all scared. Of course, then I saw the cop's headlights and I knew it was time to get the hell out. Ain't that right, Silence?"

The smaller boy, breathing heavily through his mouth,

nodded. His abnormally wise eyes were still jumping with adrenaline, his black hair was sticking out raggedly. The last thing he needed was to get arrested. His father already despised him, blaming him for his mother dying in a car accident, and he was eternally aggravated over the boy's inability to speak. *"Stop pretending like you can't talk, you little freak. The doctor said there's nothing wrong, except that you don't want to."* His father would end with a violent tirade of screaming and yelling, placing the sins of the world squarely upon his son's back-along with the heavy leather strap he used to beat him with. If he got arrested, the old man, driven by Budweiser and bitterness, would most likely beat the hell out of him.

"Silence was a quick bastard," continued Dylan. "It seemed like he passed us in a blur. Arms waving all around his head like that. Scared the hell out of me, man."

He had been called Silence ever since he had died. When he was four years old he had drowned, slipping into the water of Lake Angel. But it wasn't a slip. The fingers that gripped his ankle and pulled him down into the murky depths were icy, colder than water could ever be. The newspapers said he had been dead for seven minutes and the doctors, who really couldn't figure it out, diagnosed his silence as brain damage from lack of oxygen. His dad and the doctors were both wrong. It was the promise he had made. It was his promise never to tell that had made her let him go. She took his voice and gave him his life.

Dylan snatched the tape recorder from Silence's outstretched hand. "Let's take this back to my room and see if we got anything."

They were recording what was called EVP's, or Electric Voice Phenomenon. A few nights before, they had read about it on the Internet and listened to a bunch of samples, smiling in disbelief at the ghostly and haunting voices. The Internet site had said that if you took a tape recorder to any place that was considered haunted and just walked around recording, you would hear the voices of the dead.

"It's a good thing we didn't get caught by the cops," Dylan said as they walked down the dimly-lit street towards his house.

Craig grinned. "Damn straight. My Dad would have tanned my hide but good. And Silence's Dad would have probably lynched his ass in the front yard."

Silence agreed. He was a little nervous as to what was going to be on the tape. Since his accident, he had always felt a special kinship with the dead and he knew if any place was haunted, it was Greyson's Cemetery.

Children had been vanishing for almost 150 years in their town. Some of them were later found mutilated and murdered on the shore of Lake Angel. Many people had reported seeing Civil War soldiers marching through the cemetery as well, a confederate flag fluttering in the wind behind them as they marched through the tombstones.

"I wasn't so much afraid of the cops," Dylan said, lighting up a Marlboro. It looked out of place between his thin lips, like a child trying desperately to appear tough. "I was afraid of some sicko copying that dude Gabriel out there."

Gabriel Walker was caught making snuff films earlier in the year. He was using the cemetery as a set, mutilating and raping young women on camera. Their small town had made the national news for months after he was caught.

"I was thinking the same thing," Craig said. "I don't want to be no star of a snuff film. I was thinking how the ghosts of Gabriel's victims were probably still lurking around out there, too. If Lukas is on this tape, though, I think I'm gonna cry."

Silence had no argument with that. *If Lukas is on that tape,* he thought, *I will never sleep again.*

Lukas went into the cemetery to record EVP's, but vanished just like the dozens of other children throughout the years. They had dared him to go in alone, something they regretted after he was nowhere to be found the next day. Lukas had always promised if he died, he would come back as a ghost.

"I bet the Nightwalker got Lukas," Dylan said, his voice lowering to a whisper. Even uttering his name was considered a bad omen to any child growing up in Rawley.

Craig laughed and pointed at his tiny friend. "Look at Silence! You're freaking him the hell out!"

Silence was terrified of the Nightwalker. Over the years, he had become a sort of southern Boogeyman. The legend of the Nightwalker had been born out of the townsfolk's inability to solve all the children's disappearances. Every Rawley child had heard the phrase, *'If you don't be good, the Nightwalker is gonna get you.'* It was said his rotting flesh was covered with the faces of dead children, all of them moaning and hissing as he walked through the night.

Dylan smiled at Silence and the tiny boy shot him the middle finger. "He doesn't even want us to talk about the Nightwalker."

"The Nightwalker is fucking cool," Craig said, voice trembling with hero worship.

Silence shook his head and gave a quick glance behind him to make sure the Nightwalker wasn't lurking.

"You better watch your back," Dylan said. "If the Nightwalker catches you alone, you won't even be able to scream."

Silence shot Dylan an 'Are you stupid?' look, but smiled to show he was amused.

They tape recorded near the Fenwick mausoleum, the oldest grave in the cemetery. Edward Fenwick was the first kid to be murdered by the Nightwalker. They found his body in mangled and nearly unidentifiable pieces in the early 1900's, scattered all over the shore of Lake Angel.

They had just let the tape roll as they sat quietly on the rotting steps of the Fenwick crypt, their eyes scanning the shadowy tombstones for any signs of movement.

Silence decided he would be brave and search away from the mausoleum steps for signs of Lukas. He knew it was a stupid thing to do, but he really wanted to prove to his friends that he wasn't the coward his father thought him to be. Every time he moved his head to look in a different direction, he could swear he saw tiny figures dancing in his peripheral vision. Some of the tombstones were so white they glowed in the moonlight.

The statues that protected some of the graves looked particularly ominous by the light of the moon. Each time the cool October wind rushed into his hair, he felt he was being visited by a presence. When he saw the police headlights stabbing through the outstretched stones of the cemetery, he was almost relieved. It meant they would be able to leave.

When they arrived at the house Dylan stuck the tape into his stereo, turned on his black light, and sat back onto the bed. "I have a feeling we got something."

Craig sat on the floor nervously playing with his shoelaces. Silence was staring at the speaker like it was the giant screen of a television, his small body tense. He knew if little Eddie Fenwick were on the tape he would suffer nightmares for the rest of his life. The only reason that he had even become part of the whole thing was because he missed Lukas. Lukas and Silence had been friends since they were in kindergarten. They had even invented their own sign language, much to the annoyance of their teachers.

At first they heard nothing on the tape but the soft hiss of the recorder and the chirping of crickets. Dylan sat on the bed assuredly in the eerie blue lighting, tapping his fingers onto his skull.

The sound of a child crying filled the bedroom, a shrill and heartbreaking sob that broke the hiss on the tape. Dylan started biting his fingernails, his face giving away the fact he never believed they would really get anything of substance.

Silence stood up and paced the room, his legs threatening to give out underneath his wiry frame. The crying went on for about forty seconds and then it dropped to a low and harsh breathing.

"*Crowlin keeps us,*" a child's voice whispered. "*The black one is with Victor, but I wouldn't disturb him.*" There was a soft humming and his voice went in and out like phantom radio waves, each word seeming to come from even further away. "*...Killed...water...branches...run.*"

The child shrieked, his voice far away as if he was being pulled into a dense and thick fog.

A man's voice seemed to slither from the speakers, grave and ancient, a deep southern accent soaking each word. "*Our family is doing so well.*"

It was at this point on the tape that Silence could be heard racing through the graveyard.

"What the hell is Silence doing?" Dylan said on the tape, laughing. "He looks like he saw a ghost."

Dylan sprung up from the bed and turned on the ceiling light. "Holy shit, dude!" He held out his hand. "Look at my arm. My goosebumps are like zits!"

"I've never been so scared in my life, man," Craig said.

Silence was standing before the speaker, his diminutive body dwarfed by its massive size. He ran his hands through his dark hair. It was only at this point he realized he was not even breathing. He let his fists drop to his sides and he exhaled. The dark circles underneath his haunted eyes made him look like a dying child.

As the night went on, Dylan played the tape over and over as Silence transcribed the cryptic words into his notebook. They listened to the tape, speaking only in hushed and serious tones.

It did not take the boys long to figure out some of the clues on the tape. Silence knew immediately that Victor Cannon was one of the men killed in the snuff film that had been made in Greyson's Cemetery. Lukas was African American, so it was assumed he was the "black one" who was in the Cannon grave. The name Crowlin sounded familiar to Silence, and it was agreed he would go to the library the next day to see if he could dig anything up.

Jakep Crowlin was a wealthy local merchant in the late nineteenth century, Silence found out the next day as he perused some of the older newspapers on microfilm. At the age of seventy, Crowlin was suspected of killing some of the local children. When a customer visiting his general store saw the bonnet of the young and missing Bessy Kane, cries of *murderer!* could be heard all over town. Bessy was the fifth of seven children found missing that summer, and the town of Rawley had become paranoid and edgy.

Jakep Crowlin was found dead in his general store, hanging from the rafters, his tongue sticking out of his fat lips like a black worm. It was speculated a vigilante father had murdered him.

The next day, after an exhaustive search, they found the Crowlin Mausoleum. It was in the older part of the cemetery, snake-like weeds wrapped protectively around the its gray-green walls. The date of his death was July 27th, 1890.

Although he tried, Silence was unable see through the glass on the doors. It was covered with thick grime, almost like soot. A stone head of Christ jutted out from the top of the mausoleum doors, its eyes filled with green moss underneath its concrete crown of thorns.

A massive pine tree, decayed and rotted, loomed just over the stone building, forbidding and overbearing in its size, thick branches seeming to claw torturously towards the sky. Oddly, no needles grew from its finger-like branches. Sap poured from dozens of rotting holes in the wood like puss and termites covered its decaying base. Silence let his finger touch the sap and then pulled away quickly when an odd burning sensation stung his flesh.

"You're crazy for touching that thing, Silence," Dylan said, staring at the tree in disgust. "God knows what's in the soil underneath this cesspool."

Silence stared into his friend's eyes and frowned. Of all the things he did not want to do, digging up Victor Cannon's grave later that night was the highest on his list. Only his loyalty to Lukas kept him from retreating back to the misery that was his home.

That night, they stood over the Cannon grave and prayed, their imaginations torturing them with what they would find beneath their feet, their sweaty hands banded together. The voices on the tape made the cemetery a much creepier place than it had been the night before. Every time the wind blew, they would freeze up simultaneously, their ears and eyes straining for something that would give them the excuse to flee.

A couple of times, Silence could swear he saw some glimmer of light coming from Jakep Crowlin's mausoleum like a warning. He wanted to alert his friends, but feared they would only taunt him, and let his eyes drift back to where Dylan and Craig stabbed their shovels into the dirt. Every five minutes, Silence would turn on the flashlight to allow them to get their bearings as he shivered in the darkness.

When the shovel finally struck the wood of the coffin, they stood there for a few minutes, their bodies shaking in the cold air. None of them wanted to open it.

As far as I'm concerned, Silence thought, *the fact that we had a real ghost on the tape meant that anything could be in there. This man died in a snuff film, for God's sake.* Silence imagined Victor leaping out of the coffin, screeching dust from his throat, his decomposing body falling apart.

"We ready?" Dylan asked, his voice quivering.

Craig and Silence both shook their heads back and forth.

Dylan snickered. "Me neither," he said and stuck the crowbar into the coffin lid. "Get ready with that flashlight, Silence."

Silence wished he were the one holding the crowbar. *A flashlight isn't going to do me much good against ghosts or the undead,* he thought.

The coffin groaned under the force of the crowbar. Silence aimed the flashlight towards the spot on the wood where Victor's head would be. The coffin creaked open, a cloud of rancid air enveloping them with a *puff.*

Lukas was in the coffin on top of Victor's rotting corpse, his white eyes wide in the sea of his dark flesh. His mouth was open, his teeth jutting out above his dried-out tongue. Red lines ran from his eyes as if in his final hours he had cried tears of blood. A low ripping noise emanated from the coffin, as if something was about to tear open and throw itself upon them.

Silence dropped the flashlight and tried to scream, but all that came out of his mouth was a silent hiss of air. Craig promptly bolted into the tombstones, crying and whimpering as he ran, soon vanishing into the black night.

"Don't run, Silence," Dylan whispered, his voice taking on an inflection Silence had never heard before. "Something has my arm. I can't move."

The flashlight had fallen at the base of the reeking coffin, its light giving the newly dug hole an eerie glow. The contents of the coffin remained dark, although the whites of Lukas' eyes could still be seen glowing in the gloom.

Dylan suddenly jumped a few feet, pulled roughly as if held by spectral puppet strings, and Silence fought the urge to leave his friend behind.

"Oh God, Silence," Dylan said, his voice now a whispery whine. "Something is pulling me."

Silence grabbed the flashlight and turned the beam onto his friend's face. Dylan's eyes were so wide he could clearly see the red veins snaking around them. He let the light follow Dylan's line of site and flinched when he saw the bottom of the wrist. The outlines of fingers could clearly be seen on the arm, the thin, bony lines sinking deep into the flesh.

Dylan was suddenly pulled away from the light, an animal-like squeal firing from his lips. He was hyperventilating, his breath breaking the hushed air like a whispery heartbeat.

Dylan's scream was cut off quickly to a dull muffle. Silence aimed the shaking beam back at his friend's face and saw the indentation of fingers just to the left of his lips, his eyes so far open in his panic they looked like they were about to pop from his skull.

Silence watched, unable to move because he was so terrified. A single tear fell from Dylan's eye and rolled into the air near his cheekbone, seeming to drip over an invisible hand, floating in the air momentarily before falling to the ground.

Dylan was suddenly jerked backwards as if he had taken flight, his body hurling through the graveyard in a hazy blur. His muffled scream and boots dragging over the graveyard grass were the only sounds.

For the second time that night, Silence forgot he couldn't speak. He opened his mouth and howled with everything he had, but the only thing that came out was a sharp *Sssssssss*.

His mind shrieking for him to flee, Silence faced the direction of Dylan's muffled screams, his teeth biting painfully into his bottom lip to chase back a sob.

I'm not a coward, Daddy, Silence thought. *Someday you'll see that.*

Silence ran after Dylan into the darkness of the jutting tombstones, the jumpy beam of the flashlight cleaving through the air around him. Off in the distance, he could see Dylan's white face traveling through the cemetery like a floating orb— then it vanished with a soft splash.

Silence whimpered, his frayed nerves twitching on his face

as he moved towards the splash. Something had taken Dylan into Lake Angel, the very same place he had almost lost his life.

Silence remembered the cold and slimy hand that had clutched his ankle as a child. Not a day went by he did not recall the glowing white eyes in the murky depths of Lake Angel. He had left the lake without his voice, vowing never to go near it again.

Two drag lines led through the mud and into the water of the jet-black lake. Silence let the flashlight beam travel out into the gently undulating water and sobbed.

Dylan was in the creek about fifteen feet away, his shaven head protruding out and glistening in the light. Bubbles of water shot from his nose. Though he could not scream, his eyes did it for him, widening to the point that they looked like white shrieking mouths.

Then he was gone, pulled into the coal-black water in a quick splash. Bubbles broke the surface—an anticlimactic sound to what Silence knew was a scream sharp enough to wake the dead.

There was whispering coming from the large pine tree just above the Crowlin mausoleum, a rush of hissing from the shadowy branches. Silence turned to face the mausoleum.

It feels like I was supposed to be here, he thought, *almost like I was required to finish something that had started almost 100 years ago.*

Something grabbed his palm, a child's hand, both cold and warm. It pulled him gently toward the tree and he felt himself moving through the thick, damp air of Greyson's Cemetery. The dark windows of the mausoleum were illuminated in a dull, muddy glow.

Within the bony branches of the pine tree perched dozens of children, their legs dangling and swaying as if to their own ghostly breeze. White faces radiated in the darkness above like miniature moons. Their eyes were blots of black on their pale faces, their mouths small and pulled tight in painful frowns. One little girl cocked her head to the side slowly, almost like a dream, and studied Silence, her head drifting back and forth. Dylan's ghost stood under the tree, his ebony eyes staring ahead without emotion. Silence cried, his sobs exploding from his small body, nearly costing him his balance.

Some of the children were moaning, their mouths opening and closing. They cried out, a ghostly choir, their sad faces looking upwards as if to a Heaven that would not accept their souls.

Silence knew, then, that the children had been buried underneath the pine tree. All of the missing. Jakep Crowlin had been a clever murderer. He had known the townsfolk of Rawley would not think to look in the cemetery for their missing children.

With a rusty groan of protest, the mausoleum doors creaked open behind Silence's tiny form, a faint glow covering his body like mist. Never in his young life was he more painfully aware that he was unable to scream. The children above all turned to face the doors, low, melodic wails rustling from their dead lips. Dylan just stared ahead, his body rocking and back and forth drunkenly.

Jakep Crowlin, the Nightwalker and child murderer, stood before the open doors, a cryptic smile on his phosphorescent face, his malevolent eyes narrowing into slits. His long hair flowed around his face like underwater reeds. Craig's body was on the stone floor inside, his right arm resting over his throat as if he had struggled to breathe before he died.

Crowlin nodded and held out his long arms, his dark eyes blazing with quiet rage. Silence felt himself drawn to the figure, the wispy and ethereal forms of dozens of dead children pushing him forward and into old man's arms, their moans singing a morose lullaby.

Crowlin embraced Silence fiercely, his frosty arms wrapping around his slender frame like the loving father he never had, both inviting and suffocating.

Silence looked up into Crowlin's dusky eyes and felt dead and rancid breath blow from the decrepit mouth.

The last sound he heard before he died for the second time in his life was the harsh slam of the mausoleum doors closing behind his back in a rush of frigid wind.

Silence perched in the pine tree, his brothers and sisters lodged in the limbs around him as he clung to the dead branches. He felt oddly sad watching his Dad search for him through the cemetery. Silence could tell by looking at his father's face that he had really loved his son, and that he had many regrets. Many people had searched the graveyard for the missing children, but Silence merely watched from the tree, neither caring nor remembering why anything mattered.

Some lost part of his soul knew no one would think to look under a tree that's been undisturbed since the nineteenth century and he moaned, his small feet swinging from the rotting branch as if moved by a ghostly breeze.

SCARECROWS SCARE DEMONS DON'T THEY?

BY WESTON OCHSE

Edwin had mixed feelings about being home. It had been twenty years, and instead of returning as the conquering hero he'd bragged about so long ago, he'd returned penniless, homeless and dismarried. He liked to call it that because he'd been married several times, but for many reasons, most involving his eternal love affair with alcohol, they'd never panned out. Like being disenfranchised, dismissed and diseased, he was just dismarried. To set the record straight, he wasn't exactly penniless, either. After all, he did have his Army retirement, and half pay for doing nothing the rest of his life wasn't too bad a deal.

His main concern, however, was a place to live, and that's what had sent him out of town on this old two-lane road. The drive brought back memories. Some good ones— remembrances of hunting, fishing and the frolics of youth. And some bad ones—- demons that possessed the soul until one's only friend was oneself.

For the hundredth time this week, he wondered what had drawn him back.

Like all the roads up on the mountain, this one wound along property lines, creating a dangerous meandering path through dense forest, blind corners and switchbacks. His daddy had been a moonshine runner when he was young, and used to tell young Edwin stories about taking these roads at a hundred miles an hour in the old Chevy as Smokies tried in vain to keep up. Even so, Edwin would never be his daddy and he took it slow and careful.

There was a break in the forest up ahead as it gave way to a split rail fence, old and gray with kudzu wrapped around as if it was what kept it from falling. Edwin slowed the pickup as he approached the mailbox and read the cramped painted words, faded and flaking after years of neglect. *Jonston.* This was the place.

He examined the house, once a proud two story, now in disrepair with several differing shades of paint and tar lathered on to repair cracks and sprung seams. He could just see the silken tips of some healthy looking corn in the back yard, probably twenty acres planted with waist-high tobacco. Edwin didn't see a silo for the corn or a barn to dry the tobacco, so he supposed the old man must be either leasing the land or selling the raw product. Not as much money to be had, but still, it provided some income. Edwin figured the land had been in the old man's family since they'd originally sharecropped and other than taxes and electricity, there shouldn't be too many bills.

He'd met the old man at the Legion Hall last week when all the veterans and townsfolk had gotten together and celebrated Edwin's return. Only in a small town would they have a party for someone they hadn't seen in twenty years. It wasn't Edwin they liked anyway, it was his service record and the uniform they loved. Still, the food was free and the drink was plentiful. Then the old man had approached him and offered free room and board and three hundred dollars a month if he'd sign on as a live-in caretaker. Edwin pulled in and up the dirt drive thinking this might just be the opportunity he needed.

Old Man Jonston sat on the porch, a pitcher of iced tea breathing on the table next to him. Edwin prayed that it was whiskey, but he knew that it was only his preference. As he pulled up, the old man walked to the top of the stairs and waved. Edwin waved back and stopped behind the old man's truck— same make and model as his own, but thirty years older.

Edwin hopped out and moved up the stairs, noting how they creaked and already thinking about ways to fix them.

"Welcome, Mr. Lavern. Have any trouble finding the place?"

Old Man Jonston wore black work boots and faded denim

dungarees over a white t-shirt. Edwin held out his hand and
smiled.

"No, sir. Everything's coming back to me, and your
directions were dead on."

"I bet," said Old Man Jonston. "Here, let's sit a spell and you
can tell me about your world travels and about old Saddam."
With a liver-spotted hand he gestured toward several chairs on
the other side of the round table.

Edwin moved over and went to sit down.

"NO! Stop. Not that one, *that* one," indicated the suddenly
irate old man.

Edwin was caught in mid-sit and stood up slowly and sat
in the chair indicated. This one was old and rickety and he
discovered right away that you had to sit perfectly straight and
still or it threatened to break. He glanced longingly at the chair
he'd almost sat in and envied its sturdy lines and well-used
cushion that still held the indentations of a million sits.

The old man sat across from him in an equally comfortable-
looking chair and laid his hands face up.

"Sorry about that, Mr. Lavern. That was Henrietta's chair,
may she rest in peace. That chair is reserved for her, you know."

Edwin raised an eyebrow, then smiled. The old man was
certainly getting along in years, maybe even a little senile.
Edwin waited as Jonston lit a cigarette, noting the old ceramic
mixing bowl that was being used as an ashtray and the hundred
or so butts that almost filled it.

"It's okay, Sir. And please, call me Edwin. I've never been
called Mr. Lavern and it sounds funny."

"That's right! You went in the Army when you was eighteen.
Probably never heard anything more than Private and Sergeant
in your life." The old man's cigarette was perched in the corner
of his mouth. He reached over and poured a tall glass of tea
and slid it in front of Edwin. "And stop calling *me* Sir. I bet
you had enough of that to last a lifetime, Huh? Call me Jonston.
Everyone else does, anyway."

"Too true. Too true. Alright, then... just Jonston," he said
taking a sip of the tall glass, wishing it was whiskey. He'd a
flask in his pocket and as soon as the old man turned his

back for more than a moment, he was going to spike it proper. "Mighty good tea."

Jonston waved his hand, brushing aside the nicety. "It's my Henrietta's favorite. So you're interested in hiring on here, are you?"

"Well, I don't have any firm plans, but yes. It does seem like a good opportunity. I'd like some more details, of course."

"What's that?" asked the old man leaning forward addressing the empty chair that was Henrietta's. Jonston nodded several times, "Of course I'll get around to it, My Dear. Just let me do it in my own way."

"Uh, Jonston? Are you okay, Sir?" asked Edwin, wondering if the old man was hallucinating.

Jonston glanced at him irritably, then smiled and sat back. "Sorry about that. I'm just a crazy old man, you know. A little crazy and almost harmless."

Edwin laughed nervously and took a deep drought of the tea. *Yeah*, he thought, *drunk crazy.*

"You joined the Army in 1973. Isn't that about right?"

"Uh, yes. I mean, I finished a twenty-year tour."

"You know that's the same year my wife died."

Edwin sat back and observed the old man with compassion. Poor Jonston had never really let go, probably talked to his dead wife all the time—keeping him company in his old age.

"In fact, she told me she'd seen you before you joined up. She always said how handsome you looked in your dress greens."

"Thank you, Sir," replied Edwin. The only time he'd worn them was the day before he'd left and that day had been nothing but a bad day. "I mean, I didn't know your wife, but thanks just the same. Of course, it was so long ago and I seem to have forgotten much."

"Oh, I doubt you could ever forget her. What's that, my dear?" Jonston asked the empty chair. "All right. All right. Settle down. I'll ask him. I know you want to end this as much as I do."

"Ask me what, Sir, I mean Jonston." Edwin couldn't help but think that if he had a jug, he could see who the old man was talking to.

"Here, have some more tea," said the old man, standing and refilling the glass. "My Henrietta says there were a bunch of boys you used to hang around with. What were their names? Let me see, there was Tom Hubbard, Bobby Burdette, Little Timmy Baugh, and Clay Archie. Ain't that right?"

Edwin began to feel uncomfortable as a long forgotten memory started filtering through the years of practiced forgetfulness and alcohol. He shifted and the chair squealed in protest.

"I remember them. Haven't seen them in twenty years, but yeah. We used to hang out together. What's this have to do with the job?"

"Ah hell, boy. Give an old man a chance to reminisce. After all," he said, staring pointedly at the empty chair, "I had to be sure, now, didn't I."

"Be sure of what?"

"Be sure you were one of the bastards that killed my Henrietta. That's what."

Edwin spat out the tea he'd been drinking as the memories of that night flew to the front of his mind, his actions, the actions of everyone, suddenly in perfect clarity. He stood quickly and took one step before his legs refused their commands. He fell heavily to the wooden porch, landing on his side, staring up into the face of the old man which was suddenly filled with an almost religious fury.

"Don't try to move, son. Your legs won't work proper. And as soon as my mixture kicks in, you won't be able to even blink. It's an old recipe my granddaddy used in the Civil War when they needed to amputate. Part laudanum, part horse tranquilizer."

"But why?"

"You have the gall to ask why?" spat the old man as he stood hovering over Edwin. "You boys left her in that ditch, bleeding and broken. She was alive, you know? At least one of you bastards could have called an ambulance. She was alive for a whole day, lying there as ants and beetles crawled over her— feeding on her blood."

Alive. She'd been alive?

Horrific thoughts moved sluggishly through his mind. They

were so sure she'd been dead. After Clay had gone wild and hit her with the tire iron over and over and over, they were sure she'd died.

"Don't you worry, boy. You don't have to admit anything. Your friends all told me and Henrietta how you killed her. And we've had fifteen years to wait for you ever since I tracked down Tom Hubbard in Pikeville. Would you believe that they all blamed you? They said it was you that tore into her with a tire iron."

"No. No, it... " The words wouldn't come. He couldn't feel his legs or his arms or his face and his tongue was thicker than a bread and butter pickle.

"You won't be able to talk, now, but don't worry, you'll have plenty of time to tell your side."

Edwin watched as the world went from horizontal to vertical as the old man lifted him up and swung a limp arm around a shoulder. Jonston levered the screen door opened with his booted foot and with grunts and a few damnations, carried and drug Edwin through the house and onto the back porch. The back yard was filled with the sounds of buzzing flies and chirping crickets. The corn Edwin had noticed earlier, was thick, allowing a half-circle of grass for a back yard. The tall stalks of corn grew right up to the eaves on each corner of the house and was better than any fence for privacy.

Jonston turned and nodded to a large wicker chair, "Have a seat, my dear. This is the last one, so you best enjoy it."

Edwin watched the empty chair and saw how the cushion pressed as if someone had just sat down.

"Now, take a look," said the old man turning towards the back yard again. "Your friends have been waiting for you."

Edwin, unable to move his head or avert his eyes, saw that at the apex of the half-circle of lawn, were five scarecrows. Four really, because in the center, was an empty cross of wood, about man-sized and freshly planted.

"I saved the position of honor for you, seeing as you were the one who was in charge of the killing. Yeah, they all told me all about how you planned it, so don't go thinking I don't know the truth."

The old man limped down the stairs and drug his captive across the lawn to the empty cross. Beside it, sat a wooden crate filled with sundry instruments. The old man leaned down and gripped a strand of rope, then, almost falling with his burden, pushed Edwin against the wood. With one hand, he wrapped the rope around the upper post and around Edwin's neck, securing it with a granny knot. He stood back and grinned from ear to ear.

"Now, that'll hold you for a minute. Try and hold your breath, will you. Little Timmy over there strangled to death before I could finish and Henrietta wouldn't let me live it down for the longest time."

Edwin tried to look where Jonston had indicated and felt his head roll slowly, until the scarecrow to his right was in view. The anesthetic was beginning to wear off and he could just feel his legs and the strangling rope around his throat. While the old man secured his hands to the cross-posts with rope, Edwin examined the scarecrow. It wore a straw hat, a flannel shirt and even older dungarees than the old man wore. Fresh straw had been stuffed in the sleeves and under the hat almost completely covering the sun-bleached bones of a skeleton. He looked closer and within the straw of the head, he could make out a brown skull and the ants that still crawled in and out of the eye sockets.

Edwin turned his head and was confronted with the leering face of Jonston. He tried to scream, but only a rough sigh exited his still paralyzed mouth.

"They're still feeding aren't they. I squeeze honey into the eye sockets about once a week. Henrietta tells me it makes the boys scream. Says it itches like crazy. Funny how you can itch when you're dead, ain't it."

Edwin cried in his mind. Sobbing internally as the truth finally set in.

It had been the night before he left for basic training and the boys had thrown him a going away party. Between the shine and the whiskey and the beer, they'd all been wasted driving around in Archie's old Mercury Cougar shouting their defiance to the stars. They'd found Henrietta on the side of the road with a flat tire and stopped to help. Bobby had been the one who threw her down and ripped off her dress. At least he was the first one. They all took turns, except for Edwin. He was in the bushes puking. After Clay beat her, it was Bobby who took her car and hid it in the woods. They'd made a pact never to talk about it and until this day, Edwin had never told a soul.

"Pay attention, now, boy. This is important," said the old man holding up a hammer and what looked like a silver ten-penny nail. "This here is made of silver and has been steeping in holy water for twenty years. Prepared special-like just for you. Why silver, do you ask?"

Edwin shook his head, he'd paid for his sin. He'd paid for it for twenty years. He remembered how he'd wanted to. How he'd seen her naked and begging and felt himself throb, rubbing himself, a drunken need to fuck, to release his seed like a demon intent on conquer.

But he hadn't done anything. And it had cost him. Never a relationship, never a happy day. It was the bottle that had numbed him so he could make it to another day and another bottle. If he was guilty of anything, it was for doing nothing, not murder. He didn't want to know what the nail was for. He didn't even want to be here.

The old man ignored him and continued, "These will not only hold you up, but they will bind you. Hell will have to wait for a little while longer, because after I'm done, you'll be here until the wood rots away and the silver turns to dust. I hear they still find old silver coins from before the time of Jesus. Damn if that ain't a long time."

Edwin was beginning to feel more and more of his body and he felt the impact of the hammering and the nail entering his left hand like a dull pain. The next nail was pounded through his tricep and he could feel this one even more. On the fourth, as the man hammered the nail happily through his right hand, it was as if all his feeling had returned and his scream pierced the air, sending crows flying from the corn and stilling the sounds of the thousand crickets. It was the last nail that sent his bowels gushing. His scream erupted from his soul, soaring beyond mortal hearing, making the angels flinch in their games and the demons pause in their laughter.

"Feel that, did you? Well, don't you worry, boy. There's only one more to go and then you won't feel nothing."

The last nail was twice as long as the others and was more like a railroad spike than a nail. Old Man Jonston placed it right over Edwin's heart, and with a wry chuckle, hammered it home.

"Hey. Eddie, Wake up."

"Yeah, Ed, get your ass awake. We've been waiting for you."

He didn't know how long it had been, but he woke up, his body felt numb. His mind was fuzzy. He opened his eyes slowly and noticed that night had descended. The backyard was brightly lit by two spotlights, each affixed to a corner of the house, high under the eaves.

"Eddie. Long time no see. How was the Army, man? Did you kill anybody?"

Edwin shook his head to try and rid himself of the cobwebs, but it was to no avail. He was having trouble thinking straight.

"I told them, Ed. We told them how you killed Henrietta. You know, you shouldn't have done it."

"I was puking in the weeds. I didn't do anything," he answered automatically, turning his head to the left.

"Yeah, I know," said Clay grinning, "but they didn't."

It was Clay Archie, just the way he remembered him, except now wearing a hat and shirt and dungarees. Straw poked out from the seams almost hiding his ghostly pale face.

"Man. You got old."

Edwin spun his head to his right, and where he'd seen the skeletal remains of Little Timmy earlier, was now the painfully pale features of the little man, giggling happily. He turned and looked to the porch, twenty feet away. Old Man Jonston sat beside Henrietta, his hand resting atop hers upon the table. Like his friends, she was pale, a ghost, and he could make out her satisfied smile even at this distance.

"Tell us a story. Old Man Jonston been following your career. He told us about them wars you was in. Tell us about Grenada. Tell us about Panama. Tell us about Saddam. Tell us about all them demons you conquered," came the squeaky recognizable voice of Tom from the other side of Timmy. "Come on man, we gotta long time to kill.

WANDERING MINDS

BY DAVID WHITMAN

Carl Levine looked out the window and saw Russ Wilson's dog, Ka-pow, shitting on his front lawn.

"That goddamn son of a bitch! It's all over for that fucking dog!"

The feud had been going on for the last two years. It had started when Russ had taken to parking in front of Carl's house. *You don't own the damn street, Levine,* Russ had said. From there, it had elevated into an all out war.

Every day they could be seen shouting over the fence that separated their yards, each of them daring the other to come over and put a little action into those fighting words. Both men could often be seen sitting at the window, just waiting for the other to make the next move.

As Ka-pow did his business, he seemed to be smiling at Carl. *Here's my gift to you,* he seemed to say. The poodle didn't even try to run when he saw Carl running toward him, hands outstretched. The dog finished its business, kicked his back legs twice in a kind of burying movement, and then escaped through a trench under the fence.

Furious, Carl ran over to the wooden fence and peered over it, blue veins bulging across his bald head.

Russ was sitting on a lawn chair, wearing his favorite food stained Hawaiian shirt, scribbling on a crossword puzzle. Ka-pow sauntered over, spun around twice, and sat down next to his master.

"Goddam you, Wilson!" Carl yelled. "I told you about that

damn dog! You're not going to be happy until I kill the little son of a bitch!"

Russ looked up from his crossword puzzle, as if he heard a fly buzzing somewhere within the vicinity of his ear, and scratched his beard lazily. "That you, Levine?" He looked over at Carl. "What's the idea? I'm trying to sit here on this bench and enjoy my week off and now you're harassing me. Go back in the house, you little man."

"I'm telling you, Wilson," Carl said. "I'm going to kill that little bastard. I want you to get over here and clean up the mess he left."

Russ frowned. "What are you talking about, Levine? Ka-pow's been sitting here by me for the last half-hour. If he had gone off to relieve himself, I would have seen him go. Now go away and leave me alone."

As if listening to his command, Carl disappeared.

Russ patted the poodle gently on the head. "Good boy, Ka-pow. You're always making your Poppa proud." He loved making Levine's life miserable. It provided entertainment to his boring life ever since his wife, Mary, had left him, the miserable bitch. "Now," he said, scratching his long beard with the pencil, his concentration turning back to the puzzle. "What's a six letter word for supplant?"

Just as he started to write the answer down, a pile of dog shit landed in his lap with a disgusting *plop*. He looked up from his lawn chair, stunned.

Carl was leaning over his fence waving at him with a shovel, an enormous grin on his face. "Eat shit, Wilson! Next time that dog comes over on my lawn, I'm gonna shoot the fucker!"

Russ looked down into his shit buried lap, his mouth open in wide "O" of disbelief. *That bastard has some balls after all,* he thought, before his shock gave away to anger. He stood up from his chair, throwing his crossword puzzle book on top of Ka-pow, eyes bulging with rage. "Levine! I'm going to kill your crazy ass!"

Carl smile widened, exposing his yellow teeth. "Why don't you just come over and try it, you shit eater? I think it's about time I put you in your place."

Russ ran over to the fence and began to climb, his pudgy body dancing precariously just at the top, before he slipped and fell into Carl's lawn. He landed on his back solidly, feeling the air explode from his lungs, his Hawaiian shirt ripping open from where it had caught in the fence. His hairy belly stuck out like an obscene parody of pregnancy.

Before Russ could get to his feet, Carl brought the shovel down on top of his head, gritting his teeth as it connected with a dense thud.

The shovel wriggled in Carl's hand before it came alive with a burst of painful electricity. He could feel pulses of energy blasting through the handle and into his body. As if he was holding a live power line, Carl danced up and down energetically, spittle flying out of his chattering teeth.

The switch was sudden. Carl found himself inside Russ' portly body.

Russ let go of the shovel and looked down at himself, his mouth dropping open, bewildered to find himself in the thin and wiry frame of his hated enemy.

Carl, his ass planted firmly on the ground, looked up to see himself standing in front of him with a shovel at his feet. Ka-pow was standing off to the overgrown grass, his head cocked to the side curiously, a small whimper escaping from his furry lips.

Dazed, Carl got to his feet, rubbing his head dumbly. Something was wrong, he felt heavier somehow, and he was wearing Russ' Hawaiian shirt. He looked over at himself. He felt like he was staring at his own reflection, only he didn't have any control over what it did. In panic, he fled into his house. Russ, just as frightened, ran into his house as well.

Ka-pow watched the both of them silently and began to whine.

Mrs. Anderson, the elderly neighbor across the street, was wondering just what the hell was going on. She had just seen them fighting on the lawn and then she had seen Carl run into Russ' house and vice versa.

Carl was looking into the mirror of his bathroom and wondering what in the hell Russ Wilson's reflection was doing in it. He ran his hands through Russ' thick, curly hair, feeling for the first time in years what it felt like to actually not be bald. He began to finger his newly acquired beard inquisitively, pulling his hand away with disgust when he saw that it was dotted with food. He had never been able to grow one himself-it always came out looking vaguely like some kind of animal mange. The smell of Russ' body odor wafted into his nostrils and he flinched, his eyes wincing at the ripeness of the scent. To say something weird had happened was an understatement. They had switched bodies. His brain was actually floating in the disgusting skull of his hated neighbor.

He jumped when the phone rang, stumbling out to the living room, his mind still trying to get over the shock of what had happened.

Vacantly, he picked up the receiver. "Uh, Hello."

"Levine, you bald asshole! Give me back my body!"

"Wilson, what in the hell did you do?" Carl asked, his voice whiny and high.

"*ME!*" Russ shrieked into his ear, causing him to flinch in pain. He still felt a dull ache from when he had apparently hit himself with a shovel. "*ME!* Levine, I think we'd better get some goddamn facts straight here! First, you throw a pile of dog shit into my lap! Second, you attack me with a shovel! And now, you've somehow stolen my body from me! I just looked into the mirror and saw your chrome dome shining at me, I damn near lost my eyesight from the glare!"

Carl, finally getting his bearings, shouted into the receiver, "You big, fat, lumberjack-looking redneck prick! You think I'd want your out of shape, near death, pile-of-lard-of-a-body with egg yolk in the beard? Don't you even wash this mountain of waste?"

"So what are you trying to tell me, Levine?" Russ shot back. "You trying to say you have nothing to do with this?"

"That's exactly what I'm trying to say. What do you think, Wilson, that I'm some kind of black-magic-practicing warlock? Obviously something weird happened. We're going to have to try and switch them back somehow. Come back over, and I'll smack you over the head with the shovel again."

"What, are you crazy? Has the sun been burning into your smooth plate of a head too long? I'm not going to let you hit me with a shovel again, even if I am in your body." There was a pause and Carl heard a faint zipping sound. "Oh, and don't it figure. Let me correct that last statement. I'm not going to let you hit me with a shovel again, even if I am in your body with the little, itty-bitty dick. Jesus, Levine, it looks like a baby's broken pinky. No wonder you don't have any kids."

Carl looked into the hallway mirror and watched the bearded face of Russ Wilson turn red with embarrassment.

"You still there, Levine?" Russ asked. "I have a better suggestion. How about if I come over and hit *you* with a shovel, or actually, I mean me. Jesus, this is getting confusing!"

"No way. You're not coming near me. I'll call you back, Wilson. I need some time to catch my breath."

"Before you go, Levine, I got one last thing left to say. If this is some kind of permanent deal, I think I got myself gypped in a major way here. Almost like trading in a Porsche for a Yugo. You take care of that fine piece of machinery you got there, Levine. Because I'm going to take it back."

Carl hung up the phone and inhaled deeply. He walked over to the sofa and sat down, his tired breath escaping his newly overweight body like the hot gas of a farm animal. *At least I'm not crazy,* he thought, *because if I am, then Russ is on the same ride.*

Carl looked down at the colorful, but ugly, flowered shirt that he was wearing with strong aversion. The side of the food-stained shirt was ripped, and he could see Russ' obscenely fat stomach protruding from within the folds. All his life he had eaten well, steering clear of high fat foods and red meat. Now he was sitting here with an immense beer belly that he had acquired in seconds.

He was about to get up and call Russ and try to figure something out when an evil smile took control of his bearded face. *I probably won't be in this body permanently,* he thought. *It's time to give old Russ Wilson a little payback for the many years of harassment. It's take to take old Russ on a little adventure.*

Carl walked out of his house, whistling an old disco tune. He saw Russ, or rather he saw himself driving away, skidding the wheels of his dirty station wagon as he went. *Probably went to get himself a therapist,* he thought. *Hell, I'm badly in need of one myself.*

He got in his car and drove into town, the smile never leaving his face.

"Now, let me get this straight," the tattoo artist said to Russ. "You want me to write 'I love Jesus!' on your forehead?"

"Yes," Russ said, reaching into his pocket and pulling out his neighbor's wallet. "If you're worried about the money, I have it right here."

"This ain't about the money, pal. Don't you want to at least think about this? Okay, you like Jesus and all, but do you really need to turn your forehead into a billboard? I mean, I'm not into religion, but don't you have a better way of professin' this kinda love? Can't you just donate money to your church or something? Roll up your sleeve and I'll put it on your arm."

Russ shook his head back and forth, his perpetual grin never leaving his face. "It's for a friend."

The tattoo artist sat back against the counter. "A friend? Why don't your friend come down and get this? If you ask me, this is pretty far to go for a friend."

Russ began to get up out of the chair. "Look, if you won't do it, then I'm sure that there are people who will."

The artist put his heavily callused hand up against Russ' chest. "Sit back down, pal. I'll do it. I just wanted to make sure that you really wanted this." He pulled a waiver out from his desk. "You're gonna have to sign this, I ain't getting my ass sued."

Russ sat back in the chair and began to rub his hands over Carl's bald head. "I'll sign anything. My friend is going to love this."

The artist picked up his needle. "All right, any special color or font you want this in?"

"How about a green New Times Roman?" Russ asked. "Can you put a little red heart on my cheek too?"

When the beautician spun the chair around towards the mirror, Carl couldn't help but laugh at the reflection of his fat neighbor.

"I told you it was too drastic for you," the beautician said. "You're not the only one who is going to be laughing. Want me to at least shave off the cherry red van dyke mustache?"

"I'm laughing because it looks great. Leave the mustache just like it is, thank you very much. My friend is going to love it. This is just the way he always would have wanted it."

Carl's hair, or rather Russ' hair, was permed up into an enormously high, stiff Afro. It rose at least three feet from the top of his head and it was bluer than the waters of the Caribbean. He had gotten the beard shaved, leaving only a droopy mustache that hung down about three inches from his chin. He smirked at his reflection and then broke out into hysterics again.

"You really do like it?" she asked.

"Miss, I love it. Are you sure you didn't learn your trade in heaven? I only want you to do one more thing."

"Just don't tell anybody that you got this makeover from me, okay? What do you want?"

"Can you put a big-ass flower in it?"

When Carl, stroking his long mustache, pulled back into his driveway, he saw that Russ was still out somewhere with his body. Ka-pow was sitting on the lawn, giving out a low growl when he saw that his master looked like a clown.

Carl reached up and patted his Afro, staring at the tiny poodle. "Even you can't piss me off now, you little fuckball. Wait until your master gets a peep at his new look."

He walked into the house and threw his car keys on the front table. When he glanced up into the hallway mirror he immediately fell to the floor, overwhelmed with laughter.

He rolled to his side and got up from the floor clumsily as he was still unaccustomed to having such a rotund body. He walked over to his stereo and popped in one of his favorite discs, the *Bee Gees' Greatest Hits*. Back in the seventies, many considered him the disco king. One time he was even on *American Bandstand*. Whenever he was overwhelmed with joy, he would put in that disc and start pulling out moves from his bag of dancing tricks.

When *Jive Talkin'* began to blast through his house, he began to jiggle around, his fleshy body vibrating the floorboards. As he shook his wide ass back and forth, he realized that he was not as good of a dancer in Russ' overweight body. Deciding that he was not going to get too far moving his newly acquired heavy body, he resorted to his repertoire of dazzling hand movements, each hand flashing out with zest. He didn't hear his doorbell, or see his front door swing slowly open.

Carl looked up and saw himself standing there-mouth hung open in astonishment. His eyes widened in stupefaction when he saw the green 'I love Jesus!' tattoo written on his bald forehead. A large red heart dotted the cheek like an expressionate exclamation point. Russ returned the dismay, his mouth flapping open and closed mechanically at seeing himself with a blue Afro.

Carl grabbed his remote control and turned off the stereo. "Wilson! What in the hell did you do to my face!"

"Me! What did you do to my fucking hair! I look like a goddamn faggot! And you're dancing my body around like that only makes it look worse!"

Carl walked up to Russ and examined the tattoo. "That's not real, is it?"

"Damn right it's real, Levine! I know how much you love Jesus and all!"

Carl grabbed Russ by the shirt, which unnerved him because it made him feel like he was attacking himself. "You bastard! Tattoos are permanent! At least you can always cut this hair off!"

Russ pushed him away. "Oh well. Maybe you can get it burned off or something."

Carl screamed in frustration and ran down the hallway, his arms waving in rage, before slamming the bathroom door closed.

Russ walked over to the hallway mirror and began to examine his tattoo. "Boy, Levine!" he shouted to the bathroom door. "You should be thanking me! This tattoo is going to guarantee you a place in heaven! Old Saint Peter is going to open them gates real fast for you!"

Carl exited the bathroom, his jaw working up and down as if he was eating something. He swallowed exaggeratedly and said,

"You goddamn son of a bitch. You had to take it too far didn't you, Wilson? All I did was go and mess up your hair a little bit." Angrily he pulled the flower from his Afro and threw it to the floor. "You had to go and get me a fucking tattoo. You had to go and scar me." He turned away and headed into the kitchen.

Russ shrugged and followed him in. Carl was digging through a drawer of utensils. He pulled out a sharp looking knife and glared at him, unable to look very menacing in his blue tower of hair. "What are you doing, Levine? What are you going to do, stab me?" He began to back away fearfully. "Don't forget that this is your body that I happen to be in."

Carl put his hand down on the counter and slammed the knife down, cutting off his thumb with a thick squirt of blood. He looked over at his enemy, his face beaming triumphantly as he held the bloody hand before his face. "It's gonna be pretty hard to button your pants now ain't it, you fat fucking prick?"

Russ gaped at the severed thumb. "You bastard!" He ran over to the counter and promptly slammed his mouth against the edge, shattering it into a pulpy mass of broken teeth. He looked up and began to spit teeth out one by one. "Jesus! That hurt like hell!"

"I wouldn't know about that," Carl said, bringing the knife up and slashing his ear off with one wet slice. The ear went spinning through the air in a red arc before falling to the floor with a sickening slap. "The codeine is just starting to kick in. What did you think I was doing in the bathroom, whipdick?" He bent over and picked up the severed ear, holding it in his open palm. "It's gonna be pretty hard to shout out wrong answers to *Jeopardy* now ain't it, Russ? Unless of course you get that close captioned I've been hearing so much about. They got all kinds of things for the hearing impaired these days."

Screaming with rage, Russ picked up a chair and slammed it over his neighbor's head, totally forgetting that he was actually attacking himself. He brought the chair down again and again until he was sure that Carl was dead. It no longer even bothered him that he was staring down at his own corpse.

He dropped the chair to the floor, and exhaled dejectedly. *I guess I'm stuck in this body for the rest of my life,* he thought, trying to ignore the pain that was rocking through his shattered mouth.

"I don't think so, Wilson," Carl said.

His skin tingling with shock, Russ looked down at the corpse. Carl was still definitely dead. He gave out a pathetic little squeak when he realized that it was he himself who had spoken aloud.

Carl was back in his body, only now they were in there together. Carl and Russ were one.

It gave him another jolt when he realized that he was only in control of the right side of his body. Apparently, Carl was in control of the left. Fighting madly, Carl/Russ attacked himself, the right and left sides of the body literally under separate authority.

Carl/Russ damn near beat himself to death.

Carl/Russ sat at the table wondering just what in the hell they were going to do. Russ' body lay on the floor at their feet, reminding them of their situation. The tattoo was making Carl angrier all over again.

"Don't you go getting all pissed off," Russ said. "I can hear everything you're thinking. I didn't realize you hated me this much, Baldo."

"Fuck you, Wilson. I want you out of my body now."

"Levine, do you think I'm here by my choice? Are you forgetting that my beaten corpse is rotting on your kitchen floor?"

Carl tapped the fingers of his left hand on the table absently. He could see his reflection in the mirror. He was startled when he realized that his eyes were moving around in opposite directions, giving him the appearance of a cross-eyed cartoon character. The glaring tattoo on his forehead only worsened the situation. His right eye was looking down at the corpse on the floor, while the left was looking at himself in the mirror. It was unsettling. Was he going to have to spend the rest of his life trapped inside his own body with his enemy?

"We're going to have to bury the body. I'm-" Carl said, coming to the inevitable solution.

"Bury it?" Russ asked, cutting his enemy off. "Bury it where, you ass? In the backyard like a goddamn pet!"

"Well, actually, yes. Do you think the police are going to buy my story, you imbecile? The body of my neighbor, a person whom I hate, is lying bludgeoned on the kitchen floor. You're the one who killed your body to begin with, in case you forgot, you dumbfuck fat ass. Do you think the cops are going to believe that we switched brains and now we're trapped in my body together?"

"I don't care what they believe, Levine. I'm not going to help my enemy bury my murdered body."

"A murder in which you happened to commit, you borderline retard."

Carl's left hand lashed out and slapped him across the face. "I'm not going to put up with your lip, Levine! I've had it with you and your insults!"

The right hand whipped around in a fist and slammed into Carl/Russ' face violently. "You've had it? You've had it?"

Carl/Russ didn't stop the attack until they fell into unconsciousness.

"That cross-eyed loon in there killed his neighbor," Kenny Joe Butler, the maintenance man said, pointing through the window of the padded room.

"So what's so crazy about that?" the other worker asked. "People do that shit all the time."

They looked through the window at the straight-jacketed man with the 'I Love Jesus!' tattoo. The man was having a rather heated argument with himself.

"That's not all, bro. He's got multiple personality disorder, or something. He claims the neighbor that he killed is inside him. If you remove that straitjacket, he'll beat himself into unconsciousness."

"You don't say," he said as they continued down the corridor. "That's got to be something to see."

"Oh, it is. Every once in awhile we remove the jacket and watch him, uh, I mean them, go at it."

"Would you shut the hell up already!" Carl/Russ yelled, wriggling around in the jacket, trying desperately to break free.

"Me! Why in the hell should I shut up, Wilson! You're the one that's always babbling! This is my body you know!"

"Oh, here we go with that 'my body' shit again! Oh man,

Levine, you better hope that I don't break out of this jacket. God, will I fucking beat you, you bald bastard!"

"Please! Just shut up! I'm begging you! I can't take it! Get out of me!"

Over the years, the arguments started to get pretty redundant.

FISHES DREAM OF LONELY THINGS

BY WESTON OCHSE

*M*y mother told me to be careful by the creek. She made me promise never to swim there. She made me promise that if I saw anything strange to come running home. I thought she meant perverts or the homeless or crack addicts. I was wrong.

It was Tuesday when we decided to go fishing. The house was like *the pit of hell* as Dad always said. I wasn't allowed to use those words, but I knew what he meant and agreed. Just sitting on the couch was making me sweat through my clothes. David was with me and I was tired of kicking his butt on video games. He wouldn't give up, though. He demanded to play again and again and again. I even let him win once, but he knew it and got mad and insisted on playing yet one more time. It wasn't until Mom came in and turned it off that David finally gave in to my superior Nintendo muscles.

We were kicking around the garage, soaking up the coolness of the shaded concrete, when he spied the fishing poles.

"How about some fishin'?" he asked.

"Naw, even the fishes are hot. Anyways, remember my Mom doesn't like me playing down there."

David scoffed, or at least I think he did. I was never really sure what the word meant, but I had read it enough times to understand a little. Nonetheless, I had never seen a real person snort and look surprised at the same time so I figured it must be scoffing.

"She told you never to go swimming there," said David with

his sly look that always meant trouble. "So then don't swim. It doesn't mean you can't stick your feet in the water or wade in the shallows. Ernie said he saw a crawdaddy as big as his hand down there, and I want to find it. Besides," he said smiling. "It's always cooler in the woods. Maybe we won't melt there."

I laughed remembering yesterday when my Dad came home from work. I was in the tree and I was sure he saw me. He pulled into the driveway and stepped out of the car. He stopped at a puddle of water that ended up by the garage door, left there from when I'd gotten a drink from the hose. I watched as he dropped his briefcase and knelt down beside it. He hollered for Mom, who came running out.

"Jeffery. Oh My God, Ann. He melted. Our son melted."

My Mom smiled and so did I. It was Dad trying to be funny again. Mom would set him straight.

"Oh My God. You're right! He was just out here," said my Mom. "I just checked on him."

She fell to her knees beside my Dad and it looked like she'd started to cry. It was going too far now. I climbed down out of the tree and walked up to the puddle and stood on the other side. I put my hands on my waist like Mom always does when I've done something wrong.

"What should we do, honey?" asked my Dad. "We could get the ShopVac and suck him up. Maybe those folks at the hospital can put him back together." He stared at the puddle and it was impossible for him not to see my reflection.

"I don't think they can do that," said my Mom, her voice low and sad. "Hey. We could save him until Christmas and build a *snowboy* out of him. Like Frosty. He could come to life."

"That's it," said my Dad. "We'll move to Alaska then, where our little *snowboy* could live forever."

"Dad," I said. "Frosty ain't real. That would never work, anyways."

"We'll have to pack up his things. It's sad all his toys will go to waste, maybe David would like his Super Nintendo," said Mom.

"Mom!" I yelled. The joke had really gone too far, now.

"You know this wouldn't have happened if we had an air

conditioner," said Dad. He patted the water and said, "I'm sorry Jeffery. I am so sorry."

"Dad, Mom. Stop this. It isn't even funny."

I think it was because I started crying, but they suddenly stopped their joke. It didn't take long for us to laugh and hug, but the feeling I'd had when they pretended I wasn't there was almost too scary to stand.

She slid beneath the surface, her body slithering around mossy rocks and under submerged branches, pondering the shimmering stillness above her. It had been too long since she'd added to her loneliness, to her collection. The fishes had long since lost their fear of her, generation upon generation growing and rotting as she patrolled her length of creek. Still, they instinctively avoided her cavern: water-filled and deep, with only a thin shaft of light spearing through the narrow entrance, spot-lighting the head of her fifth victim in a translucent green halo. The milky eyes stared, seeing but immobile, fixed in a body that was lost in a forever dream.

David skittered down the hill first, leaping through the tall ferns and yelping all the way down. I followed slower, picking my way through the brush and with the back of my hand, pushing away the long green fronds that tickled my nose. I hated walking where I couldn't see what I was stepping on.

Grandpa used to tell me about the Little People before he went to heaven—stories about kingdoms within hills, toadstool houses and fairy rings. The Little People used to be everywhere, he'd said. The single greatest reason that no one ever saw the Little People anymore was because they kept getting squashed underfoot by ignorant humans.

I knew it was just my Grandpa's way of telling me to be careful. Anyways, I believed in the Little People like I believed in the Witch of Cleghorn Canyon. There had been too many stories of missing children and black cats for us to not believe in her. That is, since before we started fourth grade. When I was a third grader I believed, but I wasn't grown-up then. David said it was just a way for parents to control us. For once, I thought he was right.

"Come on, Jeffery! We're going to catch the mother of all fish, and make Derek's look like a minnow."

I smiled and sped up a little. I wasn't as competitive as David, but I would like nothing better than to show up Derek. He'd beat me up at least once every year of school. He was a fifth grader who had a new bike every year, lived in a big house with a TV in his room and caught the biggest fish ever found in Rapid Creek. No one believed there were any two and a half-foot trout in the water. Not, at least, until Derek hauled it up to the newspaper office and got his picture on the front page. David swore since the flood had washed the hatchery out back in 1972 that there had to be even more bigger fish.

I reached the bottom of the hill and broke into a run. Far ahead, David ran, holding the tip of his rod high in the air as he jumped and hooted over the pine needle-covered forest floor and fallen ponderosa pine. By the time I caught up, he was already drifting a kernel of yellow corn along the slow-moving water. Of course, he'd found the best spot. I silently cursed him and made my way downstream to the *hole*. It was where all the kids swam, but was deep enough to hide lunkers. As I turned, I caught David's smirk. No one had ever caught any fish in the *hole*, but that didn't mean they weren't there.

She watched the yellow bait drift by, and toyed with it, tugging gently on the line. She watched through the prism of water as the boy jerked his pole and inspected the now-empty hook. She smiled at her game and knew she would soon add another. She made a few bubbles, each drifting languidly to the surface, enticing the child to her spot. Tempting. Luring.

I had a few nibbles, but nothing serious, probably just some stocked fingerlings. When I was little, I loved catching them. Like my Grandpa, I was a serious fisherman, now. I was a trout man: brown, rainbow, brook, splake, cutthroat. *Cutthroats.* Now, there was a mean sounding fish—a fish that could meet a man in an alley and make him stop fishing. I had never caught one before, but with a name like that, they had to be pretty mean. Even deadly.

It was cooler near the water. I attached a bobber to my line and let it drift towards the middle. I laid back and stared at the blue sky through the long pine and imagined my corn dangling above a lunker like a bone held high above a dog. I kept my grip on the pole and closed my eyes, waiting for the fish to leap up and swallow the kernel so I could show up David and Derek and prove that I was the world's greatest fisherman.

She saw the feet, young and tender, moving slowly through the mud of the shallows, the toes wiggling as they contacted small rocks, crawdads and a snail. A boy's fleshy hand dove and pierced the mud like a bird searching for food. She slithered closer until she could examine each fine blonde hair on the boy's leg. All she needed was to reach out and touch, drag a fingernail along the instep and the child would dance with fear. She glanced toward his concentrating face, and grinned as his eyes passed over her, blinded by the glare of the sun upon the mirrored surface and his disbelief in her truth; never knowing that she was so near.

"Hey, Jeffery! Look, I got a big one."

The yell jerked me upright and my shoes splashed into the water, soaking them. The chill of the creek cleared my head of daydreams. I checked my still bobber and then glanced over to where David was wading. He held up a crawdaddy big enough to be a lobster, its claws snipping at the air and attempting to take off a few of David's wiggling fingers. It finally managed to snag one and David's scream was followed quickly by a splash and then a high pitched, "Damn."

I smiled and laid the pole carefully down, placing my butt upon the reel so if a lunker did hit, I'd have a second to keep my pole from going in. I untied my shoes and removed my soaked socks and laid them out to dry on the long grass beside me. Mom wouldn't be happy if I had wet clothes. She probably wouldn't let me down to the creek for months, if then.

I dangled my feet in the water and held the pole in my lap. The coolness ran up my legs and sent shivers of goosebumps along my skin. I watched as David splashed and fell in the shallows, chasing his Mountain Lobster. The funny scene tore through the lingering strangeness of my dream—a dream of a woman, just beneath the water watching us and waiting. My feet stilled their wagging, dead and wakeless like my bobber and I fought the urge to jerk them from the water. The urge to run. But I was a fourth grader now. The dream was just a dream.

She felt the tug of belief and allowed it to pull her down the creek and into the place where the children swam; the place where she teased their legs and toes, tickling them until they screamed with fearful laughter, each unsure if it was a leaf, or a fish or a snake, never once knowing the truth. This was the one. She felt his thoughts lurking upon her existence and sent feelers into his soul, massaging his memories and divining his needs.

When the bobber disappeared, I was so surprised at *the hole* having a fish that I stared like I was stupid. The second time, however, I jerked the pole and felt the hook set. I stood up, almost slipping into the water and held the tip of the rod high, ready for the fish to jump and lower it. It was all about being calm, my Grandpa had said. Too many as they are reeling in their catch get excited and lose.

Be calm. Breathe deep. Play it slowly.

The fish pulled hard and visions of Derek's disappointed face were foremost in my mind. This one was a lunker. Definitely the biggest I had ever hooked. Its jerks and pulls inched me forward as my wet feet slipped on the grass. There was no way I would let go, though. This was not the mother of all fishes, it was the father of all fishes and it was all mine.

Patience.

I screamed for David, but didn't look. I knew the picture of my struggle was enough information for even his dense skull. I traded tugs and whatever was at the end of my line was an equal. Maybe it was a cutthroat— one of those fish my Dad talked about. I dreamed the dream of all fisherman as they played with unknown catches. I was ready.

But I wasn't. It was a tremendous tug that jerked me into *the hole*— a tug by something immensely more powerful than me. A tug that didn't even allow me a chance to let go. Before I hit the water, I heard David's scream and then the silence of the water. As I hit, I let go of the rod, but I'd already fallen deep. My

Mom was going to be so pissed. She'd made me promise never to swim here. And no matter how much I argued, she'd never believe my fish story.

I kicked up, my clothes heavy and dragging. I looked through the green water to the sun shining brightly above and made that my goal. I was almost there when the hand grabbed my ankle. It pulled me, reeling me in. I kicked and fought for the surface, my lungs about to pop. I wanted to cry, to scream, but I knew if I opened my mouth, I would surely drown. The hand pulled down and down until I felt the muddy silt bottom. With one leg perched, I used my hands to spin me around and see what had grabbed my leg.

Of all the things I'd imagined in nightmares and dreams of dead things, the woman who gripped my leg was the worst and my last.

She hovered just above the bottom, her long red hair catching the small currents as her body wound behind her. Eyes as round and milky as dead fish examined me. Her face was old, like a great grandma, but without the necessary love. Her smile was more of a frown, but even so, I could tell she was happy—happy that she'd reeled me in.

It was then that I screamed and my lungs filled with water.

My Mom visits the spot, now. She comes almost every day. I call to her and tell her I love her, but she is closed to me. When the sun is perfect, it pierces the depths to my face and I feel its far away warmth and remember life. Especially David, Super Nintendo and my Grandfather's tales of things that couldn't be. Other than when the kids come swimming, their legs dangling just a few feet from where I sit, my Mother's visits make me the happiest. I know she doesn't understand. I know she doesn't know that I'm still here. She believes that I'm really dead—lost. It is the witch. It is her doing. She keeps me and the others so she won't be so lonely. I have spoken to them in my forever dreams and they tell me their stories. They are all like me. They believed. They were good. It is what the witch needs, what feeds her. It is our dreams of things we can't have, things dead to us. It is our dreams of dead things that allow her to live.

NIGHT OF THE HUNTERS

BY WESTON OCHSE & DAVID WHITMAN

"So then I says, 'Well, go on then, girl, see if I give a shit,'" Rolly said, staring into each and every eye around the campfire like a born storyteller. "And then she ups and throws the goddamn hammer right into the brand new television screen. She looked at me like she done caught a five foot bass—like I'm supposed to be all fuckin' impressed, and put her hands on her hips."

Mason smiled at his friend and punched him in the shoulder. He liked Rolly. The man was much smarter than he played himself to be, but tended to wear his 'Southern Boy' like a second skin. "Damn, Rolly, you're never going to be married," he said, throwing the last of his burnt venison to Get, Rolly's white poodle. "You might as well marry that damn mutt."

Rolly grinned crookedly and slapped Get's rump. "And you know something, she'd make a pretty good bride, too. That's one bitch who sits when I tell her to sit, begs when I tell her to beg, and rolls over when she wants a good rubbin.'" Rolly grinned, stared off into space for a moment and seemed to ponder the possible domestic qualities of a four-legged bitch as opposed to his normal two-legged ones, but snapped his eyes straight, then spun and glared at Mason. "Hey, Man, don't be interuptin' while I'm talkin." He scratched his balls. "Now, where was I? Oh yeah, so she's standin' there with her hands on her hips, the brand new television set smokin' behind her makin' it look like it was comin' from her ears and the top of her head—a regular demon. So, not to be intimidated, I leaned back against the wall, smiled, and said, 'It's a good goddamn thing I used your credit card to buy that set.' And then I got my fat ass out the door before she could get me with the hammer too."

The faces around the campfire, primed with grins throughout the story, erupted into howling hysterics at the newest tale of their friend's never-ending battle against the opposite sex. Billy Bob erupted into his trademark guffaws, his immense belly shaking up and down as he roared. Weasel giggled insanely. Forever Rolly's moveable laugh track and sidekick, Weasel was already so drunk his body couldn't decide which way to lean. Mason shook his head and grinned, laughing on the inside.

Just to the right of the campfire was the carcass of the bear that they had poached, its thick tongue sticking out of the side of its mouth with indignity. It had taken eight shots to bring her down and then about a dozen whacks from the baseball bat. Hunting was something that they all felt was their God-given right to do, despite any law that said otherwise. And Billy Bob, known as BB Spotlight by the sheriffs of thirteen counties, new every law there was going back to the state's reintroduction to the Union after the Great War of Northern Aggression.

The close circle of friends were still rubbing the tears from their eyes when Get stood up, yelped once, and then darted off into the woods, almost knocking Billy Bob from his log.

"Get!" Rolly shouted, staring into the dark trees. "Get your ass back here, girl!"

Mason started laughing, this time on the outside and Rolly flashed him a look of irritation. "What in the hell you laughin' at, Mason? This ain't goddamm funny, there's wild animals out there," he said pointing to the dead bear as an example. "Besides, the last time she ran off in the woods she got sprayed by a fuckin' skunk."

Weasel jumped in with squeaking titters, "And that fuckin' dog was flamin' pink for a month after you bathed her in tomato juice. You had to walk her at night, just so's the other dogs wouldn't laugh at her."

Mason laughed at the memory of Rolly, a picture of whom Joe Bob Briggs would put in a dictionary as the icon of Redneckocity, John Deere hat, lip full of Beechnut Wintergreen, tattered flannel shirt and greasy blue jeans, walking a hot pink poodle under the moonlight.

Rolly pointed a finger at Weasel, "You need to shut the hell up. And you, my edumacated friend," he added, pointing at Mason, "And you need to stop laughin' at my Get." Rolly had stood up as his blood rose. He shook his head. "Every fuckin' time somethin' happens to Get, you sit around and laugh. You can't laugh at a man's dog." He shook his head and sat down. "Never at a man's dog."

Mason slipped out a cigarette, leaned forward and lit it in the campfire. He was careful not to set the brim of his bright orange *Tennessee Volunteers* baseball cap on fire. He wore it every time they went hunting so Weasel wouldn't mistake him for deer like he did the first time they all went shooting together. He grunted, stared at Rolly, then returned his gaze to the dancing flames. "I'm laughing because your dog's name is an action verb."

Rolly spit into the fire and shook his head at his friend. "Actually, Mr. Smarty Pants, it's a transitive verb," all vestiges of his 'Southern Boy' gone. He stood up, peered into the woods and began his patented whistle, the high pitched sound slicing through the quietness of the night.

Mason shook his head, wondering how a man who looked as one dimensional as Rolly could have so many levels to his personality.

"Get! If you get sprayed by a goddamn skunk again I'm leavin' you out here in the woods!" Rolly looked over at the rest of the group. "I don't know what I'm doin' with a sissy ass poodle for a pet, anyway."

"I told you, John Wayne had pups," Billy Bob suggested. He had named his rottweiller a decidedly masculine name, not realizing that his dog was in fact a female until she gave birth. He still thought of John Wayne as a he, but it was an anachronism that Mason enjoyed.

"I ain't takin' no pups from a bitch named John Wayne," Rolly spat, looking into the woods like a mother hen. "It's un-American," he said placing his cap over his heart. "Namin' a female dog after one of America's greatest heroes. Anyways, me and Get get along just fine. Goddamn that bitch!"

"That's only 'cause she can't fit her paws around a hammer. I swear, if she had looked in a mirror and saw her pink fur, she would have broken every TV, mirror and window in your house just to let you know she wasn't as fuckin' gay as she looked," said Billy Bob.

"She can't be gay, asshole. She's a girl," said Mason, glaring at Billy Bob with one of those *I am gonna come over there and kick your ass* looks.

"Just calm down. Everyone calm down. She'll come back. She knows you take care of her and she's loyal," Mason said, moving between the two.

Rolly glanced over at Mason for any kind of sarcasm. If there was one thing that Rolly couldn't stand it was being made fun of, even by his closest friends. Mason had figured a long time ago that the whole 'Southern Boy' routine was Rolly's way of short-circuiting people. It was okay to laugh at what he pretended to be, but never the real Rolly. Never laugh at who he really was. Lucky for the world, no one really knew.

Rolly stalked back over to the log and plopped down heavily. "She'll be back. She needs to eat, don't she? It's not like she could hunt rabbit or anythin', a little white, fluffy bitch like her."

Weasel started laughing again. "That would be the shit wouldn't it, Rolly? That little bitch walkin' back into this campsite carryin' a goddamn rabbit in her little mouth. Catchin' the damn Easter Bunny. I bet even the squirrels would laugh at that."

"I'll tell you what, Weasel," Rolly said, staring into the flames with a wide smile. "That bitch may surprise your ugly ass just yet."

Billy Bob was staring off into the woods, his head cocked like he was listening to some far off music. It was the look he got when hunting. If anyone was the real hunter within the group, it was Billy Bob. The boy had hunted game from Alaska to Florida. His house was a museum to the hunt. From the alligator that greeted you at the front door, to the polar bear that seemed to hold the giant screen TV in its paws, to the wolverine toilet paper dispenser he had in the bathroom, he had over sixty stuffed animals and fish adorning the inside of his house. He was always the first one to lead the hunt, knowing exactly what the animal was thinking based on the shape and age of the tracks. He could dissect a bush in a hurricane and still be able to tell what animals had passed by, when they had passed by and the reason they had passed by. Fat old Billy Bob was their animal expert. It was almost enough to make one ignore his alcoholism and tendency to take shots at invisible things after his third six-pack.

Mason passed Billy Bob, walked over to the cooler, and grabbed himself a beer. When he noticed that Rolly was beerless, he snagged him one as well and yelled "Pull!" like they were shooting clay pigeons.

Rolly expertly caught the beer and cracked it open, forgetting about his dog for the moment. He took a long sip and grimaced. "I think what I really need is a woman. That would set me up just right."

Mason shook his head and finished up his cigarette, flicking it into the fire. He often wondered how he had found himself in the company of men like this. He owned and operated a used car lot back in town, made a decent living, but nothing spectacular. The kicker was that he had a master's degree in literature. That and a dollar bought him coffee every morning. He really hadn't done much with it other than scribble in one of his growing pile of notebooks every day. Maybe one day he would be a bestselling novelist.

Mason met Rolly and the rest of the crew at The Fish Pond, a local bar he started going to after his divorce. They had hit it off right away. Rolly may not have any college experience, or even high school for that matter, but he was smarter than a whip. Rolly was entirely self taught, reading any book that you handed him. Any book. Mason remembered the stern *shut up and never talk about this* look he got when he was helping Rolly clean out his garage and a box fell over, emptying a sprawl of romance paperbacks. To this day, Mason had respected the friendship enough to never mention it. Still, Rolly knew a little bit about everything, an aspect of his personality that was often masked by his redneck persona. Yes, Rolly was a redneck, but he was an educated redneck. *The worst kind*, thought Mason with a smile.

Weasel listed off to the side of the campfire like a boat that had tacked into a strong wind and began to piss into the grass, fighting balance, gravity and the complication of the process. Mason and Rolly watched that with amusement until Weasel did one final jig, bounced off a tree and zipped up.

"You know something, Mason?" Rolly said after taking a particularly long sip of his beer. "I got my eye on Sheela. I think I'm fixin' to make her mine."

Sheela was a waitress down at the Barbecue Pit, a favorite local restaurant, with a decidedly unoriginal name. "Shit, Rolly," Billy Bob said from where he sat perched like Humpty Dumpty on a log, thumbs caught in his rainbow suspenders. "Sheela is John Reynold's girl. John will whup your ass but good, you even so much as wink at her."

Rolly winced like he had been stabbed and looked over at Mason with a pained expression. "Why can't you shut your ass the hell up, Billy Bob? I wasn't even talkin' to you. Besides, I whipped Reynolds's ass twice already."

Billy Bob snorted. "Yeah, when we was twelve years old at fuckin' summer camp." He broke out into his trademark guffaws. "As I recall Rolly, John had his arm in a cast when you 'whipped his ass'." He started laughing again, this time joined by Weasel.

"You know something? I got something to say to you, Billy Bob," Rolly said, his face turning sober. "And you too, Weasel."

Billy Bob shook his head and smirked. "What's that, Rolly?"

"Fuck you," Rolly said nonchalantly and then shot daggers at Weasel. "And fuck you too. Fuck all of you. John Reynolds will have his ass back in a cast if he even comes near me."

Everyone started laughing, simply because Rolly had managed to keep a straight face through the whole thing. A stranger watching the conversation would probably think that a fight was about to occur. When they saw the deer, everyone suddenly stopped.

It glided from out of the trees and into the clearing, its eyes angry black slits. It snorted through its nose, a ball of red and white fur in its teeth. A huge rack of blood encrusted antlers shook with each plod of the cloven hooves. All the men stared, entranced by the deer's demeanor, their guns forgotten at their sides.

It approached the campfire and spat something into the dirt with a damp thud. A round, sticky mass of red and white hair lay on the ground. Mason thought he could see Get's teeth sticking out of the wet, furry ball.

The deer stood glaring at them in defiance as it slowly made eye contact with every one of them. Mason felt cold uncertainty slide through his veins as he stared back into the penetrating eyes.

"Ixtli!" the deer shrieked and they all jumped. Billy Bob leapt up from where he sat, turned to run into the woods screaming, and ran full speed into a low branch. He sagged to the ground in a heap. Mason had a fleeting thought that his terrified friend might think the animal had come to extract some unique punishment for killing and mounting so many of its cousins.

The deer gave one final snort of apparent disgust and darted off into the darkness. Mason and Rolly glanced at each other, their eyes wide over open mouths. Billy Bob lay on the side of the log where he had passed out, his belly threatening to burst the buttons on his plaid shirt. Weasel's mouth was opening and closing rapidly as if he had something to say, but couldn't quite bring himself to tell it.

"What in Jesus H. Christ was that?" Rolly whispered, his face ashen. He looked like he had just been punched. "I'd like to say that somebody spiked the fruit punch, Mason, but judgin' by the look on your face I'd say you just saw the same thing that I saw."

Mason looked tired. "I think that this is the first time in my life that I'm speechless. I pretty much thought it was impossible to do that to me anymore."

Rolly stood up slowly and began scanning the woods for any signs of trouble. "What in the hell did he say, Mason? It sounded like 'Ixlee.' What the fuck does 'Ixlee' mean? More importantly, what the fuck is a deer doin' sayin' it to me...us."

Mason was shaking his head back and forth, his eyes

scanning the surrounding darkness. A deer had just walked…
no, not walked…strutted. A deer had just strutted out of the
woods, spoke to them, dropped a dead dog at their feet and
paused to give them the evil eye. *Things weren't good.* With
that thought, he immediately grabbed his shotgun and began
stuffing shells into it.

Rolly, knowing a good idea when he saw it, did the same.
Weasel was too busy watching Billy Bob's belly, mesmerized by
the rise and fall of the massive plaid mound, to worry himself
with anything simple and sane like self-protection. His body
leaned forward with Billy Bob's every breath as if he was about
to be sucked into the silver dollar-sized belly button.

"What in the hell should we do, Mason?" Rolly whined.
"You're the one with the college degree."

Mason grimaced and brought the gun up, sighting into the
trees nervously. "Rolly, you'd think something would tell you
that I wasn't taught in school what to do when Bambi turns into
a fucking psycho lunatic."

Weasel started giggling insanely and fell off his log. His
chortles could be heard from the weeds like a madman in some
forgotten asylum.

"I'll tell you one thing, Mason, Bambi's one dead deer. That
motherfucker killed my goddamn dog!" He looked down at the
dog's corpse. "Oh, Get, what in the hell did he do to you?"

Billy Bob suddenly awoke and sat up. One hand went to the
bulging knot that sat in the middle of his head like a third eye
and the other reached for the thirty ought six.

"Man," he said chuckling to himself. "I just had the weirdest
dream. There was this deer you see," he said levering himself
back onto the log and grabbing a beer. "There was this deer and
he spoke to me. He said, 'You asshole. We are tired of this shit.
Prepare to die." Billy Bob chuckled again until his eyes rested
on the battered corpse of Get.

He noticed Mason and Rolly alternately staring at the
darkness between the trees and him, aiming down the lengths
of their guns. He studied the ground and saw the prints. He
squatted and ran a hand lightly over the powdery ridges, his
knuckles around the gun tightening until they were white.

Suddenly, he stood. He grabbed his pack full of shells and slung it over his back, then gripped the rifle at port arms.

"Hey guys, I am just gonna run back to the truck and check somethin," he said, his steps getting quicker and quicker. As he hit the forest edge, he broke into a run, leaving Rolly and Mason gaping at his departure.

It was a few seconds before Rolly broke the silence with a question. "What did he mean the deer said, 'Prepare to die?' All I heard was 'Ixtli' or what-the fuck."

Mason turned to answer, but they both froze as Billy Bob's screams pierced the air from far off to their left. It was silenced by a roar.

"Oh fuck, Mason, that was a goddamn bear!" Rolly shouted, his gun shaking as his eyes roamed around the dark trees, trying to penetrate the blackness. He glanced hurriedly up and noticed Mason's ass shimmying up a tree. "Where in the hell you goin', Mason? You ain't goin' to get very far hidin' up in a damn tree."

"You got a better idea?" Mason asked, not bothering to turn around as he struggled to hold onto his gun and climb up at the same time.

Rolly had to acknowledge that he didn't, and began to follow his friend. Weasel, who had sat up when they weren't looking, watched them like a little kid fascinated with monkeys at the zoo.

Rolly and Mason both managed to find a good-sized branch to perch themselves upon and began to study the ground below. Each snap and rustle made their hearts leap in their chests.

"What about him?" Mason asked, indicating Weasel, who had found the marshmallows and was toasting several over the fire, oblivious to reason and common sense.

"What about him?" Rolly replied rhetorically, checking his gun to make sure the safety was off. "If he don't have enough sense to defend himself, he ain't our problem. If we want to get out of this, we're going to have to worry about ourselves."

It's like that weird comic strip, Mason thought as he studied the ground below for signs of attack. *What in the hell was that called? The Far Side. The one where the animals were always talking like humans.*

"You know something, Mason?" Rolly asked, a crooked smile on his face. "One can't help but recognize the irony in this situation, us being hunters and all."

Mason laughed aloud and Weasel looked up at them curiously. "That's why I like you, Rolly. No matter how bad things get, you never lose your sense of humor. You lost two wives—your brother was killed last year in that motorcycle accident, Get's dead. Your mama—"

"Uh, Mason, just now might not be a good time to bring up Mama, may she rest in peace."

"Sorry, Rolly, I—" he looked down, and bit his tongue. He ignored the pain and the rivulet of blood that seeped down his chin.

A spiked buck and a black bear strolled into the clearing like two friends out for a romp, the bear walking on its two hind legs like a human. Weasel began to chuckle, clapping his hands with glee. He placed a hotdog upon a stick and held it out to his new 'friends.'

"Bambi want some pig?" he asked, giggling.

The deer leaned down and smelled the proffered gift, recoiling in almost human disgust. It glanced at the bear, who, with a quick swipe of its paw, removed Weasel's hand, sending it slapping sickeningly into the trunk of the tree that Mason and Rolly were hiding in. Weasel screamed once and then stopped as his throat was removed an instant later. The wet fountain of blood hissed red into the campfire as Weasel, a split second later, joined it, his hair crackling as his skull caught fire.

"Ixtli!" shouted the deer. "Ixtli trat!"

"So what's 'trat' mean?" asked Rolly giving their position away.

"I bet it means *Die redneck*," replied Mason, switching aim back and forth from one target to another, unable to decide which to kill first. Rolly solved the problem.

The bear looked up at them and roared, falling over, its head exploding in a spray of red mist.

"Take that you Yogi Bear motherfucker!" Rolly shouted from his branch. "You and Boo Boo ain't gonna be stealin' the picnic baskets around Yellowstone anymore, are ya!"

"Ixtli!" the deer shrieked and vanished back into the woods. Mason eyed Rolly, studying his friend. That last line about Yogi Bear was a bit much, even considering the situation.

Rolly glared back at Mason with wild eyes and a huge shit-eating grin. "Hey, Hey, Boo Boo!" He shouted out hysterically. Suddenly, he stopped, his face serious once again. "I just figured out something, Mason."

"What's that?" Mason asked, staring at his friend cautiously.

"Bears can climb trees."

"The bear's dead, Rolly," said Mason, his worry over his friend's sanity escalating.

"Ever read Goldilocks? Everyone knows there's three bears. We got one earlier. I just killed me one, now. That leaves one more," Rolly began giggling, sounding eerily like Weasel. "And I bet we taste just fucking right. Human porridge. That's what we are Mason. Human fuckin' porridge."

Mason nodded gravely at his funny farm bound friend. He looked down and patted his shotgun. "Well, he's not going to be climbing this tree, I can tell you that."

"Shhh!" Rolly hissed. "Here they come again."

What looked like the same spiked buck walked into the clearing, this time followed by three others and two bears. As the animals began to talk amongst themselves in that strange language, Rolly elbowed Mason. "See," he whispered too loudly. "I told you there was three." His smile was too wide, too happy, too insane.

"Don't shoot at them," Mason suggested with a whisper as Rolly nodded. "Maybe they'll go away after awhile. They may not know we're here."

Suddenly, Rolly, who had been shifting position, fell to the ground with a shriek and a loud *whooompf.*

The animal's conversation suddenly stopped as each turned and regarded Rolly, sprawled in a lump of arms and legs. There was a few seconds of complete silence before the animals looked over at him and began to cackle, their bodies shaking with mysterious hilarity. It was the scariest sound that Mason had ever heard.

The bear was on Rolly in a second, a mass of fur, swinging

claws and blood sprays. It was then that he finally screamed; a thin whine that went up and up until it was replaced by the wet sounds of the bears feeding on flesh. Mason watched as Rolly's head, still wearing the John Deere hat, rolled against the broken body of Get, a look of utter surprise still on the unmarred face.

The deer watched, like an audience at a ball game, every once in awhile speaking to each other and breaking out into laughter that sounded like a mixture of a human and a cat. Mason, who had been almost invisible among the leaves and kudzu, leaned down on the branch to relieve the ache in his arm and then watched with queasy fascination as his cigarette lighter fell to the ground below, hitting with an audible thud.

The animals all stopped moving at once. In an almost slow motion maneuver they all looked up, piercing Mason with their hate. He felt the urine run into his jeans with a hot rush, soaking and warming his crotch. He opened fire with his shotgun, getting two deer and a bear before he ran out of ammunition.

"Jesus wept," Mason whispered, dropping his empty gun to the ground below. "Now what?"

The animals were pouring into the clearing. A pack of wolves, several slim red foxes, a dozen or so squirrels, three white rabbits, a trio of chipmunks and a huge white possum that appeared to swagger with each step. They began to circle the campfire in a strange dance, bumping and grinding, playful bites mixed with nips and barks of glee.

"I'm fucked."

Mason watched, wishing he had written that great novel, or a book of short stories. Hell, he would have settled on being the best graffiti artist in town; 'cause he saw that one of the bears had reached into the campfire and was now holding a flaming brand before him, the flames licking promisingly into the air.

"Smoky and his buddies have just discovered fire," Mason said to his dead friends. He couldn't help but smile, despite the situation.

"People don't start forest fires. Animals do," Mason growled madly in his best Smoky the Bear impression. It was the last thing he said..

ABOUT THE AUTHORS

Weston Ochse is the author of eight novels and over a hundred short stories. He's won the Bram Stoker Award for First Novel and been nominated for the Pushcart Prize for Fiction. His work has appeared in professional writing guides, comic books, magazines, anthologies and collections. Find him online at www.westonochse.com.

David Whitman is the author of several books, including HARLAN, DEADFELLAS, and BODY COUNTING. He is also the co-author of SCARY REDNECKS AND OTHER INBRED HORRORS and APPALACHIAN GALAPAGOS: A SCARY REDNECKS COLLECTION with Weston Ochse.

David's short fiction has been published in over 100 publications over the last fifteen years, including several honorable mentions in Ellen Datlow's and Terry Windling's YEAR'S BEST FANTASY AND HORROR.

Future projects include the sequel DEADFELLAS 2: ONE STEP BEYOND and other projects, including a new novel and a possible movie adaptation of DEADFELLAS.

He lives in northeastern Pennsylvania with his son Miles.

Curious about other Crossroad Press books?
Stop by our site:
http://store.crossroadpress.com
We offer quality writing
in digital, audio, and print formats.

Enter the code FIRSTBOOK
to get 20% off your first order from our store!
Stop by today!

55844443R00129

Made in the USA
Middletown, DE
18 July 2019